Ghost Writer

Steve Higgs

Contents

Wannabe Vampire.
Monday, October 16th
1915hrs

J ANE WITHDREW HER HEAD from beneath the foliage. "Explain it again."

"The author Simon Slater was killed last year. Murdered for sure, but they haven't caught the killer."

Jane held up her index finger to make me pause. "Pinned to the wall with a sword and then set on fire, right?"

I nodded, stretching out my right arm to ease the stiffness creeping into it from lack of movement. I wriggled it around for a few seconds then switched to do the same with my left arm while I continued with what I had been saying.

"Yes. The body was identified by his wife ... soooo definitely dead."

Jane snorted a tired chuckle, we both had experience of definitely dead people turning up alive. The charred remains in this case made the perfect opportunity for it to be someone else. The wife lies and her husband's death is effectively faked. The question I usually ask at this point is why. Why would they want to fake his death? That wasn't the question I was asking this time though.

Jane was frowning because she was thinking the same question. "If the author and his wife faked his death, then why has she hired you to figure out what is happening now?"

I nodded my head. "Exactly. Until we prove otherwise, Tempest and I will proceed under the assumption that Simon Slater is dead," I stated categorically.

"So, you're asking who stood to gain from his death?" Jane asked, mostly to make conversation. We were both getting cold and pretending that we were not by refusing to talk about it.

I huffed out a breath; cases are always so confusing at the start. "Maybe. I guess it's an obvious question to start with, but I honestly expect to find Simon Slater is still alive. It begs me to ask why Mrs Slater would hire us, but perhaps she hopes to use us to manipulate the truth or create enough fog that she and Simon can cover their tracks. I'll find out more tomorrow when I meet her."

"Are the police looking to disinter his body to check if it is really him?"

I shrugged, not that she could see the gesture; Jane had her back to me, her eyes focused on the open spaces of the park.

"I doubt it," I said to give her an answer. "The police would need to show sufficient justification and they won't be taking the reports of his return from the grave seriously."

"And you said the new victims are connected to him?"

"Sort of. Some of them are. At least a couple of them are people who helped Simon on his road to success. Others though – Amy Hildestrand for one, had no known connection to the dead author."

Jane pulled her head back out of the bushes again. Turning to face me, she asked, "Do you want me to do some research into how they are connected or whether there is some linked benefit from their deaths?" When I hesitated to answer, she added, "I'm really not all that busy. I can have a crack at it tomorrow if it's quiet in the office."

I accepted her offer and thanked her, the pair of us going back to watching the park through the bushes.

If you are wondering who I am, my name is Amanda Harper. I used to be a cop, but that career wasn't going anywhere - my boss was a pain ... still is for that matter though less so since Tempest punched him in the face on live TV. Now I'm a paranormal investigator which should explain why I am looking into a supposedly dead novelist and also why I am hiding in the bushes at a public park after dark.

Jane is the third investigator at the firm. Tempest originally hired her as his assistant ... no, I need to go back a step further. Tempest originally met Jane when she was a he and a member of a Vampire Live Action Role Play or LARP vampire club. Yes, such things really exist. Long story short – Jane quit that life, asked some tough questions about where his/her life was going and what he/she wanted from it. Now I don't recall the last time I saw Jane's male persona, and I think I might find it jarring if she were to turn up as James tomorrow.

Tempest Michaels is my boyfriend and my business partner since he insisted on making me part of the firm. We both hunt ghosts and scary beasties for a living, and it has always been necessary at this point in the conversation to highlight that I do not believe in the supernatural. Tempest and I investigate the weird and wonderful because there are lots of people who do believe in it. They find macabre and paranormal explanations for events in their life which we then need to disprove or find the perfectly ordinary explanation behind.

Tempest was a soldier for a bunch of years and when he left the army, he set himself up as a private investigator. The local newspaper messed up his advert and he's been a paranormal detective ever since.

Jane and I were chatting about a case that I had taken – as a team, the three of us pick our own cases and rarely fight over the juicier sounding ones. This one was particularly interesting because of the 'returned from the dead' angle and because the series of strange deaths very accurately reflected murders described in the books of the deceased author. Simon Slater's death was no exception; the method of murder and its staging taken from his very first book.

The tabloid press was already all over the Simon Slater story as one might imagine. The general speculation was that Simon Slater had returned from the dead to enact revenge. Quite what he was supposed to be getting revenge for was still unclear, but all the victims were from the literary industry. One had reportedly been an old friend who the author fell out with some time ago and another had successfully sued Simon Slater.

My client, the deceased author's wife, Genevieve Slater, had been hounded by the press and was now holed up in her house as much as possible. She lived inside a gated suburb of Kensington, so avoiding the press wasn't all that hard, but she maintained that her husband was dead and that's where we came in - he'd been seen near the murder scenes.

Not only that, there was even CCTV footage of him passing a shop just around the corner from the second victim. All in all, it was precisely the type of case that our firm, the Blue Moon Investigation Agency, favours.

I was supposed to be investigating it with Tempest, however together with Big Ben, a former army colleague and hired muscle for the firm, my boyfriend had chosen to abscond just as we were getting started. The guys vanished in the night to play international heroes, jumping on a plane and apparently then a seaplane, of all things, to get to the British Union Isles in the middle of the Atlantic.

There they met with a woman called Patricia Fisher, an English sleuth of some renown who was having a spot of bother with some dead pirates. Tempest and Patricia had worked together on a couple of cases in the past and her office is just a handful of yards from ours in historic Rochester High Street. Together they had solved the pirate case, whatever it was.

Tempest and Big Ben were due to return tomorrow. Until then, the Simon Slater case was mine.

"Someone's coming," Jane hissed at me.

A jolt of adrenaline made my pulse rate spike slightly. The pair of us had been waiting out of sight in the darkness for over an hour, and it was excitement over the opportunity to get on with the task far more than it was fear for what might happen now that was making my heart beat faster.

Of course, you are probably wondering what it is that we are doing and who it is that we are lying in ambush for. The answer is a little surprising. We didn't exactly have a client for this case, which is to say that we were not getting paid for our time.

Under other circumstances we probably wouldn't be out freezing our butts off in the late October air, however we had received a message from a supposed vampire in which he taunted us. He claimed to be responsible for three prior attacks and dared us to stop him. He even told us where he was going to be this evening, although he wasn't generous enough to tell us when.

If you are now questioning why we hadn't involved the police and questioning if perhaps we were a little irresponsible, then I can assure you that contacting the authorities was the first thing I did.

I refer you back to the comment about my former boss. Chief Inspector Quinn is an obnoxious, petty man who holds a grudge against me for refusing to be interested in him when we worked together, and against Tempest for existing.

The chief inspector had his own investigation into the recent vampire attacks and considered our information to be dubious at best and questioned if I was being deliberately misleading. Jane and I were on our own ... well, sort of anyway.

Moving to stand next to Jane's shoulder so I could see what she was looking at, I caught sight of two young women. They were dressed for a night out in skirts and tops far too flimsy and short for the ambient weather conditions and temperature. The coats they wore and were now hugging to their bodies were little more than summer jackets, but I remembered braving the cold myself back in the day when looking the part was far more important than being warm.

They had to be almost a hundred yards from our current location at the western edge of Jackson's Field, a large expanse of greenery looking down over Rochester. Great for walking dogs, taking kids to the play park, or even teenage fumblings once the sun had set, it was a wide, open space that was filled with people by day and almost completely empty at night.

Though I worried for the safety of the two young women we could see, at the same time I wanted our wannabe vampire to attack now. Or soon. I did not want to be out here for hours and hours.

The girls, both of them illuminated by light coming from the screens on their phones as they walked, had entered the field to our left and were on a diagonal path that cut down towards the bars and clubs in the High Street.

I wanted to use my own phone to send a message, but could not risk the screen illuminating. Had I put more thought into tonight's escapade I might have picked up a radio to use for communication.

Jane asked, "What do you think?"

I scrunched up my face, squinting and debating back and forth about what to do. It was entirely possible that Chief Inspector Quinn was right, and we were just being tricked. The message we received in the form of a note through our office door could have been from anyone, and even if it was from the wannabe vampire, he could easily have been lying about tonight's location.

Truthfully though, I didn't think that was the case. The Blue Moon Investigation Agency has gained a lot of publicity over the last eighteen months of business, with several high-profile cases making national headlines. If I was right, then the idiot who lured us here tonight wanted to be able to brag that even the Blue Moons couldn't stop him.

A dozen or more people had walked through the park in the last hour, and nothing had happened to any of them. They hadn't been the right kind of target though. The two girls we could see now fit the bill of the previous victims perfectly. Was he going to strike? The girls were more than halfway across and would be gone in just a couple of minutes.

Assuming they were going to reach the edge of the field unmolested, I was about to suggest we waited just a little bit longer before calling it quits, when Jane swore loudly and burst through the branches to start running across the expanse of grass.

Echoing her sentiment with a few choice words of my own, I ran after her. A figure had emerged from a clump of trees three quarters of the way down the path. In another fifty yards the two girls would have reached the road and been safe, but the wannabe vampire - for that was who I assumed we were seeing - had chosen his ambush site well.

There was no one else in sight, and with him blocking their path, his victims would have to run back up the steep hill to get away from him. However, in their strappy, heeled shoes they would be unlikely to get away. They could yell for help, but no one would hear them above the noise of the traffic on the main road.

Jane and I tore across the grass, both experienced enough to know to wear shoes we could run in and clothes that allowed easy movement. Unfortunately, the women were almost a hundred yards from us when the vampire sprung his surprise attack, and if he was going to bite one of them - which is precisely what he had done in his previous attacks - then there was nothing we could do to stop it occurring.

I sucked in a deep breath to yell, hoping that a scream would discourage the attacker before he could injure one of the women. However, my shout died in my throat as my confused eyes tried to make sense of what I was seeing.

The wannabe vampire, a sizable man if the shady silhouette I could see was anything to go by, had not succeeded in scaring the two girls into running away. Instead, both women tossed their phones, one to the left, the other to the right, where they landed on the grass - the screens still upright to show where they were.

That the women were standing their ground was astounding, but what happened next I could not have predicted in ten lifetimes.

The male wannabe vampire rushed them. Clearly unperturbed by their willingness to face him, he raised his arms and attacked. The woman on the left hitched up her short skirt and kicked him in the face. He was barely afforded the time to reel from the blow when the other girl grabbed his jacket and drove a knee upward into his mid-section.

Jane and I both heard the outrushing of air as the man's breath left his body. Now that he was bent double, the first young lady spun on her heel to deliver another kick, this time the blow striking the side of the man's face. He managed to roll away, tumbling side over side until he could get his feet back under him.

Popping back up, he tried to make a run for it - that's how I perceived his actions, but he wasn't fast enough.

Not even close.

Just as he was attempting to come out of a crouch and into a sprint the two young women fell upon him.

They were screaming blue murder, letting him know exactly how they felt about his decision to attack them. I heard one of them ask him how he was enjoying the experience, right before she grabbed his arm and twisted it in a direction it was not supposed to go.

Out of breath, but almost there, I yelled, "Stop!"

The girls hadn't seen us charging towards them across the grass, and the sounds of their own laboured breathing and screaming had made it so they would not have heard us either. They turned to look our way now, one holding their assailant to the floor with his right arm braced against the joints and her knee in his back to hold him in place.

Her friend raised her arms and flexed her knees as she dropped into a 'guard stance', though she relaxed when she saw it was just two more women coming her way.

The fight was over, and the wannabe vampire was subdued and probably bleeding into the grass at the edge of the path. Slowing to a walk, and sucking in air to get my breath back, I pulled out my phone and called my friend PC Patience Woods.

She answered in her usual gregarious manner, "Hey, skinny white girl, did your vampire show up? Need me to arrest someone?"

Attempting to control my breathing so that this would not sound like a dirty phone call, I managed to say, "Yes, he did. Yes, I do. It's not what you might be expecting though." I finished the call without giving her a more detailed explanation, but suggested she got the lights and sirens working if she wanted to be the one to make the bust.

Ahead of me, Jane had already joined the two girls who seemed a little shaken, but none the worse for being attacked.

"The police are on their way," I let them know. Then I started to introduce myself, planning to remark on their fighting skills since the two of them had taken the vampire wannabe apart without him landing a single blow on either one of them. However, I realised that I recognised one of the two girls. "Um, Mandy, is it?" I questioned, uncertain whether I could recall her name correctly or not.

"Mindy," she corrected me. "You're both from the Blue Moon Agency, aren't you?" she nudged her friend, the one who was still pinning their assailant to the ground. "These are the people I was telling you about - the ones who came to get the ghost out of auntie's boutique. Well, not these two, actually. It was two guys, but they all investigate ghosts and stuff for a living."

I had seen Mindy when she came into the office a week or so ago. I'd been busy with another case, but Tempest and Big Ben had chosen to take it on, discovering that it was an almost routine faked haunting. Almost routine for us, that is.

The man on the ground lifted his head slightly to ask, "Can I get up now?"

He got a firm chorus of, "No!" from all four ladies.

He put his head back down, but asked, "Is Tempest Michaels here?" When no one answered him, he craned his neck to look up at me. "I was hoping I could get a photograph with him," he explained, sounding hopeful.

So that was it. The idiot wanted to get his face in the papers. Tempest was the famous one; not me or Jane. That he wanted Tempest didn't come as news; we often get clients asking specifically for him. We assure them he will take their case and then if Jane or I get it, we say he is operating in a supervisory role.

I found the idiot fake vampire's wallet and took out his ID.

"They give driving licences to vampires, do they, Jason?" I asked rhetorically. "Jason Hemmings of Larkfield Drive, Linfield, Maidstone," I reported to Jane. She would file a report in the morning and perform some basic follow up to make sure his victims were made aware. They might choose to pursue civil action, so even though we were not getting paid, it was the right thing to do, and we are all about civic responsibility.

I crouched, coming down to place one knee on the grass to get my face closer to his.

"Spit out the teeth," I commanded. There was a bruise on his left cheek and a small cut to his eyebrow just above it.

Jason let out a frustrated sigh, but when Kelly leaned her weight in to further stress his shoulder joint, he opened his mouth and did something with his tongue.

His fake vampire teeth landed on the ground a few inches from his mouth. Curling my lip in disgust, I placed my hand inside one evidence bag and used it to transfer them to another which I sealed shut. Jane filmed the whole thing for chain of evidence.

Holding the dentures up, I saw extended canines connected by a small stainless-steel bridge. They had been professionally made by a dentist. I'd seen pairs like it before, but these ones were good quality.

It was less than a minute between me making the call to Patience and the sound of sirens filling the air, but another two or three minutes before she found us. In that time, I discovered that Mindy and her friend were both what one might call martial arts experts. Not that this came as any news having seen their display. They knew each other through their dojo and were heading into town for a double date.

They were going to be late, but seemed unconcerned about it. Mindy's friend, Kelly, used her phone to update the boys on their delay, though she chose to leave out the why behind it.

"Boys don't like to know that you can beat them up if you want to," Kelly explained. "It tends to put them off."

I'd suffered the same problem myself of a sort when I was a cop. Guys generally don't want to date female police officers.

When she arrived, Patience was accompanied by her usual partner PC Brad Hardacre. I'd been partnered with Brad myself back in the day and greeted him with a smile and a wave.

"Hi, Brad."

"So this is our latest vampire idiot?" Patience asked, 'accidentally' stepping on Jason's fingers.

"Yow!" he protested.

"Oh, I'm sorry," Patience failed to move her foot. "I was just testing."

"Testing what?" Jason questioned through clenched teeth.

Brad rolled his eyes. "Stop messing about, Patience."

"What if he's a real vampire?" she asked, much to Mindy and Kelly's amusement. "We keep getting called to all these supernatural cases. I figure sooner or later we're gonna come up against something that really is supernatural. What if that's tonight? Don't you think we should do a few tests to be sure?"

Enjoying Patience's usual decision to flout procedure, I played along.

"What do you have in mind?" I egged her on.

Patience gave an exaggerated shrug and strolled a few paces away to pick up a piece of stick which she then snapped in half to produce a pointy piece.

"Perhaps I should stake him a few times, just to be sure."

Jason craned his neck to see what was going on.

"Wait, what? I'm not really a vampire!"

Patience sucked a little air between her teeth. "Can't be too sure."

"You can't kill him either, Patience," I pointed out.

Jane offered a suggestion. "You could stake him somewhere that won't kill him."

"Ooh, like in the scrotum!" gasped Patience with excitement.

The wannabe vampire freaked out, bucking and twisting as he tried to get up.

Kelly merely leaned a little more weight into his back and tugged on his right arm to keep him in place.

Brad decided he'd had enough. "All right. That's it. I'm not sure what I did wrong to get shackled with you all the time, Patience, but it falls under the label of cruel and unusual punishment."

Moments later, Jason the vampire wannabe was up and in cuffs. He was off to the local station where he would be processed, interviewed, and charged. Mindy and Kelly provided statements as did Jane and I, though all four of us would probably be requested to attend the station in the next day or so to answer some more in-depth questions about what we had seen and heard.

With the incident over and the idiot wannabe vampire still complaining that it hadn't been Tempest Michaels in attendance this evening, Jane and I started back toward our cars.

"Amanda," Patience called after me. "Hold up."

I told Jane I would see her in the morning - there was no need for her to hang around any longer, then pulled my coat tighter around myself when a cool breeze found its way through the gaps to chill me yet further.

"Everything all right?" I enquired.

Huffing and puffing from the need to chase after me and running because Brad was already calling for her to hurry up, Patience muttered, "Stupid hills. I'm going to move somewhere flat where I don't have to go up hills ever. Isn't there a country in Europe where it's all flat?"

"Holland," I informed her. "Well known for being quite flat."

"That's where I'm going then," she griped before getting to the point. "We haven't been out in ages. Seeing those two girls off on a double date on a Monday night just reminded me how lame my life's become. What are you doing tomorrow evening?"

I shot her an apologetic face. "Sorry, Patience, I'm going to be in London, I think."

"London?"

"I have a case there. With the cost and time to travel back and forth, I might as well just stay in a hotel." I expected her to look disappointed and got the absolute opposite instead.

"Yay! Nights out in the big city. What a perfectly brilliant idea!"

I blinked a couple of times and tried shaking my head. "No, that's not what I meant. I'll be there working a case. Tempest is probably coming to join me."

Patience offered me her sternest frown. "Earlier you told me Tempest was out of the country."

She thought I was blowing her off; coming up with a reason not to spend time with her and that wasn't it at all. She was right in some ways though because we hadn't spent much time together in recent weeks or months. Life had changed since I left the police.

Patience and I used to work together all the time and inevitably would plan to do things after work or when our shift rotation gave us days off. Now I saw her less and less, and whether she was trying to make me feel bad about it or whether I was feeling bad about it because I ought to, I hastily rearranged the mental image I had for the next couple of days.

"He is," I replied. He really was, though he was set to return before tomorrow night. "But hey, why don't you join me tomorrow after your shift, and we'll find time to have a few drinks or something?"

Patience's mood changed instantly.

"No need to wait for my shift to end. My rotation finishes tonight. I've got the next three days off!"

An uncharitable remark bloomed into life in my head though mercifully it stayed there and did not make it past my lips. Patience is a very good friend of mine, but she is a little bit of a handful at times. I was going to London to investigate a series of strange murders. Having Patience tag along was not going to do me any favours.

The Blue Moon Office.
Tuesday, October 17th
O823hrs

I COMPLETED MY EARLY morning run, pushing myself for the last mile or so because I felt I ought to. Alone in my apartment last night and a little bored, I guess, I'd elected to open a bottle of wine and proceeded to drink half of it with a pizza chaser.

I awoke feeling heavy and guilty which was why I was now out thrashing myself around the streets of Maidstone.

Ten minutes in the shower and some fresh fruit with yoghurt washed down by a pint of water left me feeling more in balance with my health and well-being. Dressed for the day and ready to go, my first port of call was the office in Rochester High Street, my steed to take me there a vintage Lotus Esprit.

The car was a gift from Tempest which he in turn got as a reward, quite ironically, from yet another author when he solved a mystery involving the writer's children and their attempt to defraud him out of his house. It purred and hummed in a delicious way, urging me to drive it fast around the country lanes I chose as my route rather than join the queues on the motorway.

My decision to go to the office was largely based on my desire to park the car without paying for car parking. Rochester train station is less than two hundred yards from the office front door, but I also wanted to collect a few things before I set off.

On the passenger seat was a bag, packed and ready for an overnight stay in the capital. Living out of a hotel for a few nights did not enthral me, however it was at least a three hour round trip to get in and out via train and tube, plus our cases regularly demand we work late into the night, by which time the tubes have stopped running.

As I often find, Jane was already at work; the third detective in the business is an early riser. I parked next to her car and let myself in through the back door, calling out to announce my presence as I came into the office proper from the back corridor.

"Morning."

I caught Jane and her boyfriend Jan kissing by the front door. Jan was just on his way out, the tall police officer already in his uniform and ready to start his shift. He blushed slightly upon seeing me, pecked Jane on her cheek, shot me a wave, and let himself out.

"Morning," Jane returned my salutation. "Coffee?" she asked, already making her way towards the expensive machine located in the client waiting area.

I debated her question for only a second before deciding that a hit of caffeine would do me no harm. I had been planning to pick up a to-go mug on my way to the station anyway, but reminding myself that Tempest only bought the best coffee for our machine, I went to fetch a disposable travel mug from my office.

On my way I called over my shoulder, "Sure. Thanks."

Jane was staying at the office today, holding down the fort to some extent, though we had a lady to work reception during office hours. Jane was also working a case of her own and deep into the research element of it, I knew from our discussion the previous evening.

Interrupting the quiet of our office, the sound of my phone ringing in my handbag caused me to pause and dig around for it. I usually slot it into a little pouch specifically designed to hold one's mobile communication device, however I must have missed when I was putting it in this morning because it had come to rest beneath a packet of tissues and a lint-covered Jelly Baby that must have escaped from the packet I'd been eating a few days ago.

A quick check of the screen revealed the caller to be my current client, the widow of Simon Slater, Mrs Genevieve Slater.

"Mrs Slater, good morning." I almost asked what she was calling for, but stopped talking so that she could tell me instead.

"Amanda, I think you can call me Genevieve. I see no reason for us to stand on formalities. I'm just checking to see what time you expect to get here today. I have an unavoidable meeting this morning." Genevieve was a success in her own right, following up a modelling career by starting a makeup brand that was small, but nevertheless global.

I turned my left wrist over to check the time. I had plenty of it, but not if I dawdled. The train station was only a few minutes' walk away and the trains could be relied upon to run on time. It gave me twelve minutes to get there, and I still needed to collect a few items before I set off.

"My train into London is due to arrive at Charing Cross at four minutes after ten. Am I coming to your house?"

"To my house would be best, Amanda. I would like to meet in private first. You suggested yesterday that Tempest might not be available to make this initial meeting?"

Much like the idiot vampire wannabe last night, Genevieve wanted Tempest. It was just one of those little things that would register as an annoyance if I were to allow myself to spend much time thinking about it. Everyone wanted Tempest. He was the name that people knew. I had been in the headlines too, but for some reason 'Amanda Harper' didn't stick in peoples' heads.

I kept the sigh from my voice when I said, "That is correct. However, I expect that he will join me before the end of the day. Will you be there when I arrive in London or is this going to clash with your meeting?"

Pressing the speaker button so I would hear her reply, I placed the phone on my desk and opened the cupboard in the corner. In the early days of the business, Tempest had willingly embraced the beliefs of his clients and invested in a number of ... shall we say 'props'.

He still had them - an odd selection of crucifixes, vials of holy water, editions of the Holy Bible which had been consecrated by an Archbishop. There was more - wolfsbane in powdered form, jars of salt, and other such silly paraphernalia his clients expected a paranormal investigator to carry.

Not that he had ever bought into any of it. Tempest was thoroughly resolute in his stance that the supernatural was nothing more than a lot of imagined nonsense, and as his investigations business grew, and with it his confidence, he shelved the silly 'props' in favour of more technological equipment.

Listening devices, cameras, two-way radios, motion detectors, and nonlethal weapons were just some of the items I placed into a backpack ready for whatever the case in London had to throw at us.

All the while I was continuing to converse with Genevieve Slater. Her meeting was going to run right through the morning and into the early afternoon she suspected.

That my client was not going to be available for several hours did little to change my day. If anything, it freed me up to get on with things. I had crime scenes to check out, evidence to review, and a whole bunch of interested parties to talk to.

Genevieve agreed to call me when her meeting ended, and since we both had to get going, we ended the call. I hooked the backpack onto my shoulder, looped the shoulder strap of my handbag over my neck, extended the handle of my small suitcase and started wheeling it toward the door.

"You still want that coffee?" Jane asked, nodding her head toward a mug set on the low table by the coffee machine.

The conversation with Genevieve had eaten up more time than I'd anticipated. If I didn't hustle now, I was going to miss the train and be forced to wait thirty minutes for the next one. Despite that, I ran back to my office, snagged the disposable coffee mug, and dumped the drink Jane had made me into it. It would instantly be drinking temperature as it gave up some of its retained heat to the cardboard container, but that was a good thing, not bad.

I chugged a mouthful with a wave as I ran out the door.

Kimble Publishing.
Tuesday, October 17th
0917hrs

I TIMED MY TRAIN journey into London to miss the glut of passengers on the daily work commute and thus found a seat easily in the partially filled carriage I selected. With more than an hour to kill, I opened my laptop and started going over my notes.

There had been four very recent murders, each of them mimicking the style of a murder as described in one of Simon Slater's horror novels. The first death occurred on September 12th, when Francis Niedermeyer was injected with a lethal dose of a household cleaning product. The report I had read claimed that Mr Niedermeyer fought back - his house in rural Essex showed obvious signs of a struggle which I assumed to mean upturned furniture and spilled ornaments or the like. However, the report went on to suggest that it was no more than a handful of seconds before he lost consciousness.

Niedermeyer was then arranged, the scene taken directly from *Choose Your Parents Wisely*, another of Simon Slater's horror novels. Mr Niedermeyer had acted as translator for the author's works, introducing them to the German market where they sold in great volume. However, Simon omitted to read the small print in the contract and due to German laws regarding translations, he found the bulk of the profit went to his translator.

When Simon Slater unpublished the German language books, Niedermeyer sued and won. The books were still being published and Niedermeyer was still claiming royalties from them. The suggestion that Simon was taking revenge from beyond the grave sounded viable in Niedermeyer's case.

Next it was a literary agent called Amy Hildestrand who met her end. She was discovered at home by her husband. The cause of death was a single blow to her skull with a blunt instrument - probably a hammer - but she was then stripped naked and arranged on her bed amid hundreds of sunflowers.

The death came from Simon Slater's most recent novel, *Van Gough Sunsets*, in which his central character, a private detective by the name *Quentin Quinn*, had to track and catch the victim's killer. I knew this from newspaper clippings I had read online and now questioned whether I ought to be reading Simon Slater's books. Unfortunately, the man has forty-three published works, every last one of them dark horror novels which is really not my cup of tea.

Mrs Hildestrand had no known connection to Simon Slater. She died on October 1st, leaving behind two children.

The third victim followed on October 13th. Samuel Blake was another literary agent. Naturally I assumed Simon must have been turned down by him at some point in the past, but it seemed I was wrong. The police had gone to his employers asking the same thing only to be assured Samuel Blake had never had any interaction with the famous horror novelist. Just like Amy Hildestrand, there appeared to be no connection.

In fact, there was nothing to link the victims at all except the manner in which they were killed and staged. Samuel Blake was ... well, let's just say he died horribly and yet again it came directly from one of Simon's books.

The fourth victim, the most recent one, occurred just twenty-four hours later on October 14th.

Leslie Ashe, like the three previous victims, was found dead in his home. In his case, because he was divorced and lived alone, it was his cleaner who found him. In a scene lifted directly from the book that made Simon Slater's career and ended Leslie's relationship with the author, the third victim was found dismembered inside a suitcase by the front door.

Leslie had been Simon Slater's original cover artist, producing the artwork for his first ten books. The struggling author, without the funds to pay for original artwork, had convinced a work colleague to help him. Leslie, involved in graphic design for the same marketing firm who employed Simon, thought he was doing a chap a favour, and secured conceptual payment by agreeing to a share of any profit from the books.

According to Genevieve, that amounted to a sum total of absolutely nothing until book nine was published. *In the Woods*, despite being the ninth novel Simon Slater published, was his breakout story and the one that allowed him to quit his job.

Suddenly the books were making quite a lot of money. Not just book nine, the one that started it all, but the previous eight too, as voracious readers finishing *In the Woods* went looking for something else by the same author.

The artwork for book ten was already completed, but soured by having to give unrealistic sums to Leslie Ashe for the cover artwork he'd produced, Simon Slater soon found someone new. It sparked an argument between Leslie and Simon which had never been resolved and Leslie was still receiving royalty cheques, the sum he had now been paid for his artwork amounting to more than one hundred thousand pounds.

Genevieve Slater contacted the Blue Moon Investigations Agency within hours of the fourth victim being announced. The previous deaths, while macabre, had not set off alarm bells. The police approached her after two persons reported seeing her husband in the vicinity of Amy Hildestrand's house. Not knowing the woman, Genevieve thought nothing of it.

That stance changed when Leslie Ashe's body was found.

The police had been at her house the previous day, asking Genevieve about Simon because he had once again been spotted near to the murder scene and was then captured by a CCTV camera as he passed a small parade of businesses. Not having any idea who Samuel

Blake was – she'd never heard of him and certainly couldn't attest to any connection between him and her late husband – she once again dismissed the notion.

Leslie Ashe's death changed her mind. According to my client, her husband hated Leslie more than anyone else on the planet. Leslie laughed in Simon's face when he tried to wriggle out of their deal on the cover art. Leslie still held the handwritten note the two signed so many years ago and Simon had just lost an expensive court case to Francis Niedermeyer. Had that not been the case, Simon Slater probably would have taken his old cover artist to court and won.

Genevieve called the Blue Moon office within hours of learning about Leslie's death and had been hiding in her house ever since.

It was all quite chilling and awful, and there was no denying the obvious link between the four victims. They were linked by the manner of their murders, but that couldn't be all. The four had to have something else in common. No one, including my client, appeared to have any idea what that was.

Here's the thing though; I suspected she was lying. Simon Slater had been seen alive and walking around wearing the same clothes he'd picked out for the author photograph in his books. Such things could be faked, of course, but how likely was it when we already knew he had reason to want to harm half the victims?

If I dug a little, would I discover he hated the other victims too? I would not be surprised if I did. His body was identified by his wife, who also found him. Was it really his body in the grave? Or had she faked his death?

Keeping an open mind, and accepting that Simon Slater is indeed dead, then did we have four victims or five? The first to die in a re-enactment of his books was the author himself. There was a year between his death and the current series of murders, so was it the same killer or not?

The police had investigated at the time – I had a vague memory of seeing the news reports on my television, but the killer was yet to be brought to justice. What did that mean for my current investigation?

I was still thinking about it when the train pulled into Charing Cross. As it always does, the train had gradually filled as we got closer and closer to the capital, so it was standing room only by the time we arrived, and I had to wait for the people around me to disembark before I could collect my suitcase and backpack from the storage compartment above my head.

Struggling a little with the cumbersome exit from the train, carrying my luggage, and turning down a kind offer of help from a man already carrying his own things, I took a moment to rearrange my items before setting off.

Everyone always seems to be in such a hurry in London, and I was pleased to actively resist the need to hurry along at their pace. I didn't come into the big city very often, even though it wasn't all that far to come. So far as I could see, the only reason to come here was to visit theatre land or possibly the museums.

Tempest had treated me quite recently to an evening at a West End musical. It had been utterly wonderful, my boyfriend showing his class by ordering Bollinger to be waiting for us during the intermission.

It is the little things people do that make a difference.

Once through the turnstile, I crossed the station to find the entrance to the underground. It's not far from Charing Cross to Victoria, which is a stone's throw from where I was heading, and it added only a few minutes to my journey.

I arrived at my first destination at just after ten thirty. Staring up at the front façade of Kimble Publishing, the publishing house who made Simon Slater a household name, I wondered what I would find inside.

Unexpectedly, when I pushed and then pulled the door to get inside, I found that it was locked. To my right I found a panel with a button and a little grill covering a speaker. I pressed the button, a small warbling buzzer noise echoing out from the device until I removed my thumb.

A man's voice filled the air a moment later.

"Kimble Publishing." The voice was professional and the tone inviting, yet it was also too curt to be called polite.

"Amanda Harper to see Indigo Rabner."

"Do you have an appointment?" the same curt voice asked.

"I am expected. I'm investigating the recent murders linked to Simon Slater."

There was a brief pause that made me wonder if he was about to deny me access or repeat his question about whether I had an appointment. However, a buzzer sounded, this one coming from the door lock. This time when I pulled it, the door opened.

The entrance led immediately to a reception area where the same man I'd been speaking to was now talking to someone on the phone through a headset. He placed a hand over the mouthpiece to stop his voice from reaching the caller, but mouthed the words anyway.

He wanted me to sign in, twisting a touchpad mounted on the counter so it faced me. I did as requested, remaining silent as I waited for the receptionist to finish his call. I looked around at the décor dominating the room.

It was a little scary.

The firm represented Simon Slater, that much I knew, but the horror genre had to be something they specialised in because ugly, unpleasant images filled every wall. Most were book covers, the artwork intended to tell the prospective reader precisely what they were going to find inside each book. Some, though, were film posters, where more successful works had made it onto the big screen. Or the small screen, I noted, seeing a line-up of actors I recognised from a TV series I'd elected to avoid.

Expecting the receptionist would direct me to where I needed to go, I didn't need to wait for his call to end because a door opened to my right and a woman in her sixties strode out.

"Amanda Harper?" she asked, striding confidently forward. "I'm Indigo Rabner."

I'm not sure why, but I had expected Indigo to be a man. The woman was clearly a firecracker, and this should have come as no surprise to me since she was the founding member and head of a publishing house in London.

I shook her hand, noting that her grip was strong, and she held my hand for several seconds before letting go. In contrast to all the horror around me, Indigo, a tall, thin, Caucasian woman with jet black hair dyed to eliminate the grey, was dressed for tea at the palace. Bedecked in an elegant, fitted dress, matching heels and Chanel jacket, she was the epitome of English suave and had the figure to carry it off. She was sweet and would morph into becoming one of those delightful old ladies in another decade or so.

I matched her smile with my own. "Good morning. Thank you for agreeing to meet with me."

"Oh, think nothing of it. I'm rather glad Genevieve elected to hire you, truth be told. Please, come through. We'll talk in my office. Can I have someone bring you a coffee?"

Coffee sounded good.

She paused to place her request for coffee with a tall woman as we made our way through an open plan office. I looked about, smiling engagingly because why would I do anything else. The faces in the room failed to return it.

I was being watched by almost everyone, their faces a sea of neutral expressions impossible to read.

Standing next to me, the woman Indigo stopped to address on the way in barked a single word that made me jump.

"Lucas!" When the voice of a young man replied, she barked, "Two coffees!" Turning her head to look my way she asked, "How do you take yours?"

A flustered looking man in his early twenties was already rising from his chair, a frustrated or perhaps terrified expression dominating his features.

"Oh, however it comes, thank you," I managed to reply, trying not to catch the eye of the man being addressed as a minion. It had always been one of my biggest bugbears, having my work interrupted to fetch beverages for someone else's guest when it was no effort at all for them to do it themselves. Perhaps I missed the point, but it always seemed as though people saw promotion as an opportunity to abuse those they were employed to manage.

Lucas mumbled something I didn't catch, and Indigo didn't care about. When she started walking again and I followed, the heads in the office all tracked my passage, no one blinking, no one talking.

It was unnerving and in complete contrast to the lovely woman now waiting for me to take a seat in her office. She closed the door behind me, shutting out the strange looks I was getting. If Indigo noticed them, she was playing it cool.

I found a corner just inside her office where I placed my suitcase and the backpack containing the electronic paraphernalia. It felt good to get it off my shoulders, but really it was an excuse to kill a few seconds while I looked around the room. Much like the reception area, the walls of Indigo's office were decorated with horrific images.

She caught me looking.

"Admiring the artwork?" she asked with an amused twinkle.

Unable to stop myself, I asked the question at the front of the queue, "Doesn't this give you nightmares?" I was only going to be exposed to it for a very short period and was already questioning whether it might keep me awake tonight. I could not imagine spending my days surrounded by such blood thirsty, sinister, and terrifying images.

Indigo chose to laugh. "I hardly even notice it, but honestly, I think there's real beauty in all these pieces of art."

My eyes bugged out of my head, and it's not so much that I wanted to argue, but I felt a need to challenge her. Walking a few paces across the room I lifted my right arm to point at one picture in particular.

"Even this one?" I asked, drawing her attention to what was clearly an eviscerated body being chewed on by rodents.

The head of the publishing firm gave me a one shoulder shrug.

"This is how I've made my living. By specialising in a single genre, we've become *the* name in the horror industry. Now, I'm sure you didn't come here to talk to me about artwork."

She was ready to get down to business and that suited me just fine, but before we could there was a knock at the door and Lucas was coming through it.

Indigo sighed in an annoyed manner. "How many times have I told you to use a tray, Lucas? No one wants your fingerprints all over the mugs, and look - you are spilling it on the carpet."

Lucas, his cheeks reddening, looked down at the floor guiltily where there were indeed a few spilled drops of coffee, and began to turn back towards the door.

"Now where are you going?" Indigo demanded.

Mumbling, Lucas replied, "To start again?"

Coming around the room to take the mugs from him, Indigo snapped, "Oh, just give them here."

I guess there had to be some history behind her impatience and terse tone and I questioned why it was that Lucas continued to put up with it. I knew I wouldn't. There are too many other places a person can work to suffer through the indignity of workplace bullying if that is what I was seeing.

Holding my tongue, for it would get me nowhere to say what was on my mind, I made a point of thanking Lucas for the coffee when Indigo handed it to me. I got an almost imperceptible dip of his head in thanks as he ducked back out the door.

Before the door had even shut, Indigo asked, "Now, where were we?"

My purpose for interviewing Indigo was to get a different side of the Simon Slater story. I could read what was online and in the papers, and I already had Genevieve's version, yet it was Indigo and Kimble publishing who had made Simon Slater into the household name he became.

I started with a few easy questions, covering some detail I already knew about Simon and his success. My coffee was hot when I tried to take a sip, using the motion as a pause between questions because I was heading into the meatier stuff.

"Would you say you knew Simon well?" I asked, gathering my notepad and pen again.

Indigo was holding her own coffee mug with both hands.

"Oh, yes. We were much more than just author and publisher. Simon and I were very good friends."

This was news to me, and it prompted more questions I hadn't thought to ask until now.

"How would you describe his relationship with Genevieve?"

Indigo pressed her lips together, looking at a patch on the wall to my left as she thought about how to reply.

"I will say I was surprised when he chose to marry her."

"Why is that?"

Indigo didn't have to think about her answer this time. "They have … had so little in common. No shared interests at all. I know Simon believed she would come around, but we had our reservations."

"I'm sorry, you said *our* reservations?"

"Silly me," Indigo took a sip of coffee. "I simply meant to indicate the circle of friends he and I shared." She replied casually and without needing to think about her answer. Her choice of words had seemed odd, but she gave no reason to make me believe there was anything more to it.

I probed her further on the subject of Simon and his wife, but had to conclude Indigo simply didn't like Genevieve. She wasn't going to say it out loud and if there was anything in their past, she refused to divulge what it was.

I asked about the victims and about whether Simon had any financial difficulties or any other problems that he'd been worrying about in the period before his death. I was still angling to find out if he was still alive. I held back from asking the question directly – it was too early to play my hand and I wasn't holding the winning cards yet. Had he faked his death? Would Indigo know if he had?

Indigo carried on answering my questions, never once holding back from giving me a helpful answer. She was lovely to spend time with and that made the episode with Lucas seem even more bizarre.

I was beginning to run out of questions, preliminary ones at least and was thinking about what to do and where to go next when the door to Indigo's office burst inward.

Dire Warning.
Tuesday, October 17th
1058hrs

M Y HEAD WHIPPED AROUND automatically to find the same woman Indigo stopped to talk to earlier hanging through the doorway. In her mid-thirties and quite plump around the waist, her face was flushed, and her eyes were wide as saucers.

"Kirsty, whatever is it?" demanded Indigo, her tone suggesting she was keeping her anger at the intrusion in check.

"It's Daniel!" she blurted. "He's dead!"

No one said anything for a second, but before I could ask the obvious question and find out who we were talking about, Indigo jumped to her feet. Her hands were gripping each side of her head, her knuckles turning white as the colour drained from her face.

"But we've got a meeting this afternoon," she pointed out as if that would make any difference to his condition.

Calmly, I drew Kirsty's attention my way.

"How did he die?" It was a simple question and one which I expected her to answer without feeling the need to question who I was.

Her eyes flicked across from Indigo's to meet mine and in a grave voice she said, "Dead Ringer."

Indigo gasped, and I almost questioned what the woman's reply was supposed to mean when I realised she had just named the title of yet another of Simon Slater's novels. She could have said he was murdered, or he was involved in an accident or anything else, but instead she misinterpreted my question and in so doing informed me that we had yet another victim.

"Who is Daniel?" I shot the question at Indigo. "Is he connected to Simon Slater?"

Indigo just stared at me, her mouth hanging open while her hands still clawed at the sides of her head.

The answer came from Kirsty. "Daniel McCormack. He is ... was Simon's original literary agent."

"Kirsty." Indigo said the word with little inflection, but it sounded like a warning, nevertheless. When I turned around to face her, her hands were coming back to her sides and she was looking more composed, if still a little shaken. "I'm sorry, Miss Harper, I will help you as far as it is possible to do so, but the success of my business depends on keeping the internal workings of our operation secret from our competitors. I will share them with no one."

I had a feeling the reason she'd just given me wasn't entirely truthful. Or possibly that it was truthful but wasn't the real reason she didn't want me to know more about Daniel McCormack.

I got to my feet and started jamming things back into my handbag. There was a fresh crime scene and that had to take priority.

"Where?" I demanded. "Where did Daniel McCormack die?" I was heading for the office door, forcing the woman there to back out of it.

Indigo's voice rang out before the woman could answer me.

"Where are you going, Amanda?"

I spun around in the doorway. "I'm sorry, Indigo. This is fresh evidence. It must take priority. We can pick up again later today if you can fit me into your schedule." That she was not pleased was obvious from the expression on her face. It wasn't quite a glare, but was certainly more than a frown.

Kirsty was hovering just outside Indigo's office where I found a sea of startled faces all looking her way. Her colleagues in the office had all heard her announcement and it was clear a number of them knew Daniel.

They were talking now at least, the earlier silence replaced by whispered mutterings and worried looks. I swear I heard someone say, "How could this happen to us?" It was followed by a worried gasp of, "Has he forsaken us?" It sounded like a religious question and nothing to do with the case in question.

Again, I pressed Kirsty for an answer, softening my voice so that I was imploring her to help me. "Where was he when he was killed, Kirsty? I need to know so that I can get to the bottom of what is happening here."

Indigo came to the door of her office and stopped just a couple of feet from me.

"You are not going to find the answers you are looking for, Miss Harper. Don't dig too deeply into Simon Slater's death or his life. To do so could invoke forces you cannot hope to survive."

Certain I had heard her correctly, but bewildered by her choice of words, a smile split my face. Was she joking? Professional businesswoman one moment, she now sounded like a character from one of the company's horror novels.

"Forces? Are we talking demons or ghosts?" I made a joke of it, but I was the only one who found it amusing. Looking around the office, every face was aimed at me, and no one was smiling.

With a nod of my head, I indicated my suitcase and backpack. "I'll be needing my things," I remarked, my eyes never leaving Indigo's. What had been the benign atmosphere of a publishing firm's offices, now felt like a hostile environment and I wanted to leave. Taking a page from Tempest, I was going to take my sweet time about it. They were attempting to intimidate me, and I wasn't going to show how nervous they were making me feel.

"Stay away from this case," Indigo warned once again. "For your own good."

Once I had my backpack over my shoulders and my suitcase ready to go, I met her with a level gaze. She had moved to stand next to Kirsty so that upon rejoining them in the open plan office I could see everyone.

I lifted my eyes and addressed them all.

"Investigating the weird and wonderful is what my firm does on a daily basis. Whatever is going on here will be discovered. If any of you wish to contact me for a confidential talk you can find me very easily via the internet." Speech delivered, I lowered my eyes to meet Indigo's once more. I hadn't known what to expect when I came here, but this wasn't it.

Was Indigo involved somehow? She seemed shocked by the news about Daniel McCormack, the colour genuinely draining from her face upon hearing Kirsty's outburst. Yet there was clearly *something* going on and I couldn't shift the feeling that everyone in the office was in on it.

Walking, even though I felt like running, I made my way back to reception, paused to sign myself out again on the electronic pad, and let myself out.

Only when I was a hundred yards away did I finally breathe a sigh of relief.

Evening Sorted. Tuesday, October 17th 1111hrs

S TOPPING IN A FRANCHISE coffee shop just along the road, I let my pulse rate return to normal and ordered myself a tall Americano - I had barely touched the one that Lucas brought me.

While the barista made up my drink, I moved to one side to make a phone call.

"Yo, skinny white girl!" the voice of Patience Woods blasted into my ear drum. "I'm just packing a bag, but I cannot decide between outfits. What sort of clubs are we going to tonight?"

"Um, I wasn't planning on going to any clubs tonight, Patience. I thought maybe we'd just get a couple of drinks and have a catch up."

"Oh, come on, Amanda," she whined. "Let your hair down for once. I want to get out on the town and get scarily drunk with a whole load of guys whose names I won't even remember and have to play potluck with all the phone numbers I've collected."

That sounded like precisely the sort of evening Patience would go for, but even in my wilder days I was never one for staying out till the small hours of the morning or drinking more than was sensible.

Doing my best to derail her train of thought without stomping all over her plans, I brought up the subject for which I had called her.

"There's been another murder, but I don't know where it is. Can you make a couple of calls?"

It was obvious Patience was doing stuff in the background because her reply when it came did not answer my question and had that distracted tone to it.

"I think maybe I'll just pack everything," she murmured to herself.

"Patience." I tried to break through her wardrobe concerns.

"Sorry. Yeah, I heard you. Is it still that case with the author you were telling me about?"

"Yup. Simon Slater's literary agent was found this morning ..."

"Simon Slater!" Patience blurted. "You never said the author in question was Simon Slater. I love that guy's books."

I frowned, questioning whether I had said his name last night or not when she asked me about my case in London. I guess I couldn't have because she would have reacted this way then had I done so. Equally startling though was that Patience had heard of him.

"I didn't know you read horror books," I remarked, though truthfully I was thinking I didn't know Patience read full stop.

"Ooh, yeah, I love me some gory horror."

This was news too. In my opinion, Patience is a bit of a scaredy cat. If she thinks there's something supernatural happening, she runs away, even though I am generally there assuring her that there is nothing to be scared of.

It was something we could discuss later. Right now, I needed her to find out where it was that I needed to go.

"Okay, Patience, can you find out where the crime scene is for me, please? I want to head over there now while it's still fresh."

I was still drinking my coffee when she phoned me back. One thing with being a sexually liberated woman is that Patience has a lot of male colleagues who feel inclined to do her a favour.

"He has a place by Clapham Common. I'm sending you the address now." My phone beeped as it received a message, and I took it away from my ear to glance at the screen. "I called Darius," Patience revealed.

"Which one is that again?" I asked, taking an interest even though I wasn't interested and couldn't hope to keep up with her love life.

"You've never met him," Patience replied dismissively. "It's not important. What is important though is that we hooked up a couple of years ago and I haven't seen him since. He's single and he looks like someone dipped a big bar of sex into some molten chocolate."

As descriptions go, it did nothing to provide me with an image of the man in question, yet was nevertheless sufficiently graphic to know what kind of man we were talking about.

"Also," Patience continued, "Someone is killing people in the style of Simon Slater's books!" she expressed her astonishment.

"Yes, I know. It's all quite macabre."

"You're telling me! This Daniel McCormack guy was sewn to the floor and stabbed through the heart."

"Sewn to the floor?" My stomach tightened a little.

"Damn skippy. And I don't mean his clothing was."

My stomach tightened a little more. I don't think of myself as squeamish, but there are limits to what I want to see or even hear about.

"Listen, I'm on my way," she continued. "I'm going out with Darius tonight, but he's going to get us both into the crime scene. He said it's still fresh; they've taken the body away, but the crime scene crews are still there looking for evidence."

Patience had really come through for me, and the news that she had a date tonight was a blessing since it let me off the hook.

"Don't worry," she added. "I got him to invite his brother, so you won't feel all left out and uncomfortable."

"What! Patience, have you forgotten that I've been dating Tempest for more than a year?" This was so typical of her.

"It's just a double date, Amanda. You don't have to do ... anything with him. It's not a big deal." she changed her tone from whining to upbeat when she added, "Come on, I need some fun. Patience is getting older and trying very hard not to get wiser." That she made a joke out of her refusal to date a man for more than a few days was also typical. I could continue to resist, but I knew from experience that she was going to start begging soon.

I accepted my fate and agreed to be waiting for her when the tube spat her out at Clapham Common. With that call ended, I placed one to Jane and prayed she'd had time to do a little research.

"Oh, I was just about to call you," Jane said by way of answering my call. "How's the case going?"

I puffed out my cheeks. "Too early to tell. I met the dead author's publishers, and they walk a line between scary and crazy. I'm not suggesting they have anything to do with the murders, I can't see why they would, but the boss lady warned me to stop looking into Simon's death and said I might invoke dark forces. Something like that anyway."

"Right well, you'll find this interesting then. They are one of the recipients of Simon Slater's royalties. The bulk goes to his wife Genevieve, and there are a couple of others. Here's the kicker though, two of them are among the murder victims."

"Leslie Ashe and Francis Niedermeyer," I recalled the names from my own research.

Jane hadn't been expecting me to know. "Yeah, that's right. Then there's one more; a chap called Daniel McCormack." I guess she heard me gasp because she asked, "Everything all right?"

I exhaled slowly. "Yup," I managed to reply. "Daniel McCormack's body has just been found. The information came in when I was in the publishing firm's office. They seemed shocked by the news."

"Well, they stood to gain, just like Mrs Slater. The royalties are now being divided between just the two parties by the look of it and the sales of Simon Slater's books are going through the roof from all the media attention."

Jane had done a great job as always, but the information came too late for Daniel McCormack. If I'd started the case sooner, would I have been able to save him? I cursed my luck that there were no other shareholders to investigate, for that might have allowed me to anticipate where the killer would strike next. Was this about royalties though? I already knew Amy Hildestrand and Samuel Blake didn't fit that profile.

It was all so confusing, but with more than an hour to spare, I was going to see if I couldn't catch up with Mrs Slater. She was someone who gained from the recent deaths – some of them, at least. Maybe she had something to hide.

Returned from the Grave. Tuesday, October 17th 1128hrs

"**O**H, MY GOD! OH, my God! Oh, my God!" I had wondered how Genevieve would take the news of yet another murder related to her husband and discovered the answer was that she chose to freak out. "No, no, no, no, no, no, no. This can't be happening. This can't be happening. I don't believe this."

I interrupted her to ask, "Genevieve where are you now? I've just left the offices of Kimble Publishing and I'm on my way to Daniel's house to see what information I can glean there. However, I really think we should meet as soon as possible."

"My meeting finished twenty minutes ago, I'm on my way home. Can you meet me there?" She sounded desperate now.

I already had her address, and this was the first time I could remember starting a case without having first met the client. Her house near Kensington was only a short hop on the London Underground from where I was, and I was already out of the coffee shop and on my way to the nearest tube station when we ended our call.

In previous conversations with the dead author's wife, I formed the impression that she was being guarded about what she told me. This was nothing unusual, of course. In fact, I'd go so far as to say it's quite rare when a client is wholly truthful with me. Tempest and I talk about this all the time - how we are forced to wade through the lies and the half-truths only to uncover the thing our clients wanted to remain hidden anyway. It ends up costing them twice as much, because it takes us far longer to solve their cases.

Given that there were now five murders associated with Simon Slater, and that he himself was murdered - I still suspected it to be the same person behind all six deaths or to discover Simon Slater was still alive - I was going to take a hard line with my client.

I made my way underground, returning to the surface and daylight just twelve minutes later. Outside the tube station I flagged down a cab and gave him the address I wanted. Typically, the cabbie, a rather rough looking man with a flat cap and a three-day stubble, launched into a seemingly never-ending monologue about what he'd been watching on television recently before opting to update me on West Ham United's recent run of successes.

Mercifully, it was only a four-minute drive, the meter nevertheless scoring a surprising number by the time we arrived.

Security at the entrance to Genevieve's gated street refused to let the taxi through, so I had to walk from there. It wasn't far and Genevieve had been watching for me, the front door of her elegant Georgian house opening before I could get to it. I knew what she looked like from photographs I'd found, but in the flesh the former model ... well, let's just say the pictures didn't do her justice.

She was the kind of woman other women want to hate. Blessed with statuesque curves and high cheek bones, Genevieve Slater might be in her early fifties, but she was fighting the effects of ageing better than most. Tall at five feet and ten inches, and wearing four-inch heels having come from a meeting where she undoubtedly enjoyed being taller than half the men in the room, she was dressed in bleached jeans, a high fashion label t-shirt that probably cost a month's rent, and a fitted, three-quarter length jacket. Her multi-tonal brunette hair – not a trace of grey in sight – fell to the middle of her back and could have been straight from the salon.

"Amanda?" she asked, confirming that was who she was looking at. Her voice betrayed the hope she felt that I was here to help with her situation.

With my right hand I selected a business card from my pocket and swapping it into my left I extended my right hand to shake hers.

"Yes. I'm glad we can finally meet. Shall we get down to business?" Handing her my business card, I used my left arm to guide her back into the house. As a cop I'd learned to forego small talk and chit chat unless they were necessary which, in this case, they were not. I was not here to get to know my client, merely to service her needs and solve her case.

Before I had even made it over the threshold, I was hitting her with my first question. There was one right at the top of the list that had demanded an answer ever since she first contacted the firm, yet I had held it in reserve because I wanted to see how she reacted when I asked it.

"Genevieve, you were clear when we first spoke that you believe your husband was murdered and that this is not the same killer now. Please expand on why that is."

The directness of my approach caught her off guard, her expression changing to one of mild surprise accented by a slight reddening of her cheeks.

Had she been making assumptions which she would now withdraw?

I watched her face, waiting for her to give an answer. However, none came, at least not immediately. Instead, it looked as if her gears were turning. My question had placed her on the spot, and I got the impression she was scrambling to find an answer.

After a pregnant pause that stretched out for several seconds, Genevieve finally recovered her wits to say, "I don't think it can be. You are going to ask me why, so please allow me to explain. You are aware, of course, of the rumours suggesting my husband is behind the latest spree of deaths."

I said nothing, allowing her to talk now that her words were flowing, but dipped my head in a nod that showed I agreed with her statement.

She continued, "It cannot be the same killer, Amanda, because the person doing the killings now is my husband. I don't know who killed him, but I believe he has returned from the dead and is claiming vengeance on all those who ever did him any wrong."

Okay, so I had sort of expected this. Well, maybe not this exactly, but something along these lines. The very nature of our business dictates we meet a lot of people who have convinced themselves a relative or loved one has returned from the grave. It is not, however, all that common for the undead to then go on a murderous rampage.

"You believe Simon has returned from the dead. You are the one who found him, are you not?" I already knew the answer to this question and posed it only so I could give myself a little more time to think while she was talking.

A tear formed in the corner of Genevieve's left eye, and she turned away, hiding her face as she dabbed at it. Momentarily unable to speak, she nodded her head and took a moment to gather herself.

"Yes," she mumbled. "That was almost exactly a year ago."

I levelled a question at her which I felt certain she must have been asked many times already.

"Who do you think killed Simon?"

Genevieve's mouth moved as responses formed on her lips but were dismissed before they were given air, and she shrugged one shoulder as if to suggest that she couldn't possibly guess.

Nevertheless, she said, "One of his fans probably. They were most upset with him when he killed off one of his biggest characters. That book was published six months before he died, but the hate mail at the time was getting worse and more frequent if anything. Simon said there was no such thing as bad publicity. He loved that everyone was talking about the controversy of his books. He was killed ..." she lost her voice again at this point, and I reached out a hand to touch her arm in comfort.

We were talking about how her husband had been murdered and it was a grisly affair I had no need for her to recall in detail. Yes, I had it in my head that she could very well have helped her husband fake his own death, but now that I was standing in Genevieve's house, accusing her did not feel right. I parked the notion. For now.

Simon Slater had made his fortune writing gruesome horror novels. The most famous series was about the rise of Satan and his predicted dominion over earth. Though I had not read the controversial book to which Genevieve had just made reference, I knew through online searches that his readers were expecting one thing and were given something completely different when his lead character - the leader of the church of the devil - was murdered by the soldiers of Christianity.

Seeing Genevieve's obvious distress, I suggested tea, and a few minutes later, with a steaming mug set in front of each of us, we were settled on bar stools in her kitchen.

When I thought she had sufficiently recovered, I began to probe her once again about the case.

"Genevieve, a few minutes ago you said Simon had come back from the dead to claim revenge on those who did him wrong in life. What was it that he and Daniel McCormack fell out over?"

"I don't know that they did. It was Daniel who negotiated to get Simon his big break, and they were good friends until the end. So far as I know. I realise that contradicts what I said earlier."

"Yes, it does," I agreed.

"Sorry," she apologised in a voice that was barely more than a whisper. "I know he hated at least two of them. The truth is I just didn't know my husband as well as I thought I did. I doubt I'm the first wife in history to say that."

I had no doubt she was right, but I asked, "What makes you say that?"

"Well, the other victims," she said. "I don't know Amy Hildestrand or Samuel Blake. Maybe Simon knew them, but whatever the connection is, he kept it from me. He knew Daniel for sure, though I have no idea why he would want to kill him."

I felt a natural inclination to assure my client that her husband was not back from the dead, but had learned in my early cases arguing against a person's deep-rooted beliefs, however crazy they may seem, was generally counterproductive.

Instead, I chose to confirm what it was that Mrs Slater wanted me to achieve.

In response I got a look much akin to what I might have expected if I'd asked her to remove one of her arms and hand it to me.

"Banish him back to hell. Isn't that what you do?"

Now I was in a tricky spot and had no choice but to explain. "Actually, Mrs Slater, what we do is solve crimes. Crimes are committed by the living and that is what I expect to find in this case. The killer, whatever their motivation is, has chosen to make it appear as though your husband is behind the current spate of murders. I expect to prove they have used facial prosthesis to alter their appearance. The strategic employment of copycat techniques to mimic murders your husband described in his books has captured the imagination of the public to further fuel the suggestion he is to blame."

My eyes were boring directly into Genevieve's, and it was precisely the right time to pose a question that had been burning in me since the case first arose.

"It is that, or your husband is not dead. How certain are you?" I was sorely tempted to accuse her of a hand in faking Simon's death, but this was as close as I was going to allow myself to get.

That Simon Slater might have faked his own death with the assistance of his wife to identify his body was one of the first things that occurred to Tempest when I discussed the case with him. Tempest had uncovered something very similar in an investigation a number of months ago. I was wondering if this was what had Genevieve so stressed.

Had she assisted her husband to fake his death as some kind of publicity stunt to promote his books? I had found an article online as part of my research which showed the spike in sales following his grisly murder, and an additional spike each time someone else was killed in the style of a murder depicted in his books.

Death was a real money spinner.

Perhaps she had no idea Simon was going to go on a murder spree. Maybe it had not been his original intention, but having been declared dead he saw an opportunity to settle a few scores. Unfortunately, if he was behind it all, and she knew he was alive, it begged the question why she would have hired me.

I really had no idea what she was going to say, and she caught me off guard with her adamant response.

"I can assure you, Miss Harper, that I am one hundred percent certain my husband is dead. As I said before, we are nearing the anniversary of his murder, and I fear that I may be on his list of victims."

Her statement was like getting a slap when you're not expecting it, or a glass of cold water tipped down your spine.

I blinked in my confusion before my mouth caught up with my brain.

"Genevieve you've suggested that his victims were all persons he would want to harm when he was alive. Why do you think that he might come after you?"

Not for the first time, I saw a tinge of colour coming to her cheeks and should have anticipated the admission before I heard it.

"I was cheating on him, and I think he knew."

I gave myself a few moments to absorb her revelation. It is a well-known fact that sex and money are the two greatest drivers for crime. Here I had both.

I asked a very obvious question, "Who were you having the affair with?"

Genevieve turned her face away, refusing to meet my eyes while she shook her head.

"It doesn't matter. The relationship ended shortly after Simon's death. He has been out of the picture for a long time."

"Nevertheless, Mrs Slater, these are the sorts of things I need to know to aid my investigation."

She shook her head again. "Some things must remain private, Amanda. I ask that you trust me when I say he is in no way involved with anything that has happened."

I pressed her again, but I could see she was becoming annoyed. There was nothing to gain from pushing her too far. A check of my watch confirmed that more than an hour had elapsed, and Patience would be arriving at Charing Cross very soon. I needed to get across the city to meet her at Clapham Common and I was, for now at least, done with Mrs Slater.

She saw me to the door where I had a parting comment for her, "If you really believe you are in any danger, Genevieve, you should consider moving to somewhere more secure. You live here alone, do you not?"

"Where could I go that a vengeful spirit would not find me?" she questioned, once again demonstrating how determined some people are to believe the supernatural over any other explanation.

The doorbell rang, interrupting what I was about to say, and I moved aside so that Genevieve could answer it.

There was a man outside. Tall at six feet and maybe three or four inches, he was in his late thirties, wore glasses, and suffered from premature baldness. A bit like Jason Statham, his head was completely shaved, but thereafter any resemblance to the action movie star ended.

"Jeremiah," Genevieve stepped into his personal space to air kiss him, the taller man bending slightly at the knees to bring his head down to hers. "Please, come in," she invited before turning to me.

I was looking to get out of the door, but in the relatively confined space of her hallway, there was no way to do so unless I wanted to shove Jeremiah back out into the street. I looked his way, expecting him to move, but his eyes were firmly locked on Genevieve. She had to be two decades older than the man on her doorstep, but that wasn't putting him off. Unless I was completely mistaken, whoever Jeremiah was, he was utterly infatuated with Genevieve Slater.

I wasn't going to comment, and Genevieve wasn't looking his way when she introduced him. Did she even know?

"Jeremiah this is Amanda Harper. I'm sure you remember me talking about the Blue Moon Investigation Agency. She is here to find out why Simon has chosen now to return."

I wanted to roll my eyes. It was as if she hadn't heard a word that I had said. Naturally, I didn't do that, opting instead to extend my right hand to meet his as he leaned in to introduce himself.

"Jeremiah Bramley."

I hadn't asked, but Genevieve felt it necessary to explain why he was at her house.

"Jeremiah is finishing Simon's manuscripts."

"You're an author too?" I inquired, showing interest only because I was trapped in the hallway of Genevieve's house.

My question caused Jeremiah to laugh though it sounded a little fake and forced.

"Ha! No, I have to get published to call myself an author. That's a little harder than one might think."

Actually, I imagined it was probably really quite hard to get a publishing contract or whatever such things are called, but I kept that to myself rather than find myself drawn into a conversation on the subject.

Genevieve spoke on his behalf, "Jeremiah is being modest. He's a talented writer. I'm sure it's only a matter of time before we see his titles in the book shops."

Jeremiah could have opted for modesty, but chose to leave the compliment as it was.

Genevieve continued, "Jeremiah has been with us for some time – he ran Simon's fan club, you see. When I found several partly completed manuscripts, it felt right to bring in someone who respected my husband's work enough to finish it in his voice."

"I am doing my best to meet Simon's ability to fracture the reader's mind," remarked Jeremiah, continuing his theme of modesty.

Thinking on my feet, I fished out a business card to hand to him. He quickly swapped his bag from one hand to the other so he could reciprocate.

Taking his card and pocketing it, I said, "I may have some questions for you, Jeremiah." Then, switching my attention to Genevieve, "I'm staying at the Travel Place just off Leicester Square, so I can meet you at short notice. If anything occurs to you. If you have any concerns at all, please call me." I really needed to get going, so I added, "If you'll excuse me," I took a step forward as I spoke, politely forcing Jeremiah to step away from the front door so that I could get out.

As he went inside, and Genevieve took hold of the door to close it, I caught her attention and reiterated my suggestion to seek company and security -if she really was on the list of targets, she would be much harder for the killer to find if she were not at home.

"Oh, I have a safe room," she revealed. "I've spent the last three nights sleeping in it. You'll not catch me outside at night."

Ok, well that was something. Of course, I didn't see her as a likely victim. Unless Genevieve had helped Simon fake his death, she was in no danger that I could perceive.

I bade her a good day and I got on my way. There was much to do, and I was so wrapped up in thoughts of homicidal novelists returned from the dead, copycat serial killers, and a complete lack of motivation for the current murder spree if it were not in fact the author behind it, that I failed to notice the hooded figure across the street begin to follow me.

What's that Star on the Wall? Tuesday, October 17th 1251hrs

H ERE'S THE THING ABOUT Patience: she's a plus-sized woman in a short body who has an attitude five times the size she provides for it to fit in. Consequently, that attitude spills out in a continuous stream where it habitually attacks anyone too foolish to give her a wide berth.

"Police business! Coming through! Make way!"

I could hear her voice echoing up from the underground where the escalator vanished down into the earth. Arriving almost a full minute before she came into sight, her attitude joined me in waiting for Patience by a newspaper stand just outside the exit from Clapham Common tube station.

"Ooh, a BBQ place," she gasped, looking behind me to a sign that read 'Bodean's BBQ Smokehouse' on the front façade. "Great thinking, I'm starved." She had a faraway glazed look to her eyes and an expression that suggested she was about to start drooling.

"I got you a sandwich," I announced, shoving a plastic bag into her left hand. To her disappointed face, I said, "We need to get to the crime scene before they all leave and lock the place up, remember? Also, how long are you staying for?" gripped in her right hand was the handle of a full-size suitcase; the sort you pack for a two-week holiday somewhere.

Patience tracked my eyes, a frown forming on her brow before she replied grumpily, "I just brought a few wardrobe options, that's all. Anyway, I vote we get lunch. It will be hours before they're finished with that crime scene yet."

"Have a look inside the bag," I suggested.

Standing the suitcase upright, she peered inside the plastic bag and fished out her sandwich. "Chicken, bacon, and stuffing," she drooled. "Damn you, Amanda. You always know how to defeat me."

We had worked together long enough as cops that I knew precisely how to get Patience to do almost anything. The woman loved food, and she had a few favourite dishes she simply couldn't resist. I'm certain she would still rather have gone for barbecue, but the sandwich was sufficient to weaken her resolve.

Tugging my own smaller suitcase behind me, I said, "Come on, let's get this done."

I've never really understood why people wanted to go into pathology; hanging around with dead people all day always sounded like a ghastly thing to do. A step beyond that was being one of the crime scenes people who had to deal with all manner of horrific cadavers.

Being exposed to bodies as part of my job in the police force was arguably one of the worst elements of the role, yet here I was again heading towards a crime scene where I knew somebody had died a terrible death.

Dragging along a pace behind me and mumbling around the side of her sandwich as she attempted to chew and walk and tug her own overweight suitcase, Patience jabbered about Simon Slater and her love of his books.

"... it's rumoured someone is being commissioned to write the final books in the *Devil May Care* series," she revealed. "I sure hope they do a good job, but I find it hard to believe anyone could mimic Simon Slater's work."

I almost snorted a laugh thinking about how someone was already mimicking his work - bringing it to life by murdering people in the exact manner he described in his novels. However, I chose to reveal what I knew.

"You're right. I met him less than half an hour ago."

Patience stopped walking, the suddenly absent rhythm of her suitcase wheels on the pavement enough to turn me around. Her mouth was open, the half-chewed sandwich inside threatening to fall out.

"Really? You know who it is?"

I nodded. "I'm not sure I ought to say," I teased. "Maybe if you're a good girl I will let you in on the secret." I didn't know if it was supposed to be a secret or not, but I didn't think so. Genevieve had given the information away freely enough.

Patience had to chase after me as I started walking again.

"You've got to tell me who it is, Amanda," she begged. "Is it someone famous? Is it another author I might have read? Did he tell you how he plans to capture Simon's voice in the books?"

Over my shoulder, I said, "Come along. Keep up." It was an unexpected boost to find a method to motivate Patience and I was going to milk it for all it was worth. I'd tell her eventually, but that might be a couple of days yet.

It was a short walk to the house of Daniel McCormack, his property occupying an enviable position overlooking Clapham Common itself. I could only imagine what a house in this post code might fetch on the open market, but knew for certain it was well out of my price range.

Finding it was easy enough, once we were pointing in the right direction, it was the one with all the police cars outside. A constable in uniform manned the pathway leading up to the door; I recognised the bored expression that forms after too long standing in one spot staring at the same sights.

Patience had her police identification out before we got there and her phone in her hand to call Darius and let him know we were arriving. The bored looking constable waved us by without bothering to check if I also carried credentials, and I stepped back into what felt like an all too familiar police investigation.

The house was set out over four floors and walking down the entrance hallway I had no idea on which one the murder had occurred.

"Patience?" called a voice as we passed a set of stairs. I turned my head to find a large black man crouching two steps down from the top. He was broad across his shoulders and had a light stubble and short haircut that made him look quite a bit like Idris Elba. I got what Patience has said about sex dipped in chocolate now.

Darius was yummy.

Patience had just passed the bottom of the stairs and had to back up a pace to peer around and upwards.

"Hey, babe," she purred in what I could only describe as a bedroom voice.

So that's how she planned this evening to go.

"Come on up," he gestured. "The action's all upstairs."

That he chose to employ a double entendre came as little surprise, nor did the devious grin Darius fired at Patience.

She replied with, "I sure hope so," the open flirting already making me uncomfortable before Darius chose to swing his dirty smile my way. However, whatever thoughts were in his head met with my easily deciphered glare which killed his hopeful expression in a heartbeat.

Patience parked her suitcase around the corner from the foot of the stairs and started up them. I left my bags with hers and followed.

Though Patience addressed Darius by his first name, he was, in fact, a detective inspector and this was his crime scene. The investigation into what they were now openly calling a serial killer was being led by Detective Superintendent Gary Smith.

The superintendent left no more than a few minutes before Patience and I arrived, the minor details of wrapping up the investigation on site delegated to a subordinate –

Darius. The body had been removed - something I was very glad to learn - but there were photographs available on a laptop if I wanted to see them.

I didn't, but this was not the place to demonstrate a squeamish nature.

"What's your interest here anyway?" asked Darius, his question aimed at Patience rather than me.

Patience had her head in front of the computer screen, her right index finger rolling over the mouse pad to bring up the pictures I wanted to see. Without turning away, she hooked a thumb in my direction.

"Ask her," she remarked, "she's investigating on behalf of a client, I think."

Failing to understand quite what that meant, Darius turned his attention my way, the bewildered look on his face begging for enlightenment.

I fished another business card from my pocket. "I'm Amanda Harper. I work for the Blue Moon Investigation Agency. Perhaps you've heard of us." I was being super polite and charming because he would be well within his rights to instantly turf me out of the building. I had absolutely no right to be where I was.

Darius took my card, holding it with both hands as he stared down at the information it displayed.

"You're not a cop," he observed.

"I used to be. This was more fun." It also paid considerably more, but I wasn't going to say that. "Mrs Slater hired the firm. She's concerned that this is her husband back from the dead to exact revenge on people from his past. She's also worried that he might come after her."

Darius's head flicked up to stare straight at me, his mouth half open as he wrestled with all the questions forming in his head.

"Why don't I know this? I interviewed her myself after the previous murder. That was two days ago. She never once mentioned a list of potential victims and I even asked her about possible links between them."

All I could do was shrug. "Perhaps it hadn't occurred to her before today." I didn't think that was true though. I think it occurred to her the instant she heard Leslie Ashe was killed. Why she chose to keep it from the police I could not imagine, but was probably going to have to figure out.

Patience reached behind her, stretching out her right arm and wafting it through the air until she found the sleeve of my coat.

"Amanda, you gotta see this," she tugged at my arm.

What she wanted me to see was not, as I had feared, the terrifying remains of the house's former occupant.

Patience touched the screen causing it to zoom backwards at which point the awful sight of the victim came into view.

Skewing her lips to one side, she said, "I'm not sure, but I think I've seen it on the cover of one of Simon Slater's books."

I leaned around her to take control of the mouse pad and zoomed in again. The one thing I noticed the moment I first saw it was that it looked fresh. Someone had carved it into the wood of a skirting board on the far side of the room beyond the victim's head.

By someone, I of course meant the killer in all probability.

Now that I could see it again, the rough edges where a sharp knife had whittled pieces of wood out to leave the symbol behind was quite obvious.

"Where is this?" I asked, my tone more intense than I had intended.

One of the crime scene people, working just a couple of feet away as she packed little evidence bags into sealed containers, jerked her head back towards the door.

"Across the hallway, in the living room," she let me know.

I went straight there, with Patience behind me and Darius following her. Over my shoulder I asked a question.

"Which book did you say it was from, Patience?"

"I didn't say," she replied. "But I'm sure I'm right. I've seen that symbol before. Now that I'm thinking about it, I'm sure it appears on all his books.

It took a scant few seconds to cross the room in which Daniel McCormack had met his end, taking a wide berth to avoid the rather obvious crimson stain on the carpet as I made my way toward the mark carved into the skirting.

By the time I arrived my phone had found Simon Slater's books and I was looking at the symbol for myself.

Patience peered around my arm to get a look. "Yeah, that's it. I knew I'd seen it before."

"Yes, but what does it represent?" I murmured, mostly to myself. It didn't appear on just one book cover, but was a small symbol located in the upper left corner on all the books I could find.

I wanted to say it was a pentagram, but my knowledge of such things is a little shaky even after more than a year employed as a paranormal investigator. There were fine lines drawn inside the pentagram that looked sort of like a creature's head, and tiny marks around the outside that could have been letters or symbols of some kind. I knew the creature was supposed to be a goat from seeing it more clearly on Simons Slater's book covers. Why it was here or what it represented, I couldn't say.

Dropping into a crouch, I held my phone directly in front of the symbol so that it filled the screen as much as was possible, then I took a series of photographs. There were indentations in the carpet where a piece of furniture had been sitting for some time. Scanning to my left, I found it; a small table, part of a nest of three.

"It looks like he kicked it over with his foot after the killer left," reported Darius.

I shuddered. Daniel McCormack had been sewn to the carpet and stabbed through the heart yet had still been alive somehow. The wound killed him, but not before he reached out with a foot and kicked the table over.

Rising again, I turned to face Darius. "Does this symbol appear at any of the other murder sites?"

Darius shook his head. "No. We'd have found it. It looks fresh, I'll admit, but there's nothing to suggest it was left by the killer."

I continued to stare at it, my interest bothering Darius enough that he asked, "Do you have any idea what it is? Or what it represents?"

I admitted that I didn't - there was no need to hide my ignorance. However, I chose not to mention that I knew a man who would and had already sent the photographs to him with a question.

Darius made a phone call to his boss inquiring about the symbol and thereafter was kind enough to let me quiz him about their investigation. I believe he was less guarded than he otherwise would have been because he wanted to keep me sweet. I was out on a double date with him and his brother tonight, not that the word 'date' was going to be an accurate description for the event.

I was going along only because I promised Patience I would. Tempest was due to arrive back later this evening. I hadn't heard from him in a couple of hours, and I hoped that that meant he was on his way home. How long that might take he wasn't entirely sure because he needed to take a seaplane back to Portugal before catching a commercial flight back to London.

I neither approved nor disapproved of his decision to dash off in the night to rescue someone - our relationship was such that we put few restrictions on each other. That did not, however, extend to dating other people, and I was going to tell him about my need to accompany Patience this evening as soon as I was able.

Annoyingly, Darius did not have a lot of information to share with me that was not publicly available through the media. He was able to confirm that a person closely resembling

Simon Slater had been spotted near two of the prior murders, and that his team were canvassing the local area to ascertain whether he might have been spotted here too.

The time of death recorded for Daniel McCormack was somewhere between 2200hrs and midnight last night. His cleaning lady found him this morning when she let herself in to perform her weekly routine. She had gone to hospital to be treated for shock and it was a neighbour who called the police upon hearing her desperate screams.

I could only imagine what it must have been like to find a body displayed in the way that Daniel's had been.

Quizzing Darius did provide one interesting piece of information that immediately threatened to change the course of my investigation: the police had positively identified fingerprints belonging to Simon Slater at Leslie Ashe's house. They were partials, but they were definitely his.

If the author was still alive it could only mean that Genevieve had been lying from the start. That singular line of reasoning demanded I look at everything from a different angle. But if she was guilty of being involved in a conspiracy to fake his death then why had she employed me now?

I was going around the same circle that had been plaguing me all day. I could not quite get my head around it.

Yet.

"So where are you girls staying?" Darius wanted to know.

Patience immediately turned to look at me. "Yeah, girl, where are we staying?"

Lunch. Tuesday,
October 17th 1432hrs

T HE TRUTH OF IT was I had failed to appreciate just how difficult it is to get a room in London at short notice. When I made the plan to stay in London, I hadn't thought about how hard it might be to find a room. Consequently, we were to be housed in a pokey, horrible franchise that catered to those seeking a place to lay their heads and nothing else.

When Patience said she was joining me, I had nightmare visions of having to share a bed. A swift call to Marjory, the receptionist at the office, begging her to get an extra room at all costs, had not resulted in a call back to confirm her success.

Now that I had Patience expecting an answer, I checked my phone to find my concerns were for naught. Ever efficient, Marjory had booked the extra room and sent me an email. We had two rooms in a Travel Place, just off Leicester Square.

"Ooh, super," Patience clapped her hands together at the news. It was the location that was getting her excited of course not the accommodation which was about as basic as one could find.

I had stayed in a Travel Place before and not only did the rooms have a shower instead of a bath, the towels supplied were so small and so thin I couldn't even wrap one around myself.

Still, it was only for a couple of nights.

Darius was pleased with the news too.

"There is a great little club in a basement just around the corner from Leicester Square. The doormen know who I am, so we'll not have to queue to get in."

I hid my lack of enthusiasm by expressing my desire to spend the rest of the afternoon going through the files I'd received from Genevieve Slater. Though not exactly exciting, I felt certain it would keep me out of trouble for a few hours.

Collecting our suitcases from downstairs, Patience and I set off back to the tube station again. We had gone about five yards when Patience suggested we stop for food.

"I've got to tell you, Amanda, that sandwich you bought me sure was nice, but it didn't do all that much to fill me up. I might need my energy for this evening."

I raised a critical eyebrow at her.

"You know, for dancing and stuff," she tried to bluff me.

Ten minutes later I was perusing the contents of the Barbecue Smokehouse's plastic menu and silently admitting to myself that I was actually quite hungry. The smells filling the air inside the restaurant were enticing to say the least, and my stomach growled its approval loudly enough that Patience heard me.

She raised a hand to attract the attention of a nearby waitress.

"Hey, I've got a skinny white girl here starving to death!" she called loudly enough for half the tables in the restaurant to hear her. It caused several chuckles and brought unwanted attention our way, but it did get us served faster than we otherwise might.

Patience ordered their special: an honour roll of barbecues greatest hits on a sharing platter for two. It wasn't what I had intended to get, but there seemed no need to argue – Patience would eat the lion's share anyway.

"And shots," she added. "Six each. Just to warm us up before our night out," she winked at me.

"No shots for me," I told the waitress. I could see Patience was about to complain. "I have to work still," I got in quick so she would know I wasn't just being a party pooper.

Patience frowned her disapproval before asking, "At least tell me you are going to order something to eat."

I snorted at her joke, then when she didn't smile, I wondered if she was being serious.

She sniggered at me. "Girl, I'm not that bad. You'll share it with me, right? This place smells divine, and I want to try it all, but I have a dress I need to fit into tonight. We can change the order if you want something else."

If she was trying to manipulate me by being cooperative for once, it worked. I conceded that the platter did look good and that was what we had.

While we waited for our food, I had Patience regale me with storylines from Simon Slater's books. She spoke with enthusiasm, demonstrating her passion for not only the genre but also the author. I couldn't recall ever seeing her with anything thicker than a glossy magazine, but Patience claimed to have read every last one of Simon Slater's books and even revealed he'd published a few short stories under a different name which resulted in a scandal when the general public found out.

The *Devil May Care* series was all to do with the rise of the church of Satan and his ascension to claim dominion over the earth. I found it uncomfortable to hear about, let alone read, but there was no denying an audience existed for his scary tales.

Our food arrived, a heaping, steaming platter of every kind of barbecue meat, plus on the side we had fries, cornbread, slaw, and sweet corn. It was a feast, and with a rumble emanating from my core I decided I was considerably hungrier than I had realised.

Patience attempted to divide up the food evenly, but there was no way I was going to be able to finish my half. I elected instead to tackle that which I found most enticing.

We continued to talk as we ate, Patience allowing me to steer the conversation back onto the case. I didn't have a lot to go on, as is so often the case when we start to investigate, and I was genuinely struggling to decide how I felt about my client.

"What were you saying about his publishing company?" Patience mumbled around a piece of brisket. She had sauce coating her fingers and a big blob of it on her chin. Worrying I was little better, I spent the next minute using napkins to get myself clean.

"They were weird," I told her. "The staff working in the main office all just watched me. It was bizarre." It truly had been, "The boss lady seemed nice enough, but when I went to leave, she warned me to drop the case."

Patience hitched an eyebrow. "Like a threat?"

I picked up a piece of cornbread and dunked it in some ranch dressing, taking my time to answer as I assessed that which had transpired with a critical eye.

"No," I concluded. "It wasn't a threat. It was more like she knew who I was going up against and could predict that I would get killed if I continued to investigate. She mentioned ..." I was going to say demons and ghosts, but that was wrong. It had been me who brought up those things. Indigo said dark forces.

"Dark forces," repeated Patience, her mouth properly empty for the first time in the last ten minutes. "I do not like the sound of that."

Finishing my cornbread and picking up a beef short rib, I said, "I think the woman had been spending too much time surrounded by posters and book covers from horror novels. They all have. I'd start seeing things in the shadows if I ever worked there." I chewed the rib, though to be accurate it fell apart and more or less dissolved on my tongue. Swallowing, I added, "They might be worth looking at though. There was something about them that made me feel deeply uncomfortable."

"Them? What, the whole firm?"

"Those I saw," I admitted.

Patience picked up a whole chicken leg. "You make them sound like a cult."

I didn't reply to her comment, yet it stuck with me, tickling away inside my head. Simon Slater was one of the world's most successful horror novelists and Kimble Publishing must have done rather well from the royalties he brought in. Money and sex, sex and money, they were the root cause of so many crimes. Was this one any different?

What had happened to Simon Slater's royalties when he died? Better yet, why hadn't it occurred to me to ask that question before now? Leslie Ashe had been getting a portion of them I knew, but who else? Genevieve as his surviving spouse, surely, and the publishing firm had to be invested. Were any of the other victims collecting regular pay checks from Simon's efforts?

It took me back to Jane's question about who stood to benefit. Figuring that out solves fifty percent of all our cases. My head was filling with questions, and I wanted to get on with my research.

In the Shadows.
Tuesday, October 17th
1955hrs

P USHING MY PLATE AWAY and questioning whether I might have a visible food baby when I stood up, I gestured for the waitress to bring our bill. There wasn't a great deal of anything left from our platter of food. Just a few bones, a smear or two of barbecue sauce, and the core of the sweetcorns.

I was not going to need any dinner. Or supper. Breakfast was in question too.

Another short hop on the London Underground took us to Leicester Square where the bustle of people moving with purpose carried us up, along, and out to discover a light drizzle had descended on the capital.

Neither of us had an umbrella, but according to our phones it was only a six-minute walk to get to our accommodation. The estimate proved accurate and once we were inside and out of the rain once more, Patience announced her intention to get a nap. She wanted to sleep off her lunch.

The food was making me feel drowsy too. I was not, however, going to succumb to the desire to rest. I had work to do.

Starting with the files Genevieve sent me, I dug into Simon Slater's fan club. Jeremiah had run it for the author for several years and I guess Genevieve had access because she'd sent me some of the scary emails he would sometimes receive.

Her file labelled 'potential wackos' contained more than two hundred emails, from a variety of persons who felt so strongly about Simon's work that they needed to threaten him. Two names appeared more frequently than any other and when I filtered it to see just how many these two had sent, I discovered Adrian Hargreaves featured in no fewer than one quarter of all the hate mail Genevieve saw necessary to file.

I read through a few of them, identifying a theme quite quickly. Adrian was disappointed with what he referred to as inaccuracies in Simon's description of satanic rituals and practices. The emails, which I suspected were never reaching the author because Jeremiah was handling them, became increasingly outraged that Simon was not correcting his works as Adrian suggested he should.

Adrian felt he was not being taken seriously and threatened on several occasions to demonstrate the power of the rituals when performed correctly - he was going to summon the devil himself to kill Simon Slater.

It was all very interesting, however I felt certain the police would have interviewed Adrian Hargreaves in the investigation that followed Simon's death. Since he hadn't been arrested for the murder, he clearly wasn't worth me focusing effort on him now.

I got up to pace around the room and stretch my back. I'd been sitting in the same position, hunched over my laptop for almost two hours and I was feeling stiff.

Walking around the tiny room, I talked to myself. I could believe that Simon Slater had been murdered by a crazy fan - such behaviour had been recorded before in the world of celebrity, yet why would that same person choose to start killing people associated with Simon Slater a year after his death?

There was something about the list of recent victims. Some were directly connected to the author, and those who were not – I had to question if they were and that the link simply hadn't been found yet – were all in the literary industry. In fact, of all the victims, only Leslie Ashe wasn't working in or connected to the world of books.

Outside my window when I paused to look through it, the sky was darkening. It was late afternoon in October and the sun was racing towards the horizon. Soon it would be full dark.

Turning back towards the desk and my laptop, I caught something in a shadow across the road and felt a shiver run down my spine. Snapping my head and eyes back around to stare at the patch of darkness across the road, there was nothing there.

I could hear my own breathing and feel my heart banging in my chest; the gruesome deaths were freaking me out more than I cared to admit. Forcing a deep, calming breath and berating myself for seeing things that were not there, imagine my surprise when the orange warning beacon on a passing city services truck picked out a figure hiding in the far corner of the alcove into which I was staring.

My breath caught in my throat, the sight stealing it away as a primaeval terror gripped me. The flash of amber light illuminated the figure for only a fraction of a second, yet it was enough for me to see that it was not human.

What I had seen was nothing more than a person in a costume. I knew that even though my brain was telling me otherwise. The reason I saw it so clearly was for the simple fact that the light caught on the white fur of its face. Where a person's head ought to have been, what I had seen was the face of a goat.

My feet had taken me back a pace without being commanded to do so, but coming to my senses, I exploded into action. I tore across the room, leaping the corner of the bed in my haste to get to the door. I heard it slam shut behind me, cursing that it meant I was now locked out, but moving too fast to care.

Whoever it was across the street, I wasn't about to buy that they were there by accident. I couldn't say the goat was looking up at my window - it simply wasn't possible to tell, but even in the nanosecond of strobe light, I knew it was aimed in my direction and given what I was researching, it was already too much coincidence to dismiss.

Outside in the dark looking into a lit room, they would have seen me clearly turn and run towards the door. They would be gone by the time I got to the street, of that I was certain, so to limit how far they could get, I ran as fast as I could.

Straight past the elevator, I careened through the door to access the stairs and leapt to the first landing, swung myself around on the banister and launched myself into the air again to get down to the ground floor.

Smashing through the door, my thoughts only on orientating myself so I knew which way to run, I slammed straight into Patience.

"Wahhhhh!" she yelled, juggling a carrier bag and trying to catch it as the pair of us pitched over, me toppling forward under my own momentum, and Patience falling backwards as I piled through her.

Landing on top of her and between her legs so we were face to face and staring wide-eyed at each other, the front entrance door opened to reveal two guys in their twenties.

They both broke into broad grins.

"Well now," one remarked, nudging his pal with an elbow. "Couldn't wait to get to the room, huh?"

"Don't stop on our account," said the other, leering at us. "I don't mind watching a little girl-on-girl action."

Harrumphing, mostly because the additional delay meant the goat-headed figure across the street had extra time to make good its escape, I shoved backwards to separate myself from Patience and get off the floor.

"Come on!" I yelled at her, offering a hand up. "There was someone outside my window!"

I must have almost yanked her arm from its socket, such was the energy I put into getting her upright, and I was running again before she could even get her balance.

I heard her shout, "Wait! Amanda, what's happening?" as she hustled along behind me. I didn't answer, for I was already shunting the hotel's glass entrance doors open and running into the darkness outside.

Bad News. Tuesday, October 17th 2022hrs

A BUS BLOCKED MY view across the street where it was paused to let someone off, and it started moving as I tried to run around its front end. I waved an apology to the driver, who muttered something and looked annoyed.

The dark alcove where I'd seen the figure was, of course, completely empty and the street was such that I could not see any likely hiding places.

"Are you all right, dear?" asked a voice from my left. I turned to find the person who had alighted at the bus stop – a little old lady in her eighties with a shawl around her head – staring at me quizzically. Her question came as no great surprise for I had arrived at a dead sprint and was not only a little out of breath, but also looking around frantically as if I had lost something precious.

I huffed out a breath and let my shoulders deflate.

"I thought I saw someone," I told her with a smile.

She was already hobbling off down the street away from me, her interest going no further than checking I was okay.

Patience puffed across the street, also out of breath.

"Girl, what is going on? You almost smashed the bottle of prosecco I bought for us to have while we get ready to go out."

Still staring down the street, I replied, "I think I was being watched."

I got a raised eyebrow in response. "Were you getting undressed in the window?"

"What? No!" I frowned at her. "I saw what looked like someone wearing an animal mask on their face. They were in this alcove here." I pointed.

"Animal mask, huh?" Patience reached into her carrier bag, made a rustling noise, and produced a few pieces of popcorn. "Want some?" she asked, offering me the bag. "What sort of animal?"

I hadn't told her because I know Patience and could predict how she would react. However, I was on the spot now and she would be suspicious if I failed to give her an answer.

"A goat," I admitted.

The piece of popcorn Patience had just put in her mouth rolled back out and was caught by the wind.

"A goat?"

I nodded. "I think so."

Before I knew it, Patience had hold of my arm and was dragging me back toward the hotel.

"There is way too much creepy stuff going on here, Amanda. Why you have to investigate all this spooky supernatural stuff is beyond me. Let's get back inside the hotel before the devil himself turns up to claim our souls."

"It was just someone wearing a headpiece," I argued.

"Oh, yeah?" she challenged. "What if it wasn't? Simon's books are all about devil worship and dark magical practices. What if someone has summoned a demon?"

This was fairly typical behaviour for Patience; she believed in everything supernatural despite Tempest and I disproving it constantly every time we solve a case. That she was with me at all when I was investigating the ghost of a dead author exacting vengeance from beyond the grave was something of a surprise.

Not that she was actively helping me with the case. She was here because of Darius and the chance for a couple of fun nights out.

Back inside the hotel, we rode the elevator to the first floor. I wasn't paying much attention to what Patience was doing and only looked her way when I heard her grunt in effort.

Instantaneously reacting in panic when I saw what was about to happen, I grabbed for the prosecco bottle she was trying to open. She had the neck of it gripped firmly in her left hand and was twisting the cork out with her right.

"Noooooo!" I tried to get there in time, but with a loud pop, accentuated by the close confines of the steel elevator car, the cork came free with a whole load of pressure behind it.

The fizzy wine, shaken to a state of high agitation by first being knocked to the floor and then jiggled about as Patience ran after me, burst through my fingers and hit my face. I tried to duck the fountain of wine following hot on its heels, but to be fair, there probably wasn't a safe place inside the elevator where I could have hidden.

Half a second after the cork came free, the flow of wine reduced to nothing when Patience shoved it in her mouth.

I got to watch the panic in her eyes as she did her best to swallow half a bottle in one go. She did a good job, but less than two seconds after she started, the wine ejected from her nose, and she coughed and choked the mouthful she had.

The eruption of cheap Italian wine reduced to a foamy trickle, seeping out of the bottle's mouth and running over Patience's fingers, whereupon it dripped to the floor.

I looked at her. She looked at me. We both had prosecco dripping from our eyebrows.

"I probably should have waited before opening that," Patience remarked needlessly.

The elevator pinged and the doors swished open to reveal the same two young men we'd seen only a few minutes before. They were dressed differently now; their clothing changed for a night out. The grins each wore were exactly the same as before though.

"Would you like a hand getting clean, ladies?" chortled the one on the right. Seeing him for a second time now, I chose to mentally label him 'Jason Statham Wannabe' for his shaved head and London accent. "Not that I'm saying I don't like my girls to be dirty."

His partner also had something to say. "The shower in my room is free and I can offer my personal grooming services."

They filled the doorway, effectively trapping us inside the elevator, though not for very long. I needed to get clean even before Patience showered me with prosecco. Now the need was absolute.

I was going to march straight at them, quite content to barge through them if they didn't move aside, but Patience got there first.

Seeing her place her thumb over the mouth of the bottle and give it a shake, both men chose to depart at speed, diving through the door that led to the stairs before Patience could launch her attack.

Holding my arms out to my sides as the wine dripped off my fingertips, I made my way along the corridor to my room.

Patience called after me, "There's a little bit of this prosecco left if you want some?"

"No, thank you." Patience had always been a bad influence when it came to drinking and the last thing I wanted was to get started early.

We met back at the elevator forty minutes later by which time I was clean and had shaved my legs despite selecting jeans to wear this evening. The leg shaving was because Tempest was on his way - I'd received a text message from him while I was in the shower.

He and Big Ben were both boarding a plane that would touch down in Gatwick a little less than three hours from now. Oddly, looking at my phone, I discovered I had no response to the message I sent about the pentagram I found.

The message had gone to Frank Decaux, the owner of an occult book shop in Rochester and all-around font of knowledge for anything supernatural. He was one of those truly odd characters, but a good guy, nevertheless. Tempest had a lot of time for him, for even though Frank was slightly bonkers – the man was once part of a now dissolved group called the Kent League of Demonologists or something like that – he had turned up to fight when he was needed. For that matter, he quite often turned up even when he wasn't needed and could be found in the company of four ninjas, two of whom worked in his bookshop.

It was Frank's common practise to answer almost instantly whenever I sent him a message, so the lack of response was most unusual. Assuming there had to be a good reason for it, I was giving him a little longer, but had vowed to phone him in the morning if I had not heard anything by then.

"Girl, is that your outfit for the night?" Patience asked the moment she saw me.

I knew precisely what she was asking and therefore did not rise to her baiting. She had on a sparkly sequined top that plunged through her cleavage and a skirt so short it barely covered the essentials. Her heels added a good four inches of height, and she wore patterned stockings intended solely to draw attention to her legs.

Her jacket would do little to ward off the cool October air outside, but staying warm was never the point.

In contrast, my combination of t-shirt, bleached jeans, running shoes (new and fashionable) plus a proper winter coat, made me look as if I had failed to read the brief.

Facing the elevator while I waited for it to arrive, I said, "I am not going out to pick up boys, Patience. Tempest is on his way back here and will arrive later this evening. Big Ben is going to be with him," I pointed out, reminding her of their previous liaisons.

"Big Ben is nice and all, but there's just no putting a saddle on that stallion." It sounded like something Big Ben would say himself. He was one of those guys who just didn't want to grow up. Picking up girls was easy for him so that was what he did with alarming efficiency.

The elevator returned us to the ground floor, neither of us commenting on how sticky the floor now was. Patience continued to jabber away, making up for my lack of words by employing an abundance of her own.

My mind was still on the goat figure and what that could mean. Had I imagined it? Was it paranoia that drove me to believe it was watching me? I continued to mull it over until I was made to jump out of my skin by Patience squealing.

She was not, however, as I had first feared, being attacked, but had just spotted Darius coming from the other direction. I understood her interest; the man was very handsome. As was his brother, I couldn't help but notice.

Ever exuberant, Patience flung out her arms and embraced Darius as we gathered in a gaggle in the street. It was clear from his brother's eyes that he'd taken one look at his blind date for the night and performed a mental high five. I didn't intend to glare at him in warning, but I fear that was what I did for his expression froze and his smile fell.

"I'm Amanda," I offered him my hand to shake.

"JB," he replied, his smile returning.

"I have a boyfriend."

The hopeful look had almost made it to JB's eyes once more, but this time it died for good.

Darius broke away from Patience though she looped her arm through his and fell in by his side.

"Shall we find somewhere to get a drink?" Darius asked. "It's too early to be hitting the clubs."

Walking beside Patience as we crossed the street to get to a packed bar on the other side, she leaned her head my way to murmur, "It's a double date, Amanda. You don't have to sleep with him, but you can manage to be friendly. Please?" she begged. "Don't blow this for me. I really like Darius."

How was I supposed to argue with that?

There was a cover charge to get into the bar which JB offered to pay for me. I politely declined, but remembering Patience's plea, I allowed him to fetch me a drink from the bar. He was getting a round for all four of us, which left me with Darius and Patience who were very much having a conversation between themselves.

Patience was already a little wobbly on her feet and had started to slur. She'd be fine as long as she watched what she imbibed for the next couple of hours, but was acting as if she hadn't downed six shots with her lunch and then guzzled at least half a bottle of prosecco when it exploded.

When my phone rang, I was very glad to step to one side. Fishing it from my pocket, I was pleased to see Frank's name displayed on the screen. It was noisy in the bar, but I thumbed the green button to answer the call and pressed the phone tight into my left ear while using a finger in my right ear to block out as much noise as possible.

"Frank, thanks for getting back to me," I shouted so he might hear me.

His familiar voice rumbled in my ear. "I'm sorry it took so long, Amanda. I was at a Dungeons and Dragons tournament and there were no phones allowed inside the competition hall."

"It's fine, Frank. Seriously. What can you tell me about the symbol I found?"

"There's a lot of noise there, Amanda. Where are you?"

Raising my voice, I yelled into the phone, "I'm in a bar just off Leicester Square. It's a bit noisy."

He accepted my reply and moved on. "I need to know where you found that symbol, Amanda."

"It was in the home of a man who had just been murdered, Frank. I think he's the fifth or possibly sixth victim of the same killer. I don't know if that symbol can be found at any of the other murders or if it is even connected." I could have told him it was the symbol found on Simon Slater's novels, but felt certain the bookshop owner would already know that. Also, I didn't want to draw Frank's opinion in one direction of another. Instead, I asked, "Why? What does the symbol mean?"

Rather than answer my question, Frank asked another of his own.

"How was the man killed? Was it ritualistic?"

Fruitlessly moving around the bar as I attempted to find somewhere a little quieter, I provided Frank with some background information.

"Have you read about Simon Slater, the horror author who died last year?" I didn't need to say any more.

Frank gasped with excitement. "Was this found at the site of one of his victims? Do you know how he's selecting the people he's killing?"

I sighed. I ought to have predicted Frank's reaction. Much like Patience and so many other people I meet, Frank believed wholeheartedly in the supernatural world, but more than that he believed he had the evidence to prove it.

"Simon Slater is not behind the deaths, Frank," I attempted to assure him, knowing full well he wouldn't listen. "At least, I don't think he is. Admittedly, one theory I'm working on is that Simon faked his own death and his wife helped him ..." I paused what I was saying because I'd just caught someone looking my way.

Getting stared at in a bar isn't something new, of course, but when I looked their way, they ducked back out of sight behind a pillar. They were watching me, but didn't want me to know.

The hairs on the back of my neck stood on end.

Picking up where I left off, I said, "It's that or we have a killer using scenes from Simon Slater's books to kill people from the author's life." I was doing my best to keep an open mind about the case, continuing to question whether Genevieve knew her husband was alive and planning to kill her because she was a loose end he no longer needed. Was Indigo involved in that somehow? It might help to explain her strange behaviour. However, it did nothing to justify why her staff acted so weird when I was there this morning.

Frank broke my train of thought completely when he said, "I believe Simon Slater was involved in devil worship."

Blinking, I mumbled, "I'm sorry, what now?"

"Devil worship, Amanda. The symbol you photographed is an inverted pentagram. The inverted pentagram is given meaning by the user and has been employed in many ways across the centuries. Most commonly, though, in modern practice it is employed as a religious symbol for Baphomet and Satanism."

"Baphomet?" I repeated the word I didn't recognise.

"Also known as the Sabbatic Goat," Frank explained.

For the last minute or so I had been working my way around the bar and doing my best to stay out of sight. If there was someone watching me, I wanted to know who it was. I was going to come up behind where I had last seen him standing. I paused now as the hairs on the back of my neck stood up once more, the image of the goat-headed figure shooting through my mind again.

"A goat," I questioned though I knew that was what Frank had said.

"Listen, Amanda, this is serious stuff. The Church of Satan can perform all manner of supernatural atrocities, the power of hell is more than sufficient to fuel dark magical spells. I need to know if that symbol appears where the other murders took place. If I'm right, and Simon Slater was involved in devil worship, then it could easily be the case that he *was* murdered and has returned to seek vengeance against his enemies. This is too dangerous for you to be involved in."

It was just like Frank to believe the most diabolical scenario and highly typical for him to issue a warning that we should stay away from the case.

I guess he knew me just as well for in the next breath he said, "I know you're not going to do that though."

"That's right, Frank. I have a case to solve and a murderer to catch. It might well be Simon Slater, and he could even be into devil worship, but I don't believe he's returned from the dead or can do magic, dark or otherwise."

I rounded the pillar I'd been aiming for and right there before me a tall male figure had his head craned around it in his bid to spot me.

"I've got to go, Frank. I'll call you back."

Frank attempted to yell something, his words getting cut off when I thumbed the button to end the call and stuffed the phone back into my pocket.

I was going to grab my stalker and make him tell me who he was and why he was following me. I did not for one moment think it was someone who had randomly decided they fancied me and was figuring out how to make his move. No, this was something to do with the case and I was willing to bet I would find the goat headpiece in the backpack he now had slung over one shoulder.

Just in the second before I grasped his arm, JB appeared with a drink in his hand.

"Hey, Amanda. I've been looking everywhere for you." He was coming at me from in front of the pillar, walking right toward my stalker with his eyes locked on me.

It was enough to make the stalker question who was behind him. Or maybe he heard my name. Whatever it was, he spun around on the spot, looking startled and frightened at the same time.

Neurons fired in my brain to tell me I knew precisely who I was looking at.

The Rabbit and the Bear. Tuesday, October 17th 2029hrs

JEREMIAH BRAMLEY HADN'T EXPECTED to find me standing behind him and reacted like a rabbit hearing a twig snap in the forest. Moving fast to get away from me, he took too little care about where he was going and bumped into JB.

The drinks JB held went into the air - it was an evening for spilled alcohol.

JB yelled, "Hey," but Jeremiah was already zipping through the crowded bar and the drinks had soaked a petite young woman in a little black dress whose boyfriend was instantly taking offense.

Leaving JB where he was, I ran after Jeremiah. Where did he think he was going? If I lost him, I would only find him tomorrow for goodness sake. What was the point in running?

Behind me it sounded like a fight was breaking out; shouting and cursing had grown in volume to drown out the background conversation and as I chased Jeremiah, doormen in their black suits were rushing to deal with it.

I felt sorry for JB, but I needed to catch my stalker. I could apologise to my 'date' later.

I heard Patience call out to me, "Amanda!" as I zipped by where she was cosying up to Darius, but didn't even turn my head.

Jeremiah was heading for the door, and I wanted to get to him before he made it outside. Was he involved? Was he the killer? He had access to Genevieve's house and more intimate knowledge of Simon Slater than most people on the planet.

I yelled for someone to stop him, screaming that he had taken my bag, but most people were looking at the fight and when they did look my way, Jeremiah had already passed them.

The press of the crowd made running impossible, but the same was true for Jeremiah. Unfortunately, it also meant that when he got to the free space by the doors, he would be able to accelerate and lose me.

I didn't want to have to spend the night trying to track him down.

Raging as I bumped into a guy three times my size and bounced off, I snatched the tumbler from the giant bear's hand, downed the remaining liquid, and launched it at the back of Jeremiah's head. He was less than eight feet away and my aim was true.

My face turned itself inside out when I swallowed. Cringing as the hard liquor burned a path through my body, I spat, "Ewww. Neat whisky."

"Lady, you owe me a drink," declared the bear I had stolen it from. "But I'll settle for your number."

I had no time for nonsense - Jeremiah was down, the blow to his skull enough to stop him in his tracks and make him stumble, but he was going to be up and moving in a heartbeat.

"I'll get you the whole bottle if you grab that guy!" I jabbed an arm at Jeremiah's back.

The bear needed no further encouragement, and he also had no trouble wading through the crowd who all seemed to part like the Red Sea as he advanced. Right on his heels, I was able to dart around the bear and grab Jeremiah myself while he was still getting back to his feet.

With my weight hitting him, he went down again, and I had his left arm around and into a braced position behind his back before he had a chance to figure out what was happening.

More doormen were coming my way, aiming to get involved and break up the trouble before it escalated. They needn't have worried though because it was all but over.

With a yank, I twisted Jeremiah around so he faced the bear.

"What's your name?" I asked, out of breath from exertion and adrenalin.

"Jeremiah!" yelled Jeremiah. "We met earlier. Don't you remember?"

"Not you, dummy," I snarled in his ear. "I'll get to you in a moment."

I flicked my head, inviting the bear to answer.

"Abner."

The doormen arrived.

"What's going on? Can you let him go now, miss, please?"

I didn't let Jeremiah go, and I didn't acknowledge the request either. Shunting my stalker forward, I nodded my head toward the bag over his shoulder.

"Check in the bag!" I shouted to be heard over all the noise around me.

"Miss. I'm not going to warn you again," insisted the doorman who probably wasn't used to being ignored.

Abner glanced at the doormen, but ultimately decided he was more interested in helping me than he was worried about being turfed out of the bar. He reached for Jeremiah's bag, failing to grasp it because Jeremiah was struggling against me and still trying to get free.

"There's nothing in it!" he protested. "I haven't done anything."

The doorman who had spoken blocked Abner's hand with his own. "What's in the bag?" he asked.

I wasn't sure if the question was aimed at me or Jeremiah, but I got my reply in first.

"A goat's head."

My reply got a few raised eyebrows, not least from Jeremiah who chose that moment to stop struggling.

"A goat's head?" he questioned.

The doorman raised his eyebrows, the expression a non-verbal request to check the bag still hanging off Jeremiah's shoulder. Given permission, the doorman didn't have to fight to get it because Jeremiah sloped his shoulder so it slid down his right arm.

No longer as confident as I had been about the bag's contents, I regretted calling it and started accusing Jeremiah of other crimes before they got the bag open.

"He's been stalking me. I'm investigating a series of murders and I think he might be involved."

I got more raised eyebrows, but as I now expected, there was no mask or headpiece, goat or otherwise, in Jeremiah's bag and I had a sea of faces staring at me.

The doorman spoke calmly but firmly. "Let him go now, miss."

I felt I had no choice but to comply, but when I released Jeremiah's arm and took a step back, the last thing I expected was for him to apologise.

Massaging his left arm and wincing, he nevertheless, twisted around to face me so he could say, "I'm sorry, Amanda. I didn't mean to come across as creepy. When I left Genevieve's place earlier, I decided to try to catch up with you. I know you gave me your card but for the life of me I couldn't find it. I remembered where you were staying, but when I got to your hotel, I couldn't remember your last name, and didn't want to be some weirdo describing you to the lady on reception."

"Are we okay here now?" asked the doorman, still flanked by two of his colleagues and looking to depart if there was no reason to do anything else.

I was frowning at Jeremiah, struggling to make sense of what he was saying.

"Why did you want to come to my hotel?" I demanded to know, expecting to hear he hoped to ask me out or something.

He made an ashamed face. "It's for a book."

"A book?" my frown deepened.

"Yes. You're investigating Simon's murder and the recent murders associated with him. I thought there might be an interesting angle for a follow up book or for an extra chapter at the back of Simon's final book."

I couldn't believe it.

"So how did you come to be in this bar waiting for me?" I snapped, challenging him to come up with something believable.

"I wasn't waiting for you. I was trying to figure out what to do," he replied. "I almost spat out my drink when you walked in with your boyfriend."

"That's not my boyfriend," I countered automatically.

Abner butted in, "Hey, lady, you still owe me a drink."

I flicked my eyes across and up, accepted that I did indeed owe him a replacement for the one I threw at Jeremiah's head, and motioned in the direction of the bar.

Abner started moving.

"You too," I told Jeremiah. "I haven't finished with you yet."

Publicity Stunts.
Tuesday, October 17th
2033hrs

P ATIENCE FOUND ME JUST as I was about to order drinks.

"Pornstar Martini, please," she yelled in my ear to be heard over the constant babble of drinks orders going back and forth.

"What the heck is that?" I asked.

"I have no idea," she shouted at me. "But they are delicious. You should have one. This will be my fifth. Oh, and some ice for JB. He got punched in the face and thinks he has a black eye coming."

I groaned. That was my fault. I would have to apologise and hope he accepted it.

As promised, I bought Abner a whole bottle of his favourite tipple, which he thanked me for, and took away with a fresh glass. I bought Jeremiah a sparkling water because he planned to take some painkillers for his head. I wondered if I was going to end up apologising for that too.

I really wanted to leave the bar and find somewhere quiet to grill Jeremiah. If he wasn't part of whatever was going on, then I needed to pick his brains about Genevieve. I was going to do that anyway, but it was going to be a lot harder if I had to compete with the background noise in the bar.

Taking Jeremiah with me, I headed back over to where Darius and JB were standing. Handing out drinks, I enquired as to what had happened and thankfully got the short version of events.

JB had ducked a punch thrown by the boyfriend of the girl who got the drinks down her dress. The problem was that it connected with someone else and within seconds there was a full-scale brawl. JB tried to break it up, pulling out his police identification only to have it knocked from his hand before he could speak. The doormen descended and somewhere in the melee JB took a blow to his right cheekbone.

Having been punched in the face myself in the past, I sympathised. He wasn't mad at me, but JB was curious to know the identity of my new companion.

"He's just someone who might have information about the case I am working on," I told him, keeping it brief. "I just need to ask him a few questions. I'm not being very good company, am I?" I said by way of apology.

JB waved a dismissive hand at me. "Go do your thing. I accepted I wasn't getting your number in the first three seconds after meeting you."

I pulled a face and mouthed, 'Sorry,' at him as I nudged Jeremiah toward a pair of seats against a wall. I'd been watching the couple there finishing their drinks in the hope they might be about to leave. Swooping before anyone else could get to it, I put my drink down and waited for Jeremiah to settle. The second his backside was on the stool, I hit him with my first question.

"What is Genevieve hiding?"

He took a second, examining my face to see if I was serious.

"Hiding?" he repeated. "I'm not sure what you mean."

I was not in the mood for games.

"Rubbish!" I spat. "I think she helped Simon to fake his own death and now he's evening the score against some people who got the better of him. The police aren't looking for him because they think he's dead."

Jeremiah's face had taken on an expression of stark disbelief.

"You think Simon Slater is still alive?"

I opened my mouth and closed it again while I thought about what I wanted to say.

"It's one possibility. It would explain why he has been seen in the vicinity of the murders and why his fingerprints were found – fingerprints are fairly irrefutable evidence. When I quizzed Genevieve about it today, she said this is a different killer to the person who killed Simon." I paused to run the words through my head again. They didn't fit with my theory that he was alive.

If Genevieve wanted me to believe he was dead, why would she argue that it had to be a different killer? Why was she so certain that it was a different killer? Because she knew who the first killer was!

The possibility hit me like ice water to the spine. I'd been thinking she might have helped Simon fake his death, but hadn't thought through the ramifications of what that meant. There had to have been a body. She would have identified it as his wife, and it would have needed to look enough like the author to fool anyone else who saw the body. Genevieve was either the killer or was in the conspiracy with whoever the killer was – most likely it was Simon himself.

A new thought occurred to me, causing a complete change of direction.

"What do you know about Simon worshipping the devil?"

Without needing to think, Jeremiah said, "I think it was nothing more than a publicity stunt."

I'd thrown the question at him in a way that made it seem like I *knew* for sure, but I was only picking up on what Frank said earlier. I'd expected him to question my sanity or suggest I was making it up. Instead, he confirmed there was something there to investigate.

Taking out my phone, I showed him the inverted pentagram.

"I found this near one of the recent murder victims. A very similar symbol appears on Simon's books."

Jeremiah squinted at the screen, the light from it illuminating his face in the dimly lit bar.

"Not a similar symbol. That exact symbol. The thin lines must have been too hard to get right but ..." He took out his own phone, fiddling with the screen for a second. "It should look like this." He turned it around to show me.

I was looking at a black and white image. It was the same as the one I'd seen on the book covers, except now it was far easier to make out the goat's face filling the space inside the lines. The chin filled the bottom point, the horns the two points at the top and the ears hung out on either side to fill the remaining two points of the five.

It gave me the creeps.

Now that I was looking at a cleaner image, I realised it was what I could see on the book cover. I had been looking at it on my phone and it was a small symbol mounted in a corner of the cover – far too small to make out the fine detail.

Looking back up at his face, I said, "Tell me what you know about this so-called publicity stunt, Jeremiah."

Jeremiah was familiar with the official storyline. The devil worship thing came about as a rumour that had probably, in Jeremiah's opinion, been deliberately leaked to the press when Simon's sales needed a boost. It generated a small press frenzy at the time, thrusting Simon's face into the headlines only to die down when he vehemently denied it and any notion of where the rumour had come from.

It felt like a dead end. So too did spending any more time talking to Jeremiah. I accepted defeat: he just didn't know anything useful. I quizzed him about Genevieve's affair, about possible connections to the victims who appeared to have no link to the dead author, and about Simon's obsession with the devil and all things evil.

Jeremiah answered every question to the best of his ability, but there was nothing to learn. The man tasked with finishing Simon's manuscripts and rounding out his most successful series knew how to write, but beyond that, he was of no use to me. If he was lying about his reason for stalking me, then he did so convincingly.

Trying a long shot, I asked, "Where were you last night between ten o'clock and midnight?" The details of Daniel McCormack's murder were too fresh for the press to have released them yet. If Jeremiah had to think about his answer, it could make him very interesting to me.

"I was away," he replied without missing a beat. "I go away a lot for research just as Simon did. When you are writing about a scene in a city or a place, it is much more powerful if you have been there to know how it smells and sounds. I travelled to Biggleswade yesterday afternoon. I got back when we met this morning. My overnight bag was still in the car. Why do you ask?" he enquired, an innocent expression rippling his brow.

"Just curious," I replied. Dismissing him as a possible suspect, I announced my intention to go back to my friends.

"Can I include a piece about the investigation in the final book?" Jeremiah asked, circling back to his reason for stalking me. "I really believe the readers will find it interesting."

It was something I would talk to Tempest about, but I wasn't about to commit to anything tonight. If we solved the case and found Simon Slater alive and well it would make national if not global headlines. Or if we found his killer or the serial killer behind the recent murders, whether that was one person or two, the same result might ensue.

Publicity for our business was what we wanted, but only when it reflected us in a good light.

Jeremiah accepted my rejection hoping it would change in due course.

"How's your head?" I asked, moving to get up.

He showed me a lopsided smile and rubbed the back of his skull where the tumbler struck home. Then mimed knocking on his head to show it was solid.

"It's nothing. I shouldn't have run."

I nodded. "Yes. Why did you?"

"You startled me. And then I bumped into that man and spilled his drinks and I'd been spying on you and trying to figure out what to say or how to approach you – I thought you were on a date. I guess I panicked," he admitted. "Not very manly of me, I know."

I patted his hand. "It's okay. I won't tell anyone. Now, if you'll excuse me, I'm going back to my friends. Maybe next time, just call me." I placed another business card on the table for him and walked away.

I was done for the night already and it wasn't even ten o'clock. I knew Patience wouldn't be pleased, but I just wasn't in the mood. The general hubbub of noise was starting to give me a headache, the stupidly-named drink she had me buy was too sweet for me to drink, and the thought of heading out to a nightclub in an hour or so with a plan to be there until the small hours sounded like the last thing in the world I wanted to do.

If I had known then what the rest of the evening held in store, I would have been on that dancefloor in a flash.

Ignorant Men.
Tuesday, October 17th
2151hrs

L OOKING AROUND FOR PATIENCE, I absentmindedly took another sip of my drink.

"Gaak," I pulled a face and put the drink to one side. I was thirsty, but checking the queue at the bar, there was no way I was bothering to stand in line there.

Taking out my phone, I planned to try calling Patience and if that didn't work, I was going to send her a text message and assume she would see it at some point. That plan lasted about as long as it took to bring the screen on my phone into life.

Darius appeared, touching my arm to get my attention.

I said a bad word.

He had Patience with him, but he wasn't holding her hand, he was towing her along like flotsam. The shots at lunch, the half-bottle of prosecco she gulped and the cocktails she'd thrown down her neck tonight had all combined into an ugly alcoholic mess.

"I need to leave her with you," Darius announced, manoeuvring Patience in my direction. "JB might be concussed. This evening did not go according to plan."

Not for any of us, I thought to myself.

Patience tottered over to me, a glorious grin splitting her face.

"Hey, Amanda! How's it going? This bar is fantastic! Let's get some shots!"

She swayed, lost her footing and stumbled into me. I caught her, keeping her upright by hugging her against my body. I was going to need a hand to get her back to our hotel, but when I looked again, I discovered Darius had already abandoned me.

"Darius!" I called fruitlessly through the crowd. I suspected that he heard me, though he could easily argue that my voice had been drowned out. Either way the cad had elected to escape.

Patience's left cheek had come to rest on my left shoulder though she lifted her head when I tried to move her back a pace.

"Where's Darius?" she asked, looking around with eyes that probably didn't focus.

I didn't try to sugar-coat my reply. "He left already."

She swiped an arm through the air, dismissing him as unimportant.

"Ah, we don't need him. Two sexy girls like us, we can have the pick of the men in here." To prove her point, she stuck two fingers in her mouth and whistled to get the attention of a nearby gaggle of men in their late twenties. "Hey boys! Fancy hooking up?" she enquired in a raucous manner.

Now that the guys were all looking her way, she flicked her head to make her hair move. It was supposed to be a sensuous and attractive move, but the sudden movement threw her off balance and she stumbled into me again.

The guys were laughing, and of course the group contained the two smart-mouthed men from our hotel.

I grabbed hold of Patience's arm, giving it a tug to get her moving.

"It's time to go, Patience. Let's get back to our hotel."

She tore her arm free.

"No!" she argued. "I'm having fun. You need to lighten up and let your hair down. You're always so serious."

Drawn by the live entertainment, the gaggle of men were coming closer.

Hissing insistently, I tried to grab her arm again without making a scene, I said, "I let my hair down plenty, Patience. I just don't get drunk."

Her protest was instant. "I'm not drunk! I'm ... I'm shappy," she slurred.

"These are the girls I was telling you about earlier," bragged the Jason Statham Wannabe to his friends. "All over each other on the floor of the hotel, they were."

"And again in the lift," added his partner.

Patience hiccupped, covering her mouth and pretending it hadn't happened. "Hey, guys, who wants to buy me a drink? My friend here is a little uptight, but I bet we can loosen her up with a few cocktails."

"Patience, I will leave you here," I warned. I was giving it serious consideration. She is a grown woman and capable of taking care of herself. Maybe not so much right now though. If I left her and something happened, would I forgive myself? I grabbed her arm again, this time gripping it far more firmly. When she looked at me, I said, "Please?"

The Jason Statham Wannabe didn't want the fun to end and moved to block my path.

"Stay, babe. The night is just getting started."

Dropping the pitch of my voice so there could be no question I was threatening him, I said, "Move out of my way. I won't ask again."

He turned his head to say something smart to his friends and I kicked him in the pants. Curse words flew from his mouth as he dropped to his knees, cupping his vitals, and threatening to get me.

The natural thing to do right now was escape, but I learned a few things from Tempest and Big Ben about standing my ground when it wasn't expected. Oddly, as I swivelled around to face the Statham Wannabe's friends, and gave his head a shove to send him all the way to the floor, I felt nothing but superiority and calm.

Discounting Patience, because she was a liability instead of an asset right now, I was all by myself and facing off against six men.

"Anyone else want to end their evening with a limp?" I asked, my right eyebrow hitched to encourage answers.

None came.

I waited another few seconds, making eye contact with each of the guys. Word of the ruckus I was causing had reached the ears of the bar's security team, and doormen in their black suits were heading my way.

"You again?" asked the same guy who'd wanted me to let Jeremiah go earlier.

"Don't worry. I'm leaving," I assured him.

He tilted his head with an amused expression on his face. "Damned right you are, Blondie."

Less than a minute later we were in the street outside and passing the queue of people still waiting to get in. It had been a terrible evening, and one I would have gladly avoided. Worse yet, I'd had next to nothing to drink but had spent more money than I cared to count.

It was cold out now, a gentle breeze frigid against my skin where it could find a way around or through my clothing. Hurrying away from the bar, I had no idea I was being pursued.

Kebab Compass. Tuesday, October 17th 2202hrs

THE WALK BACK TO our hotel wasn't a long one – less than five minutes probably, but predictably, Patience, now that the fresh air had hit her, wanted something to eat.

"How about a kebab?" she suggested in a tone that suggested my opinion was of value.

"I'm not hungry."

Patience nodded her head vigorously. "That's how you stay so skinny, girl. You can resist the lure of late-night snacks," she acknowledged sagely before falling silent. The silence did not last long. "How about Chinese food?"

"Really, Patience, I'm not hungry. We can stop to get you something though. I just don't want to take a big detour." I figured it couldn't hurt to put something in her belly. It would soak up the alcohol and slow down the absorption rate a little.

Of course, being in the middle of London and in one of the busier areas for bars and clubs, there were lots of eateries offering food to go. From Vietnamese to Mexican and everything in between, Patience had it all to choose from.

I steered her toward a kebab place with a short queue.

"Ooh, good choice," she remarked, eyeing up the list of options garishly illuminated on the shop's back wall.

A couple at the counter took their food and left with it in a plastic bag to take home. I was about to prompt Patience into ordering something when she stepped forward anyway.

The smells filling the small kebab shop were all meat, spices, and garlic. I was still full from lunch, but even if I hadn't been, there was nothing here that I wanted to eat.

Patience got her order less than a minute later – the speed at which a kebab could be put together another reason why I chose this place – and I steered her back out into the street.

"Mmmm nom, nom, nom," she mumbled, unwrapping her supper and taking a bite. "Mmmffmm. It'sh good," she managed to slur between bites.

"Let's walk a bit faster," I encouraged, picking up the pace because it was cool out – not that it seemed to be affecting Patience. I wanted to get back to our hotel where I could lock the door and put this evening behind me.

We crossed the road, leaving Leicester Square, and the number of people around us dropped sharply. A few minutes later and almost back at the hotel, there was almost no one around at all.

Almost no one.

There was a small, but nevertheless vital piece of information I omitted to consider when I tackled the Jason Statham wannabe: he knew where we were staying.

The moment we rounded the final corner and had our hotel right in front of us, I knew we were in trouble. The same gaggle of men I'd been forced to deal with in the bar were now blocking our path.

Statham was looking directly at me when he said, "I told you we'd get here before them." The comment was aimed at his friends and worryingly they all seemed quite willing to be here with him.

I raised my voice as we continued to close the distance to them.

"This isn't going to end the way you want it to," I warned. "My friend here is a police officer. If you touch her, you'll do jail time."

Statham shrugged. "Assuming you're telling the truth, which I don't think you are, she's a drunk police officer and won't remember a thing."

He was acting the tough guy in front of his friends, but they were looking less sure of themselves than they had a few seconds ago.

We were ten yards from them now and I was yet to slow my pace. Being threatened by a gang of men caused my body to react, fear preparing my body for fight or flight. I didn't want to have to do either, of course. Running was a poor option – Patience was slow at the best of times - and I was quite certain I couldn't fight more than one of them.

I ground to a halt a yard from the group and attempted to employ diplomacy.

"Look, I'm sorry about what happened in the bar. We are going up to our hotel rooms now. Just let us pass and nobody's evening needs to get ruined."

Statham shook his head. "I don't think so, bitch."

Up until that very moment, Patience had been completely absorbed by her kebab, but upon hearing the Jason Statham wannabe employing a word she hated, she looked up.

"Did you jussht call my friend a bitch?" she enquired in a voice that suggested it couldn't possibly be true.

Statham narrowed his eyes at her, turning back his lips slightly when he snarled, "So what if I did, bitch?"

I'm not sure if there are any circumstances where he might have got away with it, but he sealed his fate when he swatted the kebab clean out of her hand.

"Arrrrgghhh!" Patience squealed, watching it land on the pavement.

Statham's friends laughed, amused by his antics.

Patience headbutted him.

I swear I didn't see it coming and had no idea that she would do it. One moment she was gasping in horror at the loss of her supper, the next she was launching her skull at Statham's face.

He fell backwards, clutching his nose which was already leaking dark liquid, and Patience reached up to grab her head with both hands. Cradling it as one might something delicate, she wobbled from side to side drunkenly.

"Oooh, that wasn't such a great idea," she moaned.

With blood still pouring between his fingers, Statham growled, "Get them!" If Statham's friends had needed a catalyst to get them involved, then the head butt was it.

There was no time to discuss it, and no one around to help us. We couldn't get to the hotel, and I doubted we could outrun them, but we had to find more people or a safe haven and fast.

I grabbed Patience by the meaty part of her left arm and screamed, "Run!" We were moving first, but while I might have stood a chance of getting away, Patience was drunk and in heels.

We had a short head start but it wasn't going to be enough. I was about to turn and fight – I liked that plan better than getting tackled from behind and pinned to the ground, when a shadow emerged from the hotel's service yard area.

Twenty yards ahead of me, I sucked in a breath to shout for help when my brain caught up and I realised what it was that I was seeing.

The figure, now illuminated by the streetlights as it stepped out of the shadows, was clad head to foot in an embroidered black robe, the hood of which contained the same goat's head I saw earlier. Seeing it from just a few feet away now, I was shocked when the goat's eye blinked at me. Then its right ear twitched.

What the heck was I looking at?

In its right hand, it held a tall staff, a shepherd's crook, I corrected myself mentally when I observed the curling top end.

Patience screeched to a stop, her feet digging in when she braked hard to arrest her forward momentum.

"Waaaaah!" she squealed. "Waaaaah! What the heck is that thing, Amanda?"

Not that I had an answer for her; all I had were questions, but I didn't get to voice any of them because Statham's friends caught up to us.

Grabbed roughly from behind, both Patience and I were hauled from the ground. They did not appear to have even noticed the goat-headed figure standing in the street ahead; their attention entirely on the two of us.

"Hey!" I shouted at the terrifying apparition, craning my head to get a better look at it even as I struggled against the drunken idiots manhandling me. "Hey, who are you? What do you want?"

Someone cupped a boob and whether I got the right person or not I shot out an elbow and felt it connect. There was a yowl of pain, and the hand went away.

Next to me, Patience was screaming and thrashing, employing the kind of language one might associate with dock workers or lumberjacks.

Fighting off two or three men, it was inevitable that I was going to end up losing. One of the idiots finally got his arms around me and I was pinned. The same was true for Patience, but her eyes – wide as saucers – were locked on the goat-headed figure. So much so that the man facing her swung his eyes to track where she was looking.

He performed a perfect double-take, snapping his head around to stare at the haunting spectre.

"Hello, boys. Take a look at this," he invited. "The circus is in town again," he sniggered at his own joke.

I struggled to get free again, looking for an instep to stamp on, but the man holding me – who was drawing more pleasure from our closeness than I was content to accept if the lump digging into my hip was anything to go by – had on heavy boots with a steel cap and my stamping heel had no effect at all.

Statham, still recovering from the headbutt and holding his nose, caught up to the rest of us and kept going.

"Go on, freak," he growled at the human goat. "Be off with you. This is none of your business."

The upright-walking goat tilted his head slightly as if attempting to decipher some meaning from Statham's words, but did not reply and made no attempt to comply.

"I said get lost," snarled Statham, advancing on Goat Head menacingly.

The apparition lifted its right arm, bringing the staff down slowly just as Statham got within striking range.

A voice in my head screamed this was about to go badly wrong half a second before Statham burst into flame. His body blocked my view of what happened, but the logical part of my brain assured me the staff had to be loaded with some kind of pyrophoric chemical – the ones that ignite when exposed to air.

Statham reeled away, the whole front of his body engulfed in fire as he swatted at himself and shrieked in terror.

Momentarily stunned, it was only when Goat Head started towards us that Statham's friends abandoned their quest. The men holding Patience shoved her away just as the one pinning me let go. They were running away, choosing to leave Statham behind as they fled from the unnatural beast.

I grabbed Patience by her jacket and yelled, "Run!"

"Be gone," it called after us, the voice something unnatural and inhuman. It was so deep it sounded like it must have emanated from inside a cavern. "Abandon your quest or I will claim you as my slave in hell."

Patience said, "Waaaahhhh!" again and doubled her pace.

In my head I knew it was just a person in a costume. That didn't change the fact that it had just set a person on fire. I had no desire to be next.

A glance over my shoulder confirmed Goat Head was following and because I was looking the wrong way, I didn't see the obstacle until I hit it.

Tumbling, my weight pitching forward with no chance of getting my legs back under me, I could tell I had hit a person. Expecting it to be one of Statham's friends, I lashed out with a knee and tried to grab hold of an arm so I might gain the advantage when we hit the deck.

I might have gouged an eye or even bit hold of an ear had a voice not said, "Amanda?"

Hoof Prints. Tuesday, October 17th 2218hrs

IT WAS ENOUGH TO give me pause, and I looked down to find Hilary lying on the pavement beneath me.

He said, "Ow," very slowly and very carefully.

"Everyfing all right, 'Manda?" asked Basic, still on his feet and staring down at me with his usual expression of wonder.

Patience had managed to avoid running into Hilary, but seeing that I had, she chose to continue running.

Throwing myself off Hilary to an accompanying 'oooff' sound as I compressed his gut, I simultaneously attempted to get off the ground, turn around to check the relative position of Goat Head, and shout for Patience to stop running.

"Every woman for herself!" her voice echoed back as she continued haring down the street.

"It's gone," I yelled after her.

"Wass gone?" asked Basic, following my gaze as he tried to figure out what I was talking about.

"Could somebody give me a hand up, please?" requested Hilary, sounding wounded and winded.

Where the goat-headed apparition had been just a few seconds before, the street was now empty. That of course demanded I act upon the terrible injuries that Statham must have sustained.

He was slumped at the edge of the pavement where it met a wall and there was no sound coming from him.

"Patience!" I shouted at her again, this time getting her to at least look my way. I was already pulling out my phone and dialling three nines. The flames were out, but Statham was going to need an ambulance, and I needed to report the incident to the police.

I left Basic to help Hilary off the floor and went to check on the burn victim.

"What a mess," I muttered to myself, horrified at the burnt clothing and charred flesh I could see. Statham was unconscious and that was undoubtedly for the best.

Catching up to me, Hilary asked, "What's going on, Amanda? What are you doing here?"

Continuing to check over Statham for further injuries, I said, "I could ask you the same thing. I'm here pursuing a case."

It turned out that Brian 'Hilary' Clinton and James 'Basic' Burham were in the city for an exhibition and quite remarkably were also staying in the Travel Place hotel. I knew them through Tempest who in turn knew them because they lived in his village and they all drank at the same public house. It was that kind of village where there are not enough residents for the people living there to not know each other.

Basic, so called because he is as dumb as a box of rocks, used to collect shopping trolleys in a supermarket carpark, but stumbled across an idea for selling air guitars online. It's such a dumb idea it takes a special kind of person to dream it up, yet the man made so much money from it he began selling special editions.

Can you believe that? He then branched into selling wicked skids on his bike and the purchaser got a picture of the skid where he'd left the tyre rubber on the pavement. Then it was camouflage jackets, and all the person gets is a hanger.

"We're making a killing," bragged Hilary, Basic's business partner. "We've got a stall at a 'new and innovative' exhibition. It was a great chance to roll out our new line of products."

I was dying to know what they were selling now, but there was the small matter of the vanishing goat figure to investigate. Both ambulance and police were on their way to our location, so leaving Hilary to mind Statham, I tentatively retraced my steps to where I had first seen him.

"Don't go into the dark alleyway, Amanda!" cried Patience. "That's like a basic horror movie mistake."

Basic said, "Huh?"

"There is no one here," I reported back, staring into the hotel's service yard from the safety of the pavement. Quite where it had gone, I had no idea, but it was no longer anywhere in sight.

Basic and Patience came to stand beside me.

"Der was summit here?" asked Basic, struggling to grasp what was going on still.

Patience opened her mouth to answer him then started hyperventilating. Backing away with her eyes as wide as saucers again, she had a shaking finger pointing toward the ground a few yards beyond where I was standing.

I tracked her arm, frowning because I couldn't see anything that might have made her freak out. In fact, I was about to question what on earth had gotten into her when my eyes finally alighted upon a pair of footprints.

Cloven footprints.

Hoof prints one might say.

The goat-headed apparition had stepped into a puddle and left behind a pair of perfectly formed prints on the otherwise dry pavement.

The sound of sirens heading in our direction prompted a return to check on Statham once more. His friends had not returned and though I thought him to be a loathsome man with a terrible attitude, I wasn't going to let him die from his injuries.

Using my phone, I took a quick snapshot of the hoof prints and was heading back to where Patience was now gibbering quietly to herself when a police squad car burst into sight around the corner.

The ambulance was following close behind, arriving less than thirty seconds later. As you might imagine, the next half an hour was lost dealing with the aftermath of the two attacks. It had been my intention to put Patience to bed and go back to figuring out the case, but fatigue, partly due to adrenalin leaving my body after the chasing, fighting, and terror, had crept in and I wanted nothing more than to go to bed.

Basic and Hilary were quizzed about their involvement, the pair confirming my report that they arrived after everything happened. They stuck around though, waiting for me and Patience to be finished with the police.

The paramedics wasted no time in packing Statham into the ambulance. He needed urgent care and that took priority over everything else.

"A person with a goat's head?" the detective sought to confirm.

I blew out a tired breath; I'd explained it three times already.

"Yes, the head of a goat. You have the same report from Constable Woods, and you will probably get it from the burn victim when he regains consciousness. I don't know who it was, but I am in town investigating the Simon Slater case and it is no great leap to guess that the goat figure was something to do with that."

Detective Constable Priestley closed his notebook and took his time putting it away. He was employing a daft technique where he wouldn't say anything in the hope I would get bored or nervous and reveal all my secrets. I raised my eyebrows in question and stayed silent.

Like a gift from the gods my phone rang, and I blanked DC Priestly, stepping away a pace to answer it.

"Did you land?" I guessed, knowing it was Tempest calling.

"Indeed, I did," his sexy bass voice rumbled in my ear. "We are through customs already and on our way to the car. Text me the address of the hotel, I should be there within the hour. Big Ben is going to drop me off."

"You might want to bring him with you," I remarked. "There is a definite element of threat here."

Instantly concerned, I had to allay Tempest's fears, doing my best to explain the goat headed figure without embellishing it. If anything, I played the event down slightly. I didn't know for certain that it had been here for me after all.

Keep telling yourself that, Amanda.

Ignoring the know-it-all voice in my head, I promised to send Tempest the address for our hotel and said that I would attempt to book a room for Big Ben, though I knew Patience would happily have him bunk with her for the night if it came to it.

Tempest cut the call short because they were heading into the parking structure and were likely to lose signal. He was on his way to me and though I do not endorse the concept of needing a man around for protection, I will admit that I felt comforted by the knowledge that he would be here soon.

DC Priestly had no further questions, which I believe meant he couldn't think of anything to ask me - he did not come across as particularly bright. With permission to retire for the night, I thought perhaps I would fight my drowsiness and wait for Tempest to arrive.

That plan lasted about four seconds.

That's how long it took for my phone to ring with a call that changed the situation completely.

Intruder. Tuesday, October 17th 2314hrs

"A MANDA, IT'S GENEVIEVE," MY client whispered into the phone. That she was panicked about something was not in question. "I think there's someone here," she hissed, sounding terrified.

All thoughts of getting to bed vanished from my head in an instant - I was going straight over to her place, but I had to get across town to do it and the tubes were either about to shut down or had already done so. Buses ran later into the night, but I had no idea which route I wanted, and it would take forever to get there.

"Have you called the police?" I asked, biting a fingernail absentmindedly as I waited for her answer.

Genevieve's barely audible voice came back over the phone, "No, I don't want to. Can you come? I'm in the safe room. Something just moved in front of the camera," she hissed.

There it was again, her reluctance to involve the authorities. There was going to be a reason behind it, and I had to question if figuring out what it was might solve the whole case. I had wanted to confront her already and had only held back from doing so because she was my client and paying for my services.

Now that I was essentially summoned to her house in the middle of the night, it felt like a great opportunity to grill her on subjects she might find uncomfortable.

"Okay, Genevieve, I'm on my way, but it will take me a while to get there. Half an hour at least."

"Please just hurry. I think I ... arrrgh!" she screamed. "There is definitely someone outside! Message me when you get here. I'm not coming out until you do."

The line went dead, and I bit my lip as I tussled internally about what to do now. I didn't want to go alone - goodness knows this evening had been eventful enough already without encouraging further drama by being a lone woman out at night. However, even though Patience had sobered considerably in the last hour, I didn't really want to drag her along with me either.

Of course, when I announced that I needed to attend the home of a client, Hilary and Basic automatically volunteered to accompany me.

"Well, I'm not staying here alone," Patience remarked. "Where are we going?"

"A place in Kensington," I let everyone know. "The bigger question is how are we going to get there at this time of night?"

In response Hilary dug a hand into the front pocket of his trousers, retrieving a set of keys a moment later.

"I've got my van here," he announced, jangling his keys jubilantly.

Quite why he had a van with him demanded some explanation, but I let the question wait until we had all piled inside it and were moving with the traffic.

"We're at an exhibition," Hilary reiterated the explanation he'd given for being in London. Seeing my raised eyebrows, he expanded on his statement. "To transport our products."

Closing my eyes and raising a hand to stop him from saying anything more, I sought to alleviate my confusion.

"What products?" I begged to know. "Is this the new stuff you were trying to tell me about earlier? Last time I checked, you were selling air guitars, replacement strings for the air guitars, and things like camouflage jackets which, like the air guitars, take up no physical space because they do not exist."

His face alive with mischief and excitement, Hilary held a knowing index finger aloft.

"Ah, but you see, one has to maintain the mysticism of it all. We have huge boxes in which the camouflage jackets are stored. And what about the box each customer takes their air guitar home in? It is necessary for Basic and I to believe in the product. Just because it cannot be seen does not mean that it isn't there."

"Yeah," agreed Basic. "Dat's key to the whole thing. The customer's ability to imagine the physical manifestation of the items they purchase is what gives them such value."

Patience, slumped on the back seat with her head against the window, was doing a good job of pretending to be asleep. However, I heard it when she muttered, "White people are seriously crazy."

Ignoring her and trying hard not to scoff at what I was being told, I said, "You're serious?"

Basic nodded, his expression denoting how seriously he took his business.

"We ran out of invisible tattoos yesterday."

Patience's eyes fluttered open. "Say what now?"

Hilary flicked his eyes up into the rear-view mirror to look at her.

"It's our new biggest seller. We even hired two models in bikinis to show them off."

I was really struggling with it now.

"So you sell invisible tattoos, but not only that, you ran out of them."

Hilary sucked some air between his teeth, demonstrating how disappointed he still felt about failing to arrive with enough stock.

"What else?" I asked. "What other new products do you have?"

Sounding just a little ashamed, Hilary admitted, "Dehydrated water."

Patience swore, employing some colourful words to describe how she felt about that. Basic twisted around on the back seat, fishing around in the load compartment of their van. Two seconds later he settled back into his seat with a tin can in his hand.

"You've got to be kidding me." It was all I could think of to say. About the size of a baked bean tin, it had a colourful label running around the outside clearly declaring what was contained within. That the tin was empty seemed obvious, yet I needed to hold it for myself to be certain.

Shaking my head with absolute disbelief, I fixed Hilary with a questioning stare.

"Anything else?" I asked, curious to hear what other utter junk these two evil geniuses might have dreamt up.

Now looking thoroughly embarrassed, Hilary mumbled his reply.

"I didn't catch that," I invited him to repeat his answer at an audible volume.

He sighed. "Remote control toy stealth planes."

I shook my head.

"Let me guess. It's in full stealth mode and that's why they can't see it. I take it the remote control itself is invisible too."

Hilary took his eyes off the road for a moment to gawp at me in horror.

"Heavens, no. How could they possibly control it if we made the controls invisible?"

I rolled my eyes. "Well, obviously. What was I thinking?"

I found myself questioning what an alien race might make of humanity if their first contact involved some of the lunacy I was currently witness to. What tweaked my head the most was not that Basic could dream these things up, but that people would buy them. Not just one or two, but so many the two crazy people selling it all could actually run out of their imaginary product.

The opportunity to go even further down the rabbit hole with Basic and Hilary was mercifully eclipsed when the satnav announced our arrival at our destination. I hadn't been paying much attention to the roads, but looking now I realised we were just coming into the street that led to Genevieve's gated street.

Hilary rolled up to the guard, powering down his window only to discover that we were not expected. I needed to call Genevieve anyway to let her know that we were arriving, and once I had her on the phone, I let her tell the guard to let us through.

Inside, I directed Hilary around to park in front of Genevieve's property.

"Nice place," he observed with an appreciative whistle.

"We're outside," I let Genevieve know since she was still on the phone.

"Is it safe?" she asked. "Have you checked the area?"

"Didn't you get the guards to do that?" I questioned.

She made a scoffing noise. "Ha! Those idiots. They're not even rent-a-cops. They open the barrier at the front gate. Calling them guards is a joke."

I took that to mean 'no'. Basic and Hilary were already out of the van, and though Patience didn't look like she wanted to go looking for a prowler/serial killer, she also didn't want to stay in the van by herself.

Standing in front of Genevieve's house, she wanted to confirm, "Just one person lives here?"

"Yup."

She continued to stare at the house. "The wife of a dead author."

"Yup."

Patience grimaced. "I could marry someone who writes books. Especially if they were going to up and die and leave me with all the money."

I didn't say anything, but as I started my check of the perimeter, taking Patience with me while Hilary and Basic went in the opposite direction, her comment took me back to the question about who there was to gain from Simon Slater's death. Not just his death though, because there had been so many murders since.

Patience's comment about the royalties raised a good question, yet it was one that did nothing to help me. If anything, it further muddied the waters. Going back to my point about most crimes boiling down to sex or money, Simon's royalties were sufficient to motivate someone to commit murder. People had been killed for a lot less.

It could explain Leslie Ashe's murder, but what about the rest? If Genevieve was genuinely being targeted, it could be because she was now receiving Simon's cut of the takings, yet there were four victims who I was certain had no claim to his money, and what about the author himself?

I continued to go around in a circle, questioning whether Simon was still alive, then dismissing it as improbable because Genevieve had hired me. A few moments later the argument raging in my head would put the concept of Simon's faked death back on the table and I had been sailing around this buoy for two days.

Arriving at the rear of the house to find Hilary and Basic waiting for us, we confirmed not only was there no sign of anyone, but that we had also failed to find any sign of forced entry or the slightest indication that anyone had been here.

Genevieve had a camera at the front of her house, which like any modern appliance could be accessed via an app on her phone. I hadn't thought to ask her about it earlier, but putting my phone to my ear once more, and confirming we had essentially secured the perimeter of her property, it was going to be the first thing I asked her about once we were inside.

"No, I'm not coming to the door!" Genevieve babbled in a terrified tone. "I can open it automatically from where I am. I'll come out once you have checked the house."

"That is one cautious woman," muttered Patience. "How about if when we get inside, I jump out and scare her?"

I checked to see if Patience was serious, but her face wasn't giving anything away.

Concerned she might do it, I said, "I don't think that would go down very well."

I got a half shrug from Patience as we traipsed back to the front of the house. "Might be fun though," she remarked.

I wasn't really paying much attention to my surroundings truth be told. I was too busy wrapping my head around the confusing elements of the case, so when Hilary squealed and jumped in fright just as he rounded the corner of the house, it scared the bejeezus out of me.

Basic, right behind Hilary, shoved him to one side and took off.

"There's someone there!" gasped Hilary, one hand to his chest as his heart rhythm returned to normal. "Or something," he blurted between gulps of air. "It went up the other side of the house."

I twisted around and ran, giving no thought to whether the person might be dangerous.

I heard Patience yell, "Don't you leave me, Amanda Harper! I'm not getting dragged to hell by a minion of the devil because you left me with no protection!"

I could hear her chasing after me, but with Basic going anti-clockwise around the house, unless whoever it was managed to overpower him – a highly unlikely scenario – he would drive them straight into my arms. I just needed to create the element of surprise.

Racing to get to the back of the house, which was shrouded in shadow, I sucked in a deep breath and ducked behind a rose bush. Someone was coming, their footsteps fast and almost silent. Patience was coming too, but she was making enough noise to wake the local children asleep in their beds.

"Amanda where are you?" she hissed urgently.

There was no way the person coming up the opposite side of the house didn't hear her; it would make them cautious and probably ruin my chance to take them down before they saw me. However, their steps faltered for only a scant moment before trebling in pace when Basic's battle cry filled the air.

A black-clad figure shot out from the side of the house. It was short and slight, my brain telling me I was about to tackle a woman. Regardless of gender, they were about to eat grass.

With a grunt of effort, I shoved off the wall and threw myself across the patio on an intercept path. Patience caught sight of the figure and screamed, surprise and fear getting the better of her. Her yell pulled the figure's head around and a flash of moonlight illuminated the face just before I smashed into it.

Familiar Prowler. Tuesday, October 17th 2348hrs

THE FLASH OF MOONLIGHT gave me just a fraction of a second to alter my attack and had I not done so, I would have hit Frank in the face with a high elbow. I managed to pull it at the last moment, but there was nothing I could do to alter my trajectory.

I slammed into the bookshop owner, arresting my forward momentum by using it to catapult him across the garden. He made a kind of 'Waaaaah!' sound that was cut off when his head hit the grass face first. He tumbled and rolled, landing on his front whereupon he twisted his head around to look up at me with a cheesy grin.

"Evening, Amanda."

I rolled my eyes. "Frank what are you doing here?"

"BRRAARRRRRRGHHH!!!"

Oh, yes. I'd forgotten about Basic. The giant lump of a man had been ten yards behind Frank and was still pursuing him. Bellowing his war cry like a berserker and sounding like an enraged bear, he was heading for Frank, and would probably body slam him into the ground if I didn't stop him.

Mercifully, Patience saw the danger first and spread her arms and legs like a starfish to create a barrier.

"Whoa there, crazy horse! It's Frank."

Basic slowed his headlong charge before he got to Patience, peering over the top of her head to look down at the figure just starting to pick himself off the ground.

"Frank?" he questioned.

I echoed his confusion, repeating my question, "What are you doing here, Frank?"

He was back on his feet and dusting himself off to chase away the loose bits of grass now stuck to his clothing. Fixing me with a superior look, he said, "I knew you wouldn't listen, so I came in person. Simon Slater was almost certainly involved with or was himself a member of a satanic cult. That he has returned from the dead indicates that members of the cult are able to wield a significant amount of dark magic. The satanic forces involved here are going to get you all killed."

Patience came around me to get to him and I feared for a moment that she was going to sock him in the jaw or something. Quite the opposite, she flung her arms around him and pulled him into a bear hug.

"Mmmfffr, mmmuuffl, mmmumagghlly," said Frank, his face crushed into Patience's ample chest.

She released him, allowing Frank to suck in a gasp of air to refill his lungs as she gushed, "Thank you so much for coming, Frank. Finally, there is someone here who knows how dangerous this situation is. Everyone else wants to act like it's just a regular serial killer." She scanned her eyes around, squinting into the darkness. "Are the ninjas here?"

Frank waggled his eyebrows. "If you could see them, they wouldn't be very good ninjas, now would they?"

Patience's mouth formed a confused 'O'.

I rolled my eyes yet again. "They're not here, are they?"

"Um, no," said Frank, his cheeks colouring.

"What's going on?" asked Hilary. We all turned to find him peering around the side of the house. "There was a lot of noise and ... and I decided to guard the front of the house ..." he let his words trail off. "Hey, is that Frank?"

My phone rang, Genevieve calling for a panic-stricken update. I didn't bother to explain about Frank's unexpected arrival; she wasn't aware I had anyone with me. Instead, I told her I wanted to be doubly sure the house was secure and had been rechecking it.

Traipsing back to the front door, which Genevieve said she would open when she could see me outside, I quizzed Frank on his unexpected appearance.

"How did you find me?"

"I employed a tracking spell," he replied nonchalantly like it was a perfectly normal thing to say. "I picked up a strand of your hair a while back and used it as the focus to locate you."

I frowned at him.

"You really ought to be more careful," he warned, a touch of colour reaching his cheeks. "You wouldn't believe what an experienced practitioner can do with a drop of someone's blood."

I narrowed my eyes.

"Okay, okay. You always have to ruin the mysticism. I looked up Simon Slater's former address and I came here to see if there were any signs of satanic worship. The only way to stop Simon Slater's undead form is to break the spell controlling it. To do that we have to find the 'church' where the spell was cast. There will be a satanic cult behind all these deaths. If we find that, we can stop the whole thing."

I accepted his explanation – it sounded just like something Frank would do. He was as brave as a lion and willing to put his life on the line to protect others. That he was also utterly mad did not need to be stated.

Then the obvious occurred to me. "How long have you been here, Frank?"

"Oh, about forty minutes," he estimated.

"You're the prowler," I sighed.

Frank raised his eyebrows.

"What do you think we are doing here?" I demanded, impatience clear in my tone. "We came because my client spotted someone outside her house. You." I pointed out when he still didn't get it.

"Well, I was looking for signs of satanic worship," Frank defended his actions. "You know; markings on the doors and walls, that sort of thing."

"You found some, right," Patience guessed, grabbing Frank's arm so he would turn to look at her.

He made an apologetic face. "Um, no, actually. There's nothing here at all."

Under my breath, I muttered, "What a surprise."

True to her word, when we got to the front door and in sight of the camera she had there, Genevieve operated a switch, a solenoid clicked, and the front door opened.

Blue Moon is an investigation agency, not close protection. Checking houses for potential homicidal maniacs is not in the job description, but we did it anyway. Mostly this was because I was certain the scary figure Genevieve saw on her camera was Frank in his black hood as the idiot snooped around her house. It was also partly because I didn't think Genevieve would come out of her hidey hole if she had any doubt the house was safe, but also because we had to be sure and I used to be a cop, Patience still is one, and Basic looks like a shaved bear.

Seriously, Basic is one of those guys who was born a few centuries too late. He would have been right at home with the Vikings, marauding across Europe and leading armies because he weighs two hundred and goodness knows how many pounds and looks like he can run through walls. If there was anyone lurking in a dark corner of Genevieve's house, I would just have Basic eat them.

Genevieve answered the phone almost before it rang at her end. "What's going on? Did you catch him? Is he back from the dead?" she spewed her words in a torrent.

Calmly, I replied, "There is no one here. You can come out now."

"No one there? I saw ... I saw something. Are you sure it's safe to come out?"

It took another minute and a second sweep of the house, but Genevieve finally found the courage to exit her safe room. I hadn't expected it, but gathered in the central hallway running through her house, she emerged from a half-sized door under the stairs. I guess it was a clever place to put the exit because anyone visiting would assume, as I had, that it was a place to put the vacuum cleaner and ironing board.

Forced to duck as she clambered out, Genevieve looked less than perfectly presented for the first time. Her hands were shaking; that was the first thing I noticed.

Was it part of an act?

That I still couldn't decide whether to believe my client was completely innocent or entirely guilty and using me to try to cover her crimes was bugging me and that came out in an accusatory tone when I addressed her.

"What was it that you think you saw, Genevieve?"

Rising to a standing position, she didn't answer, but rushed across the space to wrap her arms around me.

"I was so scared!" she wailed. "I really thought it was Simon returning to kill me! He's going to, you know."

"Yes," agreed Frank. "Raised from the dead through dark magic, he's going to be very difficult to stop. We'll need to identify the satanic cult first and stop them ..."

Still clinging to me, Genevieve let out a horrified wail.

"Can you tone it down a touch, Frank?" I suggested in a tone that made it sound like an order.

Genevieve spluttered, "What is he talking about?"

Frank opened his mouth to speak, and I held up a hand, making a puppet mouth shape with it which I then very deliberately shut. It was enough to silence him, but I hadn't allowed for Patience – she does what she wants.

"Frank believes your husband was involved in a satanic cult," she stated.

I expected the statement to make Genevieve faint or wail again, but the effect it had was completely opposite. She stepped away from me, an angry frown forming on her brow.

"Why ever would you say such a thing?" she demanded. "Who are you, anyway?"

"This is Frank Decaux," I explained, tackling the task of introducing the new people I'd brought into my client's house. "He's ... um, he's part of my extended team," I ventured, silently checking with Frank that he wasn't going to argue. "This is Patience," I left out the part about Patience being a police officer, "and this is Hil ... Brian Clinton and James Burham. I felt your case demanded additional personnel and resources if I am to solve it swiftly, Mrs Slater."

"Will it cost me more?" she wanted to know.

I shook my head. "Not a penny. This is all from my budget."

"Very well," she made a thoughtful face, "But this one needs to watch himself," she poked a manicured finger in Frank's direction. "If I hear any more of that satanic claptrap, I'll sue him for slander. My husband was not a member of a satanic cult."

Frank mimed locking his lips, but Patience wasn't to be put off so easily.

"How do you explain your husband coming back from the dead to kill all these people then, Mrs? And how do you explain the goat-headed nightmare that attacked us tonight?"

Genevieve's eyes bugged right out of her head, and she looked terrified. "No. No, it can't be," she wailed, backing into a wall and clinging to it.

Frank's vow of silence didn't last long. "Really? Baphomet manifested in physical form right here in London?"

"Yeah," said Patience, "Scared the living crap out of me and set fire to a guy."

Frank's mouth dropped open, but it was with excitement and awe rather than shock.

"Actual physical contact! This is incredible! They must have found a way to open a portal to hell, setting him free to stalk the earth! You say he torched a person?"

Patience shrugged. "Yeah, but he was kind of a dick, so that part was okay."

Genevieve was freaking out, her hands clasped to her head like they were earlier today.

"Who is Baphomet?" she asked, her question aimed directly at Frank.

He rattled off a detailed answer, explaining about the goat thing and how he was linked directly with Satan and hell. The occult bookshop owner was in his element, but it wasn't getting me anywhere and wasn't helping Genevieve who looked paler and paler by the minute.

As he was getting to the part about the spell he believed must have been used to bring her husband back to life, he was quite tentative about suggesting again that there had to be a satanic cult behind it.

Curiously though, Genevieve didn't shout him down or threaten legal action this time. Instead, she seemed to accept what she was being told as if it somehow fitted with what she knew.

"You really think the recent murders are at the hands of this cult?" she asked, her voice quiet.

Frank nodded apologetically. "Your husband's death too, most likely. Did he ever say anything to you about devil worship?"

"NO!" Genevieve snapped, her attitude swinging through one hundred and eighty degrees yet again. Dropping her voice to a normal tone, she said, "No. Nothing like that ever unless it was to do with one of his books. Simon was a complex man with a vivid imagination, but he wasn't evil or twisted."

"He's killed five people," Patience reminded her.

"It's not Simon," Hilary added unhelpfully. "It's just his reanimated corpse."

Further discussion of the subject was cut short when my phone pinged.

"Tempest just arrived," I announced, heading for the door. I would be glad to see him under any circumstances, but right now ... he was my sanity anchor and I needed him close by.

I kissed him on the doorstep and held him for a few seconds. He'd only been gone two days, but I had missed him.

Behind him Big Ben yawned and waited and when I turned to go inside with Tempest, he followed, but protested, "Hey, no hug and kiss for me?"

"Not a chance, sex pest, I don't know where your lips have been."

"Everywhere," he grinned. "They've been everywhere, babe."

Ignoring Big Ben's remarks as he knew I would, I led both newcomers into Genevieve's living room.

"Genevieve this is Tempest Michaels," I introduced him, and was about to do the same for Big Ben even though I knew he would then hit on her, but when I turned to look, I discovered he wasn't there.

Regardless, I stepped back so Tempest could do his thing. He is charming and handsome and employs those attributes along with his confident personality to instill calm where none exists. He exudes confidence and that makes people trust him.

With him to reiterate my words, the conversation changed course.

"I can assure you, Mrs Slater, that if your husband is dead ..." we had swiftly discussed some of my suspicions on the doorstep.

"He is," she insisted.

"Then it is someone else behind the murders." Shifting to a thoughtful expression, Tempest said, "Amanda tells me you believe the recent murders are being committed by a different killer even though they are re-enactments of scenes from your husband's books and that is how he died. Can you tell me what makes you so sure?"

I had asked the same question myself.

On the spot, she didn't sound anywhere near as certain as she had earlier today.

"Well, despite what you say, I still think it is Simon back from the dead. Since he couldn't have killed himself, his killer must be someone else."

Tempest pursed his lips and nodded his head, acknowledging her statement. There was no point arguing with her; her beliefs were too deeply ingrained. Only by catching whoever was really behind the murders would we convince her.

It was late in the day and since her prowler turned out to be Frank – not that we told her that - there was no immediate danger to Mrs Slater that I could perceive. I needed sleep and I was certain Tempest did too. In the morning, fresh and rested, we would examine what we knew, and push forward. Right now, everyone was tired, and it was time to call it a day.

Announcing our intended departure, Genevieve's immediate response was, "You can't all leave me! I need someone to stay here!"

"I'll do it," volunteered Big Ben.

His voice echoed in from outside the room where he'd chosen to relax in a large wing-backed chair.

Surprised to hear a voice and unaware there was yet another person with us, she was looking in the direction of the door when Big Ben came through it.

His lips split in a wolf's smile.

What Big Ben Does Best. Wednesday, October 18th 0029hrs

WITH EVERYONE SHUFFLING TOWARD the door, there began a swift discussion of who was going to ride in whose car: Frank's jalopy or Hilary's van.

I found myself pulled to one side by Big Ben.

"Looks like I'm providing close protection tonight," he stated, without almost no inflection. I say almost because there was a definite huskiness to his voice - Big Ben was going to have Genevieve's pants off within minutes of us leaving. "What's the deal here? Did I just hear that her husband was killed a while back?"

Questioning whether he was asking just to determine if an enraged spouse was going to kick the bedroom door in, I said, "Simon Slater's murder was staged to be a re-enactment of one of the crimes from his books. It made all the papers at the time," I added, surprised Big Ben didn't already know about it.

"You think I have time to read the newspapers?" he quipped.

I rolled my eyes. "You could watch a TV news channel."

"That sounds boring. There're no naked women. Although I did date this reporter chick once and she wanted me to ..."

"Stop!" I demanded. "I have no desire to be regaled with any of your sleazy sex stories."

He sniggered at me. "Sure thing, PC Hotstuff," he employed an old nickname Tempest had for me when we first met.

I huffed out a breath and considered kicking Big Ben in the trousers.

Big Ben, AKA Benjamin Winters, stands six foot and seven inches tall, looks like a cover model from a fitness magazine, and is one of those boys who simply refuses to grow up. By which I mean he still plays with toys every day, but his toys are now women.

He is very nice to look at but thereafter all interest on my part ceases. I'm with Tempest and quite happy, but if I were not, Big Ben would still never make it into my bed because he is a man slut. Tempest employs him as muscle on a casual but semi-regular basis and for that task he is perfectly suited.

I have seen Big Ben wade into seemingly insurmountable numbers only to emerge the sole man standing just moments later. According to Tempest, fighting Big Ben is like trying to catch a running lawnmower and the injuries sustained approximately the same.

Whatever the case, he was staying here with Genevieve – a situation that appeared to meet with her wholehearted approval.

Outside in Frank's car, I nudged Tempest.

"How long?"

He raised one eyebrow. "Until he has her in bed? Less than fifteen minutes is my bet."

I snorted a tired laugh, but couldn't argue. I countered with, "I'm going to say ten," and I lost because it was exactly thirteen minutes before Tempest's phone pinged with a picture of Genevieve wearing distinctly less than when I last saw her.

I rested my head against Tempest's muscular shoulder and shut my eyes. They flicked open two seconds later when something itched at my brain.

"Was that a scar on her back?" I asked.

Tempest took out his phone and tapped with his thumb to produce the picture again. The picture was taken pointed downwards at Genevieve's naked back. She was facing away from Big Ben and ... well, I'm sure you don't need the full description to figure it out. Anyway, at the base of her spine was a scar.

Six inches across and roughly circular, I couldn't figure out what could have caused it. It wasn't a burn – they always leave such terrible scars.

"It's a tattoo," Tempest replied, his eyes closing as he laid his head back. "I think."

The moment he said it, I knew he was right. What I was seeing wasn't a scar at all, but the discoloured tissue left behind by laser tattoo removal. Do professional models have tattoos? I suspected the answer was yes, but not in general because it would limit the photoshoots they could do. Ok, she was no longer a model, but she'd had a tattoo and then chose to remove it.

Why?

The question went on the list with the two hundred others I had no answers for.

Height Difference.
Wednesday, October
18th 0615hrs

D ESPITE THE LATE FINISH to the previous day, the lure of an unresolved mystery had me awake at an early hour. I sat up in bed, rubbing my eyes and looking across to the other side of the bed only to find it empty.

You might be thinking that returning to our hotel, given that Statham's friends and the goat-headed apparition knew we were staying there, might be dangerous and you would be right. Tempest had the same thought and worked his magic to find us rooms elsewhere.

Of course, getting a room in London after midnight is no easy feat, but Tempest had a contact at ... you won't believe it, but ... the Ritz. Even though it cost an arm and both legs, that was where we were staying.

Patience had gawped at the palatial entrance lobby when we arrived and continued to stare open-mouthed at everything as a bellhop led us through the corridors to our rooms. I'd stayed there before; with Tempest of course, so it wasn't new to me, but there was no denying the opulence of our surroundings.

He'd booked two rooms, one for us and one for Patience. Frank took my room at the Travel Place rather than make the drive home tonight, which left the guys at one location and us at another.

Tempest was at the hotel room's grand writing desk, working on his laptop.

I crossed the room, my skin goosepimpling from the sudden drop in temperature.

"What're you working on, champ?" I put an arm around his shoulders and kissed his ear. On the screen of his computer was a picture I recognised; a still taken from the CCTV footage that supposedly captured Simon Slater mere yards from the second murder scene.

"It looks like him," Tempest remarked. "But unless he did fake his own death," something I haven't ruled out yet, "then we can assume it is someone else doing a good job of pretending to be him."

"Yes. But who and why?" I voiced the obvious questions. "I mean, the why is so they can kill a bunch of people and have everyone believe it is a dead person doing it. That's obvious. But why kill *them*?"

Tempest sucked on his cheek. "That is a very good question. The victims, Simon Slater included, are all linked to some extent by the publishing industry. Some of them, as Jane discovered, are linked by Simon's royalties. Others stick out though because they do not share that link."

"What are you thinking?" I asked, glad to have a second brain working on the problem. "The royalties are just too obvious to dismiss. I feel like it has to be a motivating factor. With the deaths so far, if Jane's list is correct, there are only two parties left to claim the money: Genevieve and Indigo's publishing house."

"Exactly," Tempest leaned his head to one side to kiss my fingers. "I can't see it being Genevieve herself ..."

"She's hiding something," I insisted. "Guilt is dripping off her. I'm not suggesting she's behind the murders," I quickly pointed out. "Her terror feels genuine, but I'm still not convinced she didn't help her husband to fake his death and that means she was complicit in the death of whoever they buried in Simon's place."

Tempest didn't argue. What he said was, "It leaves Simon's publishers as the probable perpetrators. I know that fails to deal with the deaths not associated with the royalties, but it's where I want to focus our efforts for now. You said there was something screwy about them?"

I snorted a laugh. "Absolutely. They were all just weird, like they were using a single brain for everyone in the office."

"Like a cult," Tempest remarked, ominously. He twisted around to look at me. "I'm not sure Frank is wrong about the satanic cult, babe." He was being serious. "It would explain the symbol you found and the goat-headed figure last night."

Getting on board with the idea, I told him, "Genevieve was very quick to blast Frank when he suggested her husband could have been a member." I thought about that for a moment. "Then she calmed down and listened to what he had to say. That happened when she learned about Goat Head. She knows more than she is willing to admit."

"A cult," Tempest remarked. "I think we need to take a very close look at Kimble Publishing, but first I want to visit this place." He jabbed a finger at the screen. "Fancy breakfast out?"

Thirty minutes later, I discovered the secret meaning behind Tempest's question. We could have enjoyed the wonderful breakfast at the Ritz, or we could have walked a few yards down the street to find a plethora of restaurants from which to choose.

We certainly didn't need to take the tube across town to find food, but that was what we did because the CCTV picture of Simon had an Armenian food place in the background.

We exited the tube at Perivale, one of the westernmost stations on the Central Line and had to walk almost a mile to get to our destination. Tempest was yet to explain why he wanted to visit the place, but I found out soon enough.

"How tall was Simon Slater?" he asked.

I had no idea what the answer was, but I instantly knew why Tempest was asking.

"The guy in the footage is what? Too tall or too short?" I asked.

Tempest had stopped in front of a signpost. "Too tall."

"How tall was Simon?" I repeated Tempest's question, suspecting he already knew the answer.

"Five feet ten inches." Tempest opened his laptop and brought up the photograph again. Then he measured himself against the pole of the signpost, licked his finger and made a mark on it. "That's six feet."

Taking his laptop from his bag, he booted it into life and brought the CCTV picture up. Even using my eyeball as a measuring device, I could instantly tell the man in the photograph was taller than Tempest. It made him several inches taller than Simon Slater.

I let a laugh slip from my lips and smiled. "The police haven't picked up on that." They would have reported it to the press to show they were making progress if they knew.

"They probably dismissed the picture as misleading. If they believe Simon Slater is dead, the CCTV footage can be considered as nothing more than a coincidence – someone who looks like him. So too for the other photograph they have."

A flash of memory sparked to life. "They found his fingerprints at the latest crime scene."

Tempest showed me a surprised face. "Really?"

I told him how Patience leveraged Darius' interest in her to get us into the crime scene and that he gave me all kinds of juicy information because we were meeting for drinks later that day.

Tempest folded his laptop and put it away. "I bet that's confusing them," he said, zipping his backpack closed. "Breakfast?"

The Armenian place served some mean pancakes which we both ordered with hungry excitement. Waiting for our food to be served, we drank piping hot, fresh coffee. Dark and unctuous, it gave off a heavenly aroma that made me want more even before I took my first sip.

"I want Big Ben to snoop around Genevieve's house," I announced with a shudder as I took my first swig of the dark brew and imagined the caffeine hitting my veins. "Whatever she is hiding, it has to be connected to this case."

Tempest agreed. "That tattoo removal must be recent. I believe it takes several sessions to remove most tattoos."

"Well, there's nothing left of it now," I remarked.

"Which is unfortunate, but not insurmountable. There might be photographs of her somewhere online that reveal what it was. Or Big Ben might find something on her phone."

"It could be nothing," I tried to decide how important it was.

"It could be."

I took another sip of my coffee. "But we won't know until we know."

Tempest picked up his phone, planning to call Big Ben I guessed. "Exactly."

My phone began to vibrate at that very moment, the name 'Big Ben' displayed on the screen. I showed Tempest, turning the phone so he could see the screen before I thumbed the answer icon.

Tempest put his phone down again and leaned across the table so he would hear what Big Ben had to say – there were people around us, and kids, so I wasn't going to put the big idiot on speaker because the chances were he was about to brag about his night of top-level shagging.

"Amanda, can you hear me?" he whispered, being uncharacteristically discreet.

"Yes. I have Tempest with me. If you are about to regale me with last night's run down of all the rooms and positions you did it in, please don't bother."

There was a beat of silence before he said, "When do I ever talk to you about sex, Hotstuff?"

I rolled my eyes. "All the damn time, Ben. Listen, I have a job for you."

He cut over me, "You need to hear this first. Genevieve just got a call – they are going to exhume her husband. She is freaking out. She's downstairs somewhere now shouting at her lawyers. I think it's her lawyers anyway."

This was big news.

"That must be because they found his fingerprints." In my head I punched a fist into the air. "She knows they are going to discover it's not his body and that will land her right in it."

I heard Big Ben making a thoughtful clicking noise with his tongue. "I don't know," he began to say. "She wanted to talk about it all last night and I'm not so sure her husband is alive. If she helped to fake his death, then she is a great actor. She convinced me."

An unwelcome mental image of Genevieve 'convincing' Big Ben to believe her story flashed into my head.

Pushing it away, I asked, "Okay, so what's going to happen now? I need you to snoop around her house. Is there any chance you can do that? Is she going to kick you out or do you think you can convince her to let you stay there tonight again? Maybe when she's asleep ..."

"Hotstuff, that woman doesn't sleep. I've never known an older woman with so much energy. Last night she ..."

"La-la-la-la-la-laaaa," I sang with my fingers in my ears much to Tempest's amusement. He said something to Big Ben and gave me the nod that it was safe to listen again.

"Oh, hold on," said Big Ben, the sound of his feet on the floor echoing back through the phone as he went somewhere fast. "She just went out."

"And left you there?" I questioned.

"Apparently so."

Frowning, I said, "I guess she forgot about you."

"Babe. She isn't ever going to forget about me. The number of times I made her ..."

"Stop talking!" I insisted, my fingers heading for my ears again. The sound of his laughter caused me to stop while I could still hear – the evil git loved teasing me.

"My guess is she is heading for wherever her husband is buried with a plan to stop them digging him up," Big Ben suggested. "Whatever the case, it would appear that I have some time to snoop. What do you want me to look for?"

Proof. Wednesday, October 18th 0758hrs

FOR COMPLETENESS AS MUCH as anything, I was going to call Genevieve. She was going to be tied up for a chunk of the day, of that I felt certain, and needed to get a call into her quickly. If she was guilty of faking her husband's death, I was going to hear it in her voice.

Shockingly, while I was deliberating how to word my careful accusation, she called me.

"Genevieve, good morning," I answered guardedly.

"Amanda, hi," she was a little out of breath. Was that fear of discovery affecting her heart rate?

"I understand you are having quite the start to your day."

"So, you know then," Genevieve remarked. "Is nothing sacred? A person ought to be allowed to rest once they are in the grave. Listen, I ran into Jeremiah on my way out of the door. I sent him away because your friend, Benjamin, is still in my house. It would have been ... awkward, I guess, if they'd bumped into each other. Jeremiah has something of a crush on me, I think."

He did, I'd seen the way he looked at her.

"I don't suppose I could beg you to send him a message for me, could you. Benjamin that is, not Jeremiah. Just to let him know I'm sorry for just running out like that. I don't have his number, I'm afraid."

"I can send it to you," I offered, flicking between apps. "It's on it's way to you now."

Genevieve thanked me and made it clear she wanted to get off the phone. I dearly wanted to ask her what they were going to find when they opened Simon's coffin, but I couldn't find a way to do it without levelling an outright accusation. I almost did it, but lost the chance when she snapped out a swift 'Goodbye' and ended the call.

Even then I toyed with the idea of calling her back.

Tempest put a hand on my shoulder. "You should let it go for now. The truth about Simon is coming out today whether she likes it or not. Her lawyers will not be able to stop the exhumation. He is either dead as she claims, or alive, in which case she is in a whole heap of trouble."

He was right. Letting her maintain the pretence until the truth was out there for all to see was the most sensible strategy to employ.

I pocketed my phone, and making a silent bet with myself that we wouldn't have a client for this case by the end of the day, I followed Tempest down into the London Underground again.

It was still early when we arrived at the Travel Place near Leicester Square. Next on our agenda was to explore another of the murder locations, but first Tempest wanted to 'have a little chat' with Frank. The well-meaning crazy man was a mite unpredictable, as demonstrated by his unexpected appearance at Genevieve's place last night. He wanted to be involved, convinced as he was that we were up against the forces of hell, but his good intentions were likely to just get in our way.

We bumped into Basic and Hilary as we came into the hotel's excuse for an entrance lobby.

Tempest greeted them, "Just heading out guys?"

Basic grinned, "S'right."

Hilary said, "It's the last day of the exhibition. One last chance to draw attention to the business."

"Last chance to sell the stock," I teased.

"S'right," agreed Basic, the irony of my statement going straight over his head. To be fair, I could make fun of them all I wanted, they were making a fortune with their innovative, non-existent products. It was the kind of money that could attract a gold-digger, and for a while I know Tempest had been concerned about Basic's girlfriend. Maisy had a master's degree in Engineering and might be considered ill-suited for a relationship with Basic, yet the two had been dating for more than a year and there was no sign that she was trying to lock him into anything for her own financial gain.

We wished the guys luck and rode the elevator up to Patience's room. Frank was up and dressed and keen to be part of whatever we had planned for the day.

"But you need me," he protested when Tempest advised we were setting off without him. "I know you don't believe in anything magical or supernatural, but this is an actual satanic cult we're talking about. Whether you wish to accept the truth of their ability to wield dark magic or not, you have to believe that there are real people involved."

We conceded his point, but it didn't really change anything. I left it to Tempest to deliver the bad news.

"Sorry, Frank, old boy, if what you say is true then I'm afraid we really don't want you with us. I promise to call you for advice and opinion as I so often do, but if there is a satanic cult behind these murders, the last thing I want to do is put people, such as yourself, in danger."

Frank hung his head a little, unwilling to make eye contact with either one of us.

"No, I understand. You don't want the scrawny, ninety-pound bookshop owner messing things up for you and getting into trouble if things get exciting." He was taking it badly and knowingly overreacting.

Tempest placed a hand on Frank's shoulder. "That's not it at all, Frank. I'm not suggesting you can't handle yourself; goodness knows we've been in enough scrapes together. At the moment though, Amanda and I are still trying to figure out who's behind this. I, for one, will feel more relaxed if I know you are back at your business in Rochester."

Frank nodded his head, still unwilling to take his eyes off the carpet, as he grabbed the edge of the door and began to close it.

"Don't worry, I understand. I won't get in your way. I guess I'll see you around sometime."

He was taking the rejection badly, and I know Tempest wanted to say something to make him feel better, but Frank stepped out of the room to shake Tempest's hand, a forced smile returning to his face.

"Good luck the pair of you. Call me if you need anything. I'll be in the shop." He offered me his hand too and a winning smile to go with it. "I'm just going to grab a shower, if you don't mind," he said while backing into the room and closing the door.

We were essentially dismissed, but message delivered, and Frank carefully extracted from the case before he could lead Genevieve down any more worrying rabbit holes, it was time to get on with things.

Amy Hildestrand had lived in a big house not far from Wimbledon. It was news to me, but Wimbledon, the tennis mecca, is not accessed from Wimbledon tube station. How weird is that? Instead, one alights at Southfields and walks along the road to get to it. Tempest knew this because he has been there. I had not.

Leaving behind three children and a husband, who was unfortunate enough to be the one who discovered his wife's body, we were lucky enough to find Mr Hildestrand at home.

He introduced himself as John and said, "I'm an independent literary agent," to explain his ability to work from home. "You say this is about Amy's murder?"

I could only imagine how raw it must still feel to him; the event was only weeks ago.

Taking the lead, I said, "Yes. We have been hired by Genevieve Slater, Simon Slater's widow. We have a few questions about the nature of your wife's relationship with Simon, but if you will permit us, we wish to inspect the room where you found your wife."

"We believe the killer may have left a mark," added Tempest.

"A mark?" John questioned. "Is that what the police were here looking for yesterday? They were very thorough in their examination. I don't think they would have missed it." Mr Hildestrand wasn't blocking our access, but his body language wasn't inviting either.

That the police had returned to look for the symbol came as news, but it wasn't surprising. Finding the symbol at Daniel McCormack's house demanded a swift follow up on their part.

Left with the belief John was undecided about what he stood to gain by indulging our request, I said, "We specialise in cases of this kind, Mr Hildestrand. It's been weeks since the killings started, and the police are yet to arrest anyone. You want your wife's killer to be caught. We all want the killer behind bars. The angle we are exploring is one the police have probably failed to consider." He was listening, so I dropped the bombshell. "Simon Slater's grave is currently being exhumed."

"What!" John spluttered, unable to believe his ears. "They think he's still alive, don't they? Did he fake his own death so he could kill my wife?"

Tempest stepped in to calm him down.

"We don't know that yet, sir. It is one possible explanation. When the police interviewed you, did they ask you about possible connections between your wife and either Francis Niedermeyer, Leslie Ashe, or any of the other victims?"

"Yes, they did. To my knowledge, Amy had never heard of any of them. She knew of Simon, but only because he is a literary giant. I don't think the two ever met."

In a soft voice, I repeated my request, "Can we see the room?"

John, still muttering angrily about what he was going to do to Simon Slater if he proved to still be alive, led us through his house and up a wide flight of stairs. He stopped outside a closed door.

"I haven't been back in here since ... since it happened. The kids are still staying with their aunt in Margate. I'm only here because I have client meetings. I can't wait to be rid of the place."

Tempest and I had both observed the estate agent's sign outside the house, neither one of us particularly surprised that the victim's widower wanted to move on. Silently, I questioned how hard it might be to sell a house where a murder had recently taken place.

"It's not locked," John told us as he backed toward the stairs and started to descend them. He didn't want to see inside, so we waited until he was out of sight before opening the door.

If I was expecting to find the remnants of the crime scenes teams' investigation left behind because nobody had been in here since the murder, then I was to be disappointed. The room was tidy and clean, the large double bed where Amy Hildestrand's body had been found was freshly made up and one could be forgiven for questioning how anything awful could have ever happened here.

Wordlessly, I began looking around the room. We both knew what we were looking for and given how well hidden the previous symbol had been, the pair of us were peering behind furniture and in obscure places.

Five minutes later, after shifting all the furniture away from the walls and carefully returning it to its original positions, we were questioning where it was that we had not looked, and whether the appearance of the symbol might prove to be a red herring.

Tempest puffed out his lips and scratched the side of his face.

"We are missing something," he remarked.

I sighed and slumped to sit on the corner of the bed. "What if the reason we cannot find a connection between the victims is that there isn't one. The police are stumped too." I checked to see what face Tempest was pulling. "Do you believe that?" I asked.

He took a moment to consider his answer, sucking in a lungful of air and letting it go slowly.

"No."

"Me neither. Whether it really is Simon Slater killing these people or someone else, they have to be connected. We just cannot see what the connection is."

Tempest had a perplexed expression, his forehead creased where he was frowning hard.

"This is where Amy Hildestrand's body was found ..." he murmured.

I shot off the bed. "But it's not where she was killed!"

We had both read the newspaper reports; Amy was attacked when she opened the front door, blood splatter on the wall telling a story the crime scenes guys could easily read. Tempest darted for the bedroom door, and I went after him, stopping and racing back to straighten the bed clothes when I saw the dent my backside had left.

John heard us coming down the stairs and appeared in the hallway just as the pair of us started our search.

I found the symbol before John could ask what we were doing. A tug on the arm of Tempest's jacket turned him around.

In the corner where the interior wall met the front of the house, behind a small chest of drawers with a rubber plant in a pot on top, the killer had left his calling card. Etched into the skirting board and hidden from the world when Amy's killer moved the chest of drawers back to its original position, the crude inverted pentagram was undeniable.

"What is that?" asked John, peering around me to see what Tempest and I were looking at.

I tore my eyes away from it and gave him a single word answer. "Proof."

Being Watched.
Wednesday, October 18th O912hrs

I T WAS PROOF, BUT what was it that it proved? Amy had been targeted by the same killer as Daniel McCormack. That was in little doubt anyway, but ruling out the possibility of a copycat killer was important. The press didn't know about the symbol, and neither did the police until yesterday, so there was no chance a copycat could have targeted Amy – the presence of the symbol was enough to convince me we were dealing with a single killer.

I took out my phone.

"You're letting the cops know?" Tempest sought to confirm, using his own phone to take a picture of the symbol."

"Patience," I replied, lifting my phone to my ear. "She needs a gift to offer Darius after last night's double date went so badly wrong. Plus, I want her to be getting informed when they open the coffin and find the remains inside are not Simon Slater's."

I got a raised eyebrow. "Double date?" he asked, his voice filled with sugar.

"Really? All that stuff I just said and what you heard was 'double date'?" I made a dismissive face and turned away when the call connected. In the background, I could hear Tempest talking to Mr Hildestrand.

"Amanda, is that you? What is wrong with you, girl? Why can't you leave me to sleep?"

"I have something for you," I teased.

"Is it breakfast?" she asked, sounding hopeful. "Because I might forgive you for waking me up if it is. I never did get supper last night and I'm starving."

"It's better than breakfast," I claimed, doubting she would see it that way. "I have evidence you can use to get a second date with Darius."

"Oh, I told him where I was staying and he's joining me for lunch. Apparently, he's never been to the Ritz." She said it like it made him strange or something.

"Neither had you until a few hours ago," I pointed out.

"Yeah, well, he doesn't need to know that. I'm going to tip a couple of the wait staff and have them address me like I'm a regular. Have them escort me to my 'usual table' maybe."

I chuckled, her antics so often amusing to me.

Remembering why I called, she asked, "What's the evidence?"

I told her where we were and what we had found.

"No copycat then," she concluded. "What about Mr Goat Head? Anything more from him? I'm sure glad we didn't stay in that pokey hotel last night. That thing gave me the creeps. I sure won't be reading any Simon Slater books any time soon."

"Nothing, but look, can you get Darius to check for CCTV footage in the area? I want to know if a camera picked up where it came from or where it went. If we get lucky, we might see them getting out of a car, or putting on that stupid goat head."

"I'll ask, but I don't think Baphomet uses a car, babes."

I left it at that, certain Patience was going to abuse Tempest's generosity and exploit her stay at the Ritz to the maximum. Treating Darius to lunch to make up for the previous evening was a good move, but not one she was paying for. Tempest could write the costs off as business expenses against his tax return, but even so ...

By the time I ended the call, Tempest had explained to John Hildestrand what was likely to happen next and apologised for the certain return of the police. Once they got wind of the symbol in his house, they were going to be all over it again.

We could have told them ourselves, but doing so would tie us up when they demanded we answer questions. Letting Patience handle it was a better solution and meant she was earning her keep.

I thanked John for his time and avoided falling into the trap of offering condolences – he would have heard it enough by now and be sick of the constant reminder. Heading back to the tube station, I called the office to catch up with Jane.

"Hi, Amanda, I was just about to call you," she revealed. "I just got a mysterious email." I had the speaker on so Tempest could hear her too.

"Isn't that the only kind we get," he joked.

"This one is more cryptic than most. I'll just forward it. Sorry, but it was in our spam box, and I only just checked it. This was sent two hours ago."

The email icon flashed on my screen a heartbeat later. A dab with my index finger opened it.

'*Must talk to you! We met yesterday. Being watched at all times. Meet me outside the fried chicken place in Victoria Station at eleven o'clock. It's about the murders.*'

"Being watched at all times," Tempest read from the screen, stopping to look around. If we were under surveillance, they were good enough to not get caught by Tempest. He was one of the most alert people I had ever met.

"Any idea what it means?" asked Jane. "Or who it's from? Who did you meet yesterday?"

"Lots of people," I replied, skewing my lips to one side as I tried to find some meaning in the sender's email address. It was numbers and letters rather than a name. "I don't know who this is."

"But we have little choice other than to go to the meeting point."

"Trap?" I asked his opinion.

He shook his head. "Too public unless they intend to kill us and have a sniper set up somewhere."

I choked on my next breath. "Nothing to worry about then."

Tempest started walking, heading toward the tube station still. "If we want to get there ahead of time, we'll have to hustle." I knew why he wanted to be there early. He was going to find a vantage point so we could watch. If someone I recognised showed up, we could pounce.

I thanked Jane, and was about to hang up, but she stopped me.

"There's something else while you are both on the phone." I told her to carry on. "There was a vampire stabbing last night."

I didn't reply for a few seconds as my brain processed the news.

"What I mean is, someone was stabbed, and it's someone I know from my days in the LARP club. The attacker used a wooden stake and damned near killed him."

"Wowza," I remarked. "Did they catch the attacker?"

"There's a tube just pulling in," called Tempest. A few yards ahead of me, he'd seen the train arriving. This far out from the central hub of the capital, if we didn't get this one, it was a ten minute or longer wait for the next.

"Jane, I've got to go!" I yelled at her.

"No problem. No, they didn't catch anyone," Jane spoke quickly. "We might have a case though. I'll tell you more about it later."

I stuffed my phone into my pocket and ran.

Boy did I regret that later.

Snooping. Wednesday, October 18th 1038hrs

B IG BEN WASN'T USED to snooping around another person's house, but equally, doing so didn't bother him. It was a task that needed to be done and he was best positioned for it.

He'd waited ten minutes for Genevieve to remember he was there and either return or call. When she didn't, he got started.

The first place he looked was in the kitchen, specifically inside the refrigerator. He didn't find any clues per se, but he did find eggs, butter, milk, and bacon. A glass of milk satisfied his thirst while he opened drawers and cupboards looking for the utensils he required to make a decent breakfast.

With bacon under the grill, slices of bread in the toaster and eggs bubbling in a skillet, he chugged another glass of milk and poked in a few more drawers.

He found what one might expect, including the obligatory junk drawer filled with old keys, half dead batteries, plasters, pens, and other paraphernalia.

Chuckling to himself, he sent Hilary and Basic a picture of the open drawer questioning whether they had considered selling a junk drawer starter kit. Putting his phone down because his food was ready, he took his plate to the breakfast bar.

Finding the leather seat cold against his bare buttocks, Big Ben found a tea towel to act as a barrier. He liked walking around naked; it made him feel like *Arnold Schwarzenegger* when he first appears in each of the *Terminator* movies.

Five minutes later, with the dirty plate, glass, cutlery, and everything else loaded into the dishwasher, he wiped his lips on a piece of kitchen towel and restarted the search, this time doing it properly.

Genevieve's house had a sitting room, a drawing room, a library, a games room with a full-sized snooker table, a dining room, and office ... it was a big house. He looked at photographs on the walls, none of which had Genevieve's husband in them, he noted. They also didn't show the tattoo on her back.

He'd noticed the skin on her back, of course, but hadn't put any thought to it – his mind was otherwise employed having fun. He wanted to find a computer and did so no sooner than he started looking. It was in the office, obviously.

Twenty minutes later, he gave up trying to guess the password. He knew he could call Jane and she would most likely reveal some clever hack to get around it, but that required admitting that he couldn't do it by himself, and he wasn't ready for that yet.

Surmising that if there was something to hide, it would be in an obscure location, Big Ben set about looking where he didn't think it would be.

Under the couches all he found were dust bunnies and a pound coin. He would have pocketed the coin if he'd been wearing any clothes. Placing it on a coffee table, then changing his mind because Genevieve might question where it had come from, he put it back under the couch.

It took more than half an hour to find the door leading down to the cellar. Initially, he'd dismissed the door because it looked like a broom cupboard, but having looked everywhere else downstairs, he figured he ought to eliminate it.

That was when he noticed the door had a lock on it.

None of the other doors did. It was a Chubb lock and there was no sign of the key. He put his nose to the edge of the frame and sniffed. The air was laden with the earthen mustiness he associated with underground spaces.

"Perfect place to hide things," Big Ben remarked to himself, setting off for the kitchen.

In the junk drawer, a single Chubb key promised hope and proved to be the right one for the only locked door in the house.

The darkness spilling out from inside reminded Big Ben of how foreboding he'd found the cellar at his grandparent's house. He'd been young and small, and his imagination conjured monsters in the shadows. Now that he knew he was the most dangerous thing around, dark places held nothing to fear.

The steps leading down were stone and cool beneath his feet. They were also dusty, his feet leaving a fresh trail of footsteps going down.

"No one has been down here in a while," he remarked into the darkness. The temperature dropped several degrees as he descended, goose bumbs surfacing on his skin by the time he reached the bottom.

There, he found a short corridor and a door. The door was a solid oak thing – too sturdy for him to hope to smash his way through, and it was locked. Big Ben shook the handle just to see if the door had any give, and slammed a shoulder into it, but if he wanted to see what was on the other side, he was going to need tools.

A noise coming from above his head caught his attention. Genevieve was home. Cursing in his head, but hoping he could get back upstairs before she got her coat off, he ran. Using his long legs to take the steps three at a time, he was back on the ground floor four seconds later. He carefully pressed the cellar door shut, thankful the hinge didn't squeak, and placed the key on top of the door frame where it couldn't be seen.

Confidently, he strolled out into the central corridor to greet the lady of the house, his naked body enough, he believed, to distract her from asking any questions.

It wasn't Genevieve.

Victoria Station. Wednesday, October 18th 1054hrs

WE MADE IT TO the station with time to spare, positioning ourselves fifty yards apart with overlapping angles from which to watch the front of the fried chicken place.

The line about us being watched was bugging me because it wasn't true, not unless they had a team on the job. We had been across London in two different directions on the tube this morning, there was no chance we had a tail and we hopped on board the tube at Southfields just before the doors shut – anyone tailing us would have been left behind.

Now waiting to see if anyone I recognised showed up, I understood that we had been brought to a set place at a set time. If someone wanted to know where we were, this was how to do it.

So was this a trap or a con or was there a genuine person with information about the murders on their way to meet me?

"Anything?" asked Tempest, his voice coming over the tiny two-way radio in my hand.

"Nothing so far."

I rolled my arm over to check my watch: there were still a couple of minutes before I was supposed to meet whoever it was. I was going to give it until a couple of minutes after the hour and then wander over if no one showed. It could be that they were doing the same thing as me and hiding out of sight.

Thinking that, I started to look around. Victoria Station, like all the other transport hubs in London, was full to the brim with people going in every direction. It was impossible to keep track of them, but chance or luck aimed my eyes at the one face among the ten thousand that I had seen before.

Stepping out from my hiding place behind a billboard, I made a beeline for him, desperately racking my brain for a name. None came, but I knew who he was – the man who brought me coffee at Kimble Publishing.

Indigo had been hard on him, dispelling the sweet lady demeanour she'd shown until that point. Now he was here, and he had secrets he wanted to reveal. Closing in on him as he walked toward the fried chicken place, I could see how nervous he was. Constantly checking over his shoulder and checking his watch.

With a jolt I remembered Victoria Station was walking distance from Kimble Publishing. Lucas ... the name popped into my head, was on a break, or doing the office junior's lunch run for sandwiches or something like that. He'd squeezed in meeting me and was pushed for time.

"Lucas," I called out to catch his attention, but I was going to have to shout to make him hear me above the noise of the crowded station. That would just draw attention to us, so I quickened my pace and touched his shoulder.

He flinched so hard I thought he might snap a bone and swung his head around to see who was there.

"It's me. Relax," I frowned at him. "What's got you so spooked?"

"If they see me with you, I'm as good as dead," he blurted.

"They? Who are we talking about? The people at your office?"

"I don't have much time," Lucas warned. "There's a house in the countryside. It's down in Kent. I've never been there. Not yet anyways, but I know it's there. All your answers are there. They are performing rituals, summoning the dark lord. That's why people are dying. It's Indigo. Without Simon Slater to write more books the company isn't making half as much money. She needs all the other people out of the way so she can claim all the royalties."

"Wait, slow down." He was jumping from one thought to the next, spitting his words out in a jumbled mess and his eyes had never stayed in the same spot for more than half a second. Someone or something – I remembered the goat-headed apparition – had him terrified almost out of his mind. "You are telling me that Indigo is behind the killings?"

"All of them are," Lucas blurted his answer. "Together they summon the dark lord to do their bidding in return for their loyalty and to aid their recruitment."

"Recruitment?" He was introducing a new idea every time he spoke. I needed to steer him back on track.

"This house, Lucas. Where is it?"

"I don't know," he wailed and flinched again because he thought he saw someone. I had to grab his arm to keep him in place. "I've never been there, but I do know they are going tonight. They plan to summon the dark lord again."

"Lucas you are safe now. You don't have to go back to them."

He laughed at me but there was no mirth in it, only dreadful fear and acceptance.

"You don't know them. There is no way out. Once you are in, that's it for life."

Dismissing the argument as either futile or pointless, I steered him back to what I needed to know.

"Did Indigo kill Simon too?"

"No. I mean, I don't think so. Look, I've not been with them for very long. That's why I've never been to the house. It doesn't make any sense for them to want Simon dead. He was the one keeping the business afloat."

"Okay, Lucas. I'm going to need you to work with me. I can get you protection, but I need to know more. I need the names of the people involved," I was in full cop mode now, hoisting my phone from my pocket to record what he had to say. "I need to know who it is that dressed themselves up in a goat head outfit last night and set fire to a man ..."

"What?" The question fell from Lucas's lips in a horrified gasp. I looked up from sorting out my phone to find he was backing away. "Baphomet was here?"

"What? No. It was just someone in a costume, Lucas." I started after him, but right before my eyes every drop of colour drained from his face, and he froze.

It only lasted for a second, replaced by a cry of petrified horror and denial so loud it was heard by everyone within a hundred-yard radius.

I followed his gaze, seeing nothing, until through a gap in the crowd I spotted the goat headed figure again. It sent a spike of adrenalin straight into my veins.

"Noooo! Nooo!" Twisting off one foot, the Kimble Publishing office junior made a break for the nearest exit. He ran blindly, knocking into people and bowling more than one of them over in his panicked desire to get away.

Tempest's voice came over the radio.

"I saw it! Get the kid. I'll get the goat!"

I didn't see Tempest moving or have any idea how far away he was from Goat Head. I couldn't think about it either. Lucas had a twenty-yard head start and was ripping through the crowd at a speed I doubted I could match.

Releasing a grunt of effort, I threw myself into the pursuit as behind me I heard Tempest bellowing for people to clear a path.

I had already lost sight of Lucas, but I could tell where he was from the angry shouts. Aiming for the wide opening that formed one of the main exits from the station, I was hampered by my need to avoid knocking people over.

He was outside already and turning onto Victoria Street. I knew where we were from a recent trip to the Apollo Theatre to see *Wicked the Musical*. If I didn't catch him soon, he would vanish into the rabbit warren of London's back streets.

Racing through the exit, I was coming out of the structure and the acoustic effect amplifying the noise inside would drop away – if I shouted, he would hear me.

I heard a squeal of brakes and a blast of horn. They drove an icy lance right through my gut, but it was the cry of horror and the awful, sickening crunch of a human body being hit at speed by a car that stole my breath.

I ran on, rounding the corner to find the traffic slowing to a stop and pedestrians leaping the barriers at the side of the road. They were all heading for one spot at the front of a London cab. I didn't want to see for I already knew I was going to find Lucas lying on the tarmac.

Fighting against the revulsion rising like bile in my throat, I made my way along the edge of the cars to get to the crowd of people and pushed my way into them, tapping shoulders and begging to be let through.

My breath caught in my throat, and I had to look away. I've seen dead people before. As a cop I was required to attend murder scenes and accidental deaths. Road accidents too, but none of them had ever been someone I was talking to just a few moments before.

A man in his fifties was bent over Lucas's body. He clearly knew what he was doing – an off-duty paramedic perhaps. When he stopped trying to help and closed Lucas's sightless eyes, it was all I could do not to vomit.

A hand gripped my shoulder.

"Babe?" Tempest pulled me into his arms and took me away from the scene.

"The goat?" I asked.

"Sorry. He vanished into the crowd. I saw him once, but I think he ducked out of sight to take off the cloak and mask. I never even came close to catching him."

I didn't know where we were going; I was just putting one foot in front of the other, unable to shift the image in my head. Tempest led me into a bar. It was too early in the day to be drinking, but the neat whisky he put in my hands went down without a fight.

He had one too, holding my hand across the table and waiting for the adrenalin to work its way out of my system.

When I finally found my voice more than fifteen minutes later, I said, "He was terrified. Utterly terrified. Kimble Publishing *is* the cult. That's what he led me to believe. I met Lucas when I went there yesterday – he was the office junior, I guess. He brought me coffee." I swiped angrily at a tear. Tears wouldn't do Lucas any good. Bringing Indigo and the rest of them down would though.

"What else did he tell you?" Tempest calmly focused my mind.

"That we can catch them at a house in the countryside and that they are going there tonight. I think that is what he was trying to tell me. He didn't have enough time to explain, however he made it sound like that was where we could catch them red-handed."

I didn't need to explain the worth of finding irrefutable evidence. We couldn't raid their office; the police tend to frown on that sort of thing. However, if we found proof – anything that would tie the people at Kimble Publishing to the murders – everything would change.

"You're going to tell me Lucas ran before he had the chance to tell you where the house is," Tempest guessed.

I shook my head, looking into Tempest's eyes so my brain wouldn't keep going back to the image of Lucas lying in the street.

"No, he didn't know where it is. He said he was a recent recruit and hadn't been there yet. We can find it though. It will be listed as a company asset."

Tempest sucked some air between his teeth. "It might be. Let's get Jane on it. If it's owned by the company, it will be on their filings at Companies House. We need a back-up plan though."

"Stake out?"

He nodded. "Stake out. It can't be us though. They definitely know who you are, and I probably just got spotted too. Let's get Big Ben involved."

Lock Picking for Dummies. Wednesday, October 18th 1115hrs

A FTER AN HOUR IN bed, Genevieve's cleaner (Big Ben couldn't recall if he'd even bothered to ask her name), insisted that she needed to get on with cleaning the house. He didn't fight her – she argued that she couldn't afford to lose her job which she most certainly would if her employer came home to find her naked in bed when she ought to be mopping the floors.

Big Ben chose to get a shower – he'd learned long ago that women can smell another woman on a man from ten paces away. Not that Big Ben felt Genevieve had a legitimate claim to complain if she caught him with her cleaner, but he felt it was good form to chase the sweat and ... Isabella! Her name flashed into his head. He thought it was good form to remove the scent of Isabella from his skin.

Showered and dry he chose to put some clothes on. Between Genevieve and ... nope, Big Ben lost the other woman's name again – between the two of them he was feeling a little fatigued and expected to be required to perform again later when the lady of the house returned.

Snooping around the house was impractical with whateverhernamewas cleaning it, so he found the remote for the television in Genevieve's living room, made a coffee, and parked himself in front of the big screen.

The cleaner, unable to trust that she would resist a second round if she saw him again, chose to call out that she was leaving before hurriedly running out the door. Big Ben heard it close and gave her a minute.

Content that she wasn't going to change her mind and come bursting back through the door, ripping her clothes off in a cloud of lustful ardour, he returned to the task of exploring the house.

Big Ben was going back down to the cellar, of course. He wanted to know what was behind the locked door, but he was going to have to find the key first or some tools. Forcing it open would be a last resort to be employed if Tempest believed it was necessary.

He considered sending Genevieve a text message – just to check she wasn't on her way back. He wouldn't word it like that, obviously; there were more subtle ways to obtain an answer. Opting to employ an old favourite, Big Ben dropped his trousers and sent her a picture of 'the General'. The old fella had enjoyed a number of promotions over the years, each based on a secret list of objectives he was yet to share with anyone.

Task complete; the picture accompanied only by the words 'He's waiting' and a winking emoji, the Blue Moon Investigation Agency's hired muscle went back to the task of searching the house.

The junk drawer in the kitchen did not yield a key as he hoped it might. Nor did any of the other places he looked. While weighing up his options, Big Ben's phone pinged with a message from Genevieve.

'I'm so sorry! I left without saying anything this morning. I will be back as soon as I can. Please make yourself at home until I return. XX Geni.'

"Super," Big Ben remarked to himself. He clearly had some time before Genevieve would return. Could he pick a lock?

He typed 'how to pick a lock' into the search bar on his phone and got pages of hits back. It occurred to him that he could probably call an emergency locksmith out and have him open the lock, but suspected a professional's method might involve drilling the old lock to remove it – not the result he wanted.

With phone in hand, a desire to be recognised as a guy who gets things done and not just the big muscular, pretty one, Big Ben selected a few tools lying randomly in the junk drawer and headed back to the basement.

There, he discovered the stupid phone signal didn't work and the lockpicking instructions had gone away. He'd seen a couple of the pictures though; it genuinely didn't look all that hard.

Kneeling on the floor, he set to work.

Communications Issues. Wednesday October 18th 1126hrs

T EMPEST STARED AT HIS phone, frustration ruling his features.

"No answer," he explained unnecessarily – he'd tried to make contact with Big Ben about eight times.

I was about to ask what else we could do or if we ought to try wearing disguises to stake out Kimble Publishing, when my own phone rang.

I glanced at the screen, my eyebrows lifting in surprise when I saw it was Hilary's name displayed.

"Amanda!" he trumpeted excitedly. "We've sold out already. There was a mad rush to get all our products this morning. We sold everything so fast we can barely believe it."

"All the imaginary stock," I remarked a touch more sarcastically than I intended.

"Yes. And the real stuff too, of course," he said, reminding me that they actually had remote controls for the stealth plane and a few other ridiculous gimmicks. "And you won't believe the genius idea Big Ben came up with. We're going to have to pay him commission for sharing it with us first."

"You've heard from Big Ben?" I questioned needlessly. "How long ago? We've been trying to get a hold of him."

Hilary said, "Oh, um, maybe two hours ago. It was a while back. You want me to try calling him now?"

I considered his offer, but said, "No." I couldn't see why he would answer to Hilary and not Tempest. "Hey, what did you call for, anyway?"

"Just to say we are finished for the day. We've got a couple of things to load into the van, but otherwise we are free. Basic suggested you guys might need a hand."

Basic's voice rumbled in the background, "S'right. Friends, help friends."

I couldn't argue with that, and their offer came at the timeliest opportunity.

They found us forty minutes later. I was drinking strong coffee by then to chase away the hard liquor and we'd grabbed a bite of lunch to keep us going. Jane had drawn a blank on the house in the countryside – there was nothing listed as a company asset, which meant it had to belong to someone who worked there, or that they had access to it somehow. Either way, finding its location was proving tricky. We told Hilary and Basic about our plan to watch the publishing firm.

"That's it?" questioned Hilary. "That sounds easy enough."

"It is easy," Tempest agreed. "But I'm sure you remember the last time I asked you to do a quick stakeout." Tempest had been good enough to regale me with the story of Hilary trying to watch a table of witches in a coffee shop.

"No focusing on the cake this time," Hilary promised. "We have pictures of the staff from their website," he held up his phone to demonstrate, "and if we see them leaving the publishing place on foot in the direction of Victoria Station, we are to let you know."

"That's all you do," I reinforced the notion that all we wanted was observation.

Hilary performed a salute – badly, like civilians who have never been taught how to do it always do. Basic copied him, smacking himself in the side of his head with his catcher's mitt sized hand.

"Roger. All understood," Hilary confirmed again. "We just drink tea and eat cake and watch out the window. If we see people leaving, we let you know. Where are you guys going to be?"

It was a pertinent question which I fielded.

"Not far away. If they head for the station, we need to be able to react and find out which train they take. Lucas said they are going to the house in the countryside tonight and that is where they will do whatever it is that they are doing."

Hilary frowned. "What *are* they doing?"

I puffed out my cheeks and pulled a face. "That's the part we don't know. Lucas said they are behind the deaths," I found it curious that he said death and not murders, but I couldn't quiz him about it now, "and we are fairly sure this is to do with Simon Slater's royalties. The income from his books was being divided between a bunch of people, many of whom got a share from contracts he entered into early in his career when he had no money," I explained. It meant that if Indigo was behind it, she had arranged for the murder of Daniel McCormack – one of her own employees. "It looks like Kimble Publishing is trying to eliminate all the people who had a share so they can keep it all for themselves. That's the why of it, and if, as Lucas claimed, they are all in on it, then catching them in the act is almost the only way we can bring them down. Otherwise, they all get to provide alibis for each other, and the murders could each be committed by a different person."

Hilary raised his hand to ask a question.

Tempest hiked an eyebrow, making Hilary lower his arm.

"Why aren't we involving the police?" he asked. "Surely, they could use their resources to find the house in the countryside. If we have the confession from this Lucas fellow, he can tell them what he knows, and they can swoop."

"Lucas is dead," I stated bluntly. The comment made Hilary's eyes flare with shock. "Even if he were not, without evidence ... without catching them in the act or discovering something that will tie them to the crimes, we have nothing to take to the police. You know we don't have the best relationship with them." It was something of an understatement, especially when we were talking about the Kent Police.

Tempest continued where I had left off, diverting the conversation away from Lucas's death before Hilary could ask a question and make me relive the experience.

"Following them will be tricky, but we think we can disguise ourselves well enough that we are not recognised. We plan to plant a couple of trackers in pockets."

Tempest was deliberate in making it sound easy – it wasn't going to be, and a dozen things could go wrong. He also didn't mention that we were heading to Genevieve's house next to see what had happened to Big Ben. Not that we were overly worried; the big doofus could take care of himself and was most likely asleep having been awake and 'performing' for most of the night.

I wanted to check in on Patience. The moment she had Darius on her side, I needed to know what had been found in Simon Slater's coffin. It had been several hours since we discovered the order had been given to dig it up, so it would be at the morgue by now.

How long does it take to determine the identity of a body? I didn't know the answer and the subject was too macabre to be looking up on my phone. I would get an answer from Patience when I could and the confirmation that Simon Slater wasn't in his grave would shift our investigation yet again.

So too the police, who would have some hard questions for Genevieve.

Sending Hilary and Basic on their way with a wish for good luck, I touched Tempest's arm. He was just pocketing Hilary's spare keys. The van would get towed if left where it was and having it gave us greater mobility – provided we could negotiate London daytime traffic.

"You realise we might not have a client," I remarked.

He checked traffic before starting across the road toward Hilary's van. "It had occurred to me. However, if Simon Slater *is* dead, it simplifies things a little."

It certainly would. Right now, I had nothing but confusion in my head. I could see Simon as the killer, going around bumping off people from his past. I could also see the scary people at Kimble Publishing as responsible for the deaths because the firm stood to gain. However, neither likely culprit – Simon or the people at Kimble Publishing, had any known reason for killing Samuel Blake or Amy Hildestrand. What were their deaths about?

In the van, as Tempest joined the slow-moving traffic, we talked about the missing elements and how we had to keep plugging along until we got a break. We had only been on the case for a couple of days; figuring it out was going to take some time and possibly a little luck.

I pulled up the number for Patience in my recently dialled list and thumbed the green button. Annoyingly, just like Big Ben, I got no answer. I tried again, then sent her a text to check she was okay.

Giving up on her, I tried calling Big Ben again, getting the same nil response as before. It was as if he'd switched his phone off – something I do when Tempest and I are in bed – or had gone where there was no signal. In the nation's capital, I couldn't come up with many places that could happen. Even the Underground had coverage.

Hilary and Basic.
Wednesday, October
18th 1213hrs

"THIS IS FUN," SAID Hilary, not really meaning it.

Basic stared at him. One thing James Burham was not known for was conversation. He didn't make small talk. He barely talked at all unless prompted to do so by a direct question. Occasionally a question would pop into his head that demanded an answer, but for the most part, he stayed quiet and let the world go by.

They were on a stakeout, watching the building opposite; he understood that much. However, the why of it vanished in a fog of difficult to follow words when Amanda explained what was going on. It seemed to have something to do with a goat. Not that he needed a long-winded explanation to get him to help; his friends needed him and that was good enough.

Sitting opposite him, Hilary understood only too well that they were watching a building that might contain not only a murderer, but a whole firm of them. Having agreed to help, he hadn't realised that would mean operating on his own. It wasn't too bad getting involved if Tempest was around, or even better if Big Ben was there. Big Ben was good at making sure anyone wanting to do Hilary harm would soon find themselves unconscious and bleeding. It was thoroughly reassuring.

Of course, Basic possessed the ability to do precisely the same to any would-be attackers, but he wasn't intuitive enough to pre-empt a strike. Hilary worried he might find himself being kidnapped by a murderous satanic cult before his business partner chose to react.

The waitress brought them their order – a pot of tea and a layered dish of delicate cakes and finger sandwiches. Attempting to pour the tea, he found his hands were shaking.

Basic took over.

"Everyfing, all right?" Basic enquired.

"Yes, fine. Just peachy," Hilary lied.

"You need the toilet?"

"What? No!" Hilary replied automatically before wondering if a visit to the establishment's smallest room might be in order after all.

Basic selected a cucumber sandwich, his meaty fingers each significantly bigger than the carefully prepared morsel. Hilary watched as his partner removed the piece of cucumber and devoured the rest in a single bite.

Using both hands so his cup wouldn't rattle on the saucer when he lifted it, Hilary sipped at his tea. From the corner of his eye, he spotted when someone emerged from the front door of Kimble Publishing. They stopped to hold the door open, waiting on the pavement until another person appeared.

Hilary made a tapping noise with his tongue, watching the two people – a man and a woman – walk down the street. Was it time to call Tempest and Amanda? The couple were probably on their way to lunch, right?

The door opened again, two more figures in office wear and coats stepping out and heading the same way as the first two. This time the door didn't swing fully shut before a hand caught it. Now half a dozen people exited, and Hilary grabbed for his phone.

By the time it connected, a further eighteen people had left the building and Hilary was starting to worry. A quick check of the firm's website confirmed they only employed forty people. More than half had already walked down the road toward Victoria Station, and more were coming.

Tempest swore, his voice loud in Hilary's ear.

Amanda said, "We are stuck in traffic. It's going to take us a while to get back to you."

That they had not anticipated the firm all leaving this early was clear, but they both agreed with Hilary's opinion that they were most likely heading for lunch somewhere. They knew about their dead colleague, Lucas; Amanda said they had to because they spooked him into running in front of a car, but her opinion was that they were not stopping work for the day in honour of his death as one might at any other firm.

"I've just seen Indigo leave," announced Hilary, checking her picture against the woman he could see walking down the street. "What do we do?"

Tempest asked, "Are the lights still on inside the office?"

Hilary diverted his gaze. "Yes."

"And they haven't all left yet?"

"No. By my count there has to be five or maybe six still inside." Hilary waited, straining his hearing because Tempest and Amanda were discussing something between themselves.

When Amanda spoke again, she said, "Sit tight and let us know when they come back. We think you are right and what you are seeing is just the usual office routine of cutting out for an hour's lunch break."

"What if they don't come back? What if the others leave too? Oh, hold on. Another one did just leave. He's heading in the direction of Victoria Station as well."

"Then we try to figure out where they went," said Tempest. "The stakeout was always a longshot. We'll come back for you as soon as we have confirmed Big Ben is okay."

They ended the call, leaving Hilary clutching his phone and fretting.

"Do you think we should follow them anyway?" he asked Basic's opinion. "You know, just to be sure. If we find them having lunch, we know there's nothing to worry about and we can come back here."

Basic scooped half a dozen of the tiny sandwiches, shoved them in his right coat pocket, and then went back for cake. Stuffing two pieces into his mouth, he stood up.

Hilary, seeing that the decision to follow had been made, fished out a twenty pound note, tucked it under his saucer and drained the rest of his tea.

Replacing his cup, he noted that his hands had stopped shaking. They were doing something now, and though it felt infinitely more dangerous, it was, at the same time, better to be in motion.

Outside the little coffee shop, they found their exit had coincided with yet another of the Kimble Publishing staff leaving. Did that leave anyone inside?

They had no way of knowing the answer, but strolling nonchalantly in the same direction on the other side of the street, they both failed to notice a black-clad figure step out from behind a shop display and begin to follow them.

Tiddlywinks. Wednesday, October 18th 1259hrs

"THERE HAS TO BE some kind of roadworks or an accident ahead," moaned Tempest, displaying an uncharacteristic show of impatience.

We were stuck and hadn't moved in ten minutes. The ten minutes prior to that all we did was creep forward a few yards. Horns beeped periodically, as if that would make any difference to the situation.

Big Ben still wasn't answering the phone and though we both stated that we were not worried, I could not deny the unease I felt rising. Tempest's old army buddy was tough, but he wasn't unkillable. If someone came at him with a gun or an axe ... or if Genevieve poisoned him ...

I chose not to voice my worries out of fear Tempest would be thinking the same thing. It would do neither of us any good to fret.

A call from Patience changed things.

"Hey, girl, you called me like ten times," she observed sounding so chipper I knew precisely why she hadn't returned them until now.

"Darius there, is he?" I enquired sweetly, my words laced with false saccharin. "Been getting to know one another, have you?"

"Ha!" she spat. "We haven't been playing tiddlywinks!"

"Okay, that's all the description I require, Patience. Now that you are firmly in his good graces, I need you to quiz him about Simon Slater's grave. Have they been able to identify the body yet?"

"Oh, yeah. They did that hours ago, babes. I thought I sent you a text message. Did you not get one?"

"NO!" I snapped. "I didn't!" While I was trying to figure all this out, she was sitting on the one piece of information that would determine the course of today's investigation. It wasn't the only thing she'd been sitting on by the sound of it.

"Okay, stroppy knickers," Patience chuckled, her mood buoyed by a current of endorphins and undentable for the time being. "I'm sorry," she lamented. "Truly I am, but ... well, I don't know if you noticed how big his hands and feet are ..."

I knew where she was going with this and steered her back on track. Meanwhile, the traffic was finally moving again, and Tempest gunned the van's engine to get through a gap before it could close.

"Focus, Patience. Simon Slater. Whose body was in his coffin?"

"Oh, yeah, right, sorry. His was."

"I'm sorry, what?" I wasn't sure I'd heard her correctly.

"The body in the coffin *was* Simon Slater. You expected it to be someone else, right?"

I looked across at Tempest, who risked a quick glance my way. He didn't want to take his eyes off the road for long, but gave me a shrug of acceptance before he looked back at the car in front.

I let my mind reel for a few seconds. Simon Slater was dead. The impact of that single statement changed everything.

To start with it meant Genevieve wasn't being targeted by her husband in a bid to tie off the final loose end that might reveal the truth. It also meant she hadn't lied and wasn't an accomplice to a murder. All my theories about his faked death fell apart in an instant but the next conclusion went off like a bomb in my head.

"Kimble Publishing *is* behind it all," I blurted as my breath caught.

"That would be my guess too," agreed Tempest.

They were the only ones left. I still had no idea why they had killed Amy and Samuel, but being in the dark was hardly a revelation.

"Is Darius there?" I asked. "I need to include him in some information."

I heard Patience shout, "Babes! I've got Amanda on the phone. She needs to tell you something."

He came on the line, Patience putting her phone on speaker. In a four person conversation, I told him about Lucas and the house in Kent. It wasn't much to go on; we all knew that, but it was what we had and enabled Darius to steer effort in that direction – if his boss would agree to it.

Officially, Darius had the day off. He'd been hard at the case for weeks and probably needed the break, but new information coming to light, combined with his own ambition, were going to get him back into his office today.

I heard Patience ask, "You're staying to have lunch with me, right?" and I heard his apology. "Damn you, Amanda Harper," Patience swore at me. It was meant in jest, but she was undoubtedly irked all the same. The prominence of the case dictated Darius put it first.

Tempest's phone beeped with an incoming text message. Rather than read it himself – the act demanding he take his eyes off the busy road, he extracted it from his pocket and handed it to me.

I was just ending the call with Patience, and a good thing too because my jaw dropped open when I read the words on the screen.

"It's from Hilary and Basic!" I told Tempest, my tone urgent. "The pair of them are on a train with all the cult members!"

Destination Unknown. Wednesday, October 18th 1407hrs

I T WAS TOO LATE to stop them from doing it; the event was already in the past.

"Send Hilary a reply," Tempest requested, "and ask if he is free to talk."

The fact that Hilary chose to send a text rather than call suggested otherwise, which was the point of checking, of course.

Tempest's phone pinged again, and I read from the screen, '*Only if I move. We are in a carriage with about a dozen of the people from Kimble Publishing. They're all silent. No one is talking at all. It's really spooky.*'

Tempest peered at his phone as my fingers flashed across the screen, adding a reply. When the message left with a whooshing sound, I explained, "I just asked them where they are going."

Tempest rushed to get through a junction before the lights could change and pin us in place again.

The answer from Hilary was almost instant. Reading again, I told Tempest. "They are on the Faversham line. Calling at all stations. What do we want him to do?"

I looked at Tempest when I answered Hilary's question. "We won't have any idea where the cult members are going unless Hilary and Basic stay with them until they get off. Indigo and her staff must all be going to the same place. The boys should be safe enough on the train, don't you think?"

Tempest checked his rear-view, flicked his indicator and changed lanes. "Probably," he grunted, his attention on negotiating the road to get across another lane and I saw what he was doing. Ahead was an overhead sign dictating which lane was going to go which way. He needed to get all the way across to the right to aim for the M2 motorway – he was heading for Kent.

"What about Big Ben?" I asked.

Gritting his teeth because he didn't like the answer, Tempest said, "Hilary and Basic have to take priority. We know the killer isn't Simon which makes any involvement in anything on Genevieve's part highly unlikely. She could be a target. However, if the cult members are planning to kill her too, they are clearly not about to do it in the next few hours. I think Big Ben is safe for now."

"Then why isn't he answering his phone?" I begged to know, worried for what it could mean.

Tempest had no answer for me, but said, "It could be anything. Dead battery, he dropped it in the bath ... anything. I doubt he's in any trouble."

Lock Picking for Dummies Part 2. Wednesday, October 18th 1415hrs

B IG BEN WASN'T IN trouble, but he was getting annoyed. Convincing himself that he could pick the lock, he'd set to work with a fork, three small screwdrivers, a can of WD-40, all courtesy of the kitchen's junk drawer, and a paring knife he took from a block of knives on the counter.

Hours later, his knees were protesting, his eyes were beginning to ache from squinting into the keyhole, and his fingers sported several small cuts.

The stupid lock continued to defy him even though he was convinced he could feel the parts inside moving. It almost turned once, he was certain of it, but the stupid fork – one tine of which he'd bent to an improbable angle and would need to hide – slipped and his combination of implements tumbled to the floor.

Aware that he could go back upstairs to the ground floor where his phone would have signal and he could consult again the plethora of information on the internet, he chose instead to just keep going.

A rumble from his stomach suggested it was well after noon. A silent promise that he would give up in five minutes and forage for a sandwich remained unfulfilled fifteen minutes later because the lock almost turned again.

He was close. Surely, he was close. The trick, he told himself, was to mimic enough of the key so the barrel would rotate. He also told himself he had no idea what he was talking about, but with a bead of sweat hanging precariously off his right eyebrow to invade his vision, he carefully slid the paring knife alongside the fork. There were four implements jammed into the small hole, each threatening to jump out at any moment as they already had about six dozen times.

Big Ben curled a little finger around the whole bunch to keep them in place, then flexed his arm muscles, trying his hardest to turn the whole thing as one unit.

It started to turn, but as it had so many times before, they went a few degrees and then stopped. Determined not to be beaten, he increased his grip and shifted a leg to gain better leverage.

Did it just move?

Big Ben sucked in a lungful of air and shouting an angry insult, he twisted with all his might.

The knife blade snapped, the broken end with the handle skewering his right hand as the tools came free. Uttering an obscenity at a volume he suspected the neighbours might have heard, he fell back and rolled onto the floor, clutching his hand protectively.

With the momentum of his effort expended, Big Ben shuffled around to sit upright and examined his hand. The knife was buried all the way to the hilt in his palm with the broken end protruding through his metacarpals.

"That's going to leave a scar," he remarked to himself. Tutting and cursing, he started to get up, intending to return to the kitchen where he already knew he would find a first aid kit. However, he had only just begun to rise when he spotted it.

In a dark corner back by the stairs, hanging beneath a shelf was a key one could only see if lying on the floor. There was nothing on the shelf set at knee height; it was one of a series of four shelves each bolted to the wall and each as devoid of items as the others.

He'd dismissed them, but there it was, and it had to be the right key.

Sure enough, when the scrabbling fingers of his uninjured left hand found the key, it fit the lock perfectly.

"I'll just tell them I picked the lock anyway," he said to the air. With a turn the door unlocked, and he gripped the handle wondering what could be on the other side and hoping it was going to be worth the effort.

He yanked it open and stared.

After a few seconds of staring in disbelief, he said, "Well, that just beats anything I could have come up with."

The Chase Begins. Wednesday, October 18th 1448hrs

WE MADE DECENT TIME getting out of the capital, but the train had left Victoria Station heading south almost an hour ago. It was nearing the end of its journey and the guys were still on it. Reporting every time they reached a new station and no one got off, I was beginning to believe Indigo and her colleagues were staying on all the way to the end.

This was not good news. For a start, Hilary and Basic would have to get off with the satanic cult. The plan had been for them to stay on, reporting where Indigo and her people got off before the train then whisked them safely onwards. If they went all the way to the terminus, they would have no choice but to get off at the same time. The second problem is that Faversham was more than an hour from our current location.

"Text them," Tempest agreed with my thoughts on the matter. "If the cult members stay on at the penultimate station, Hilary and Basic can get off and we will still know where Indigo and her crew are heading."

I sent the instruction away, staring down at my phone and waiting impatiently for the reply to come back.

'Get off at Sittingbourne?' Hilary wanted to confirm.

'Yes.'

'We just left there. Too late. Sorry.'

"They already went by it, didn't they?" Tempest guessed from my reaction. "Tell them under no circumstance are they to attempt to follow them once they get off the train."

I relayed his words precisely as he said them and got a confirmation from Hilary that he understood.

What We do for Friends. Wednesday, October 18th 1506hrs

ALIGHTING ON PLATFORM TWO of Faversham's station, Hilary and Basic did their best to look like they were not watching what the staff from Kimble Publishing were doing. They moved with the foot traffic, following the crowd up and over an old steel bridge that connected the platforms and led to the exit without the slightest thought for anyone's physical ability.

That the concept of the old and infirm or physically handicapped might wish to also travel via rail had not been a consideration when the tracks were laid, and the stations built. Only in the last decade or more had funding been assigned to correct such short-sightedness.

Hilary wasn't able to pick out many of the people from Kimble Publishing, but he didn't have to. Given the number of people staying on until the final stop, a small town in the heart of Kent, most of them had to be the ones he and Basic watched leaving Kimble Publishing.

They were still not talking; the whole lot of them acting as though they had sworn a vow of silence. Unnerved by it, but keeping that to himself, Hilary did as Tempest said he should and let the staff of Kimble Publishing sweep around and ahead of him as he and Basic dawdled.

Handing over their tickets at the turnstile, they exited the station into the October sunshine and edged to the left where a rank of taxis sat waiting expectantly.

"What now, Hilary?" asked Basic, trying to remember that he was supposed to avoid watching the people.

Hilary was about to answer when Indigo, the one person he recognised because Amanda pointed her out to him on the website, paused just outside the station's exit. She looked directly at him, causing his heart to stutter, but moved on a moment later, continuing to stare, not at him, as he first believed, but at something behind him.

He twisted around, breathing a sigh of relief when he spotted a billboard displaying the latest Simon Slater story, a book released posthumously. The author finished it long before his demise, the manuscript found with four other partially completed stories.

This was the first of them, the publicity circus behind it hyped to maximum by the promise of terror that would claim your soul if you ever closed your eyes again.

Allowing his erratic heartbeat to return to a normal rhythm, Hilary said, "Now I think we find a pub and wait for Tempest to get here with Amanda. I could do with a pint."

Basic didn't disagree and the pair got directions from the chap in the ticket office. It was a pleasant afternoon, the sun slowly dipping toward the horizon when Hilary sent a message to Tempest's phone to reassure him.

'We are on our way to The Prince's Head pub. It's half a mile from the station. See you there. The cult people all walked down the hill and have gone.'

Basic had been considering the plan as it was for more than a minute when he offered his opinion.

"I fink we should follow them."

Hilary cranked an eyebrow. "What?"

"Dose people. I fink we should follow them. Tempest and 'Manda won't know where they went. I can see them still."

Hilary couldn't see them at all and was jolly glad about it. However, before he could dismiss Basic's claim, his intellectually challenged companion jabbed an arm across the field to his right and there Hilary saw a procession of people wending their way along a country road.

That they couldn't be going far was obvious – they'd ignored the taxis, not that there was enough to take them all, electing instead to walk to their final destination. Some of the women were wearing heeled shoes, which again dictated that wherever they were going couldn't be far away.

Grimacing, mostly because he wanted to argue and knew he would sound cowardly if he did, even to his own ears, and because ultimately Basic would go by himself if Hilary chose to head into the pub, he accepted his fate.

"Okay, but we keep our distance and when we know where they have gone, we come back to the pub, yes?"

Basic thought about it for a moment. "Okay." Hilary was a good friend and Basic recognised the value of such things. From being a person he saw in the pub most weeks, to becoming business partners, Brian Clinton had steered him on a path that led to more money than Basic could count. Not that this was saying much because numbers had always been a bit tricky for him.

Basic was having fun in his new career and was glad to have someone to share it with. It had all been getting a bit confusing; the numbers of online sales skyrocketing when his air guitar product took off, but Hilary took all such worries away, taking on the financial side of things to, as Hilary put it, give Basic the freedom to express his creativity.

Now walking down the hill in the direction the cult members had gone, Basic could feel his partner's discomfort and made a pact with himself to make sure no harm could come to him.

Had he looked over his shoulder, instead of checking through the trees to make sure he could still see the people they were following, he might have spotted a dark shape moving between the trees just off the path.

Another Brick in the Wall. Wednesday, October 18th 1515hrs

W ITH HIS INJURED HAND cleaned and bandaged, Big Ben had found the liquor cabinet in the living room and allowed himself a healthy shot of Scottish whisky. There had to be pain meds in the house, but he hadn't found them yet and had given up looking, opting for an alternative method of numbing the throb coming from his wound.

Concocting a few stories in his head to account for the blood – which he'd done his best to clean up – and the wound, he'd settled on a tale involving a trick for opening bottles. It was one of those old army things where one might not have a bottle opener to hand but did have beer and wasn't going to be denied.

There were cold bottles of Corona in the fridge, one of which he emptied into the sink rather than drink it – he'd noticed a slight gain in body fat recently and wanted to reverse it quickly. He then broke the top off it, being careful to manage the broken pieces of glass.

Evidence trail taken care of and wound suitably bound, he returned to the basement.

At the bottom of the stairs, he collected his phone from where he'd left it and went back up to the ground level. As expected, it began to ping madly the moment it reacquired a signal. Most of the incoming traffic was automated messages to advise he'd missed calls, but there were text messages too.

The bulk were from Tempest and Amanda, questioning where he was and threatening various penalties if he wasn't answering just because he was in bed with someone.

Placing the phone on the counter, he thumbed the button to connect him with Tempest and waited for someone to answer.

"Ben?"

"Yup. What's up?"

"What's up? We are investigating a series of grisly murders and have you snooping around the home of a person who we suspected either could have been involved at some level or was a possible target for the killer and we haven't been able to get hold of you for hours. That's what's up," moaned Tempest. "Can I assume you are in perfectly good health?"

"A few scratches," Big Ben replied, meaning his hand, and playing down the knife wound going all the way through it. At the other end of the line Amanda rolled her eyes, guessing incorrectly that Big Ben was referring to wounds inflicted by Genevieve's fingernails at the height of passion.

Picking up on what Tempest said, Big Ben asked, "You said *could* have been involved. Past tense. Has there been a development?"

Tempest blinked in his confusion. "Simon Slater is dead. That's the development. How do you not know that?"

"How? No one has told me. I've been snooping just like Hotstuff asked me to. Genevieve hasn't returned home yet ..."

"Hold on," Amanda cut into the conversation. "She hasn't returned? She's been gone for hours. Ben, I need to call her."

Hearing the worry in Amanda's voice, Big Ben was quick to say, "She's fine." He fiddled with his phone to bring up the recent message he had from her. "She's on her way back to the house and apologises for leaving me here all day by myself. Actually, I'd better go. I need to clear up the evidence of my snooping." Big Ben was referring to the blood on the floor in the basement, the dust had soaked it up and he was sure no one ever went down there because his footprints were the only ones in the layer of dust he found. Nevertheless, he knew it was good practice to cover his tracks.

"Did you find anything?" Amanda enquired, curious to hear if his search had unearthed anything interesting.

Big Ben frowned deeply, unsure how to describe his discovery.

"There's a basement," he started. "And it leads to a locked door. I found the key but guess what is behind the door."

In the van, unseen by Big Ben, Tempest and Amanda met each other's eyes, a silent question passing between them. They had no idea what might be in the basement of Simon Slater's house, but something scary and incriminating seemed like an obvious answer.

Big Ben supplied the answer, "A brick wall."

"A brick wall?" Tempest repeated.

"Yup. Someone bricked up the doorway and did a pretty good job of it. I've no idea what is behind it, but whatever it is, the bricks are recent. If I had to guess, I'd say they were added in the last year."

Tempest voiced the obvious conclusion, "Genevieve bricked it up after Simon died? Why would she do that?"

Big Ben heard Amanda's reply, "I don't think it matters. If the Kimble Publishing people are behind the deaths like Lucas said, and I was wrong about Genevieve being involved, whatever interior decorating she wishes to do is none of our business."

It was all Big Ben needed to hear. "Fair enough. Anything else I need to know?"

He listened to the update, surprised to hear they were heading for Faversham, a point not far from where they all lived and worked.

"Does this mean you're going to end up dealing with Quinn?" he asked, certain he already knew the answer.

Tempest sighed and chuckled, "Probably."

Amanda told him, "I'll handle Quinn. You can be somewhere else."

Big Ben wished them luck and disconnected the call. The message from Genevieve to say she was on her way home had been sent half an hour ago – he expected her to arrive any minute. If he wanted to deal with the mess in the basement, he was going to have to hurry.

Of course, because life is like that, he heard the front door opening before he could move an inch. A mental check reassured him he'd left the cellar door shut. If there was a chance to lock it and return the key to the junk drawer later, he would, but he doubted it really mattered.

If Genevieve wished to engage in 'activities' he would most certainly oblige. His injury would add a new element, forcing her to take on a more superior role. Excited by the prospect, he checked his reflection in the door of the microwave and gave his biceps a quick pump.

Choosing to wait for her where he was, he called out, "In the kitchen."

Footsteps approached, soft on the carpet in the hallway. He moved to meet her, stepping out of the kitchen to playfully startle her.

It backfired.

Mostly this was because it wasn't Genevieve at all.

He almost got his hand up to block the blow aimed at his head.

Almost.

Time to call the Police. Wednesday, October 18th 1529hrs

"**Y**OU DID WHAT?" EVEN though they had found the satanic cult's secret hidden base, Hilary kind of expected Tempest to be displeased. "You said you were going to the pub," Tempest pointed out.

"Well, we were," Hilary replied, his tone dripping with apology and regret. "But we could see them walking through the countryside and figured they couldn't be going all that far. Basic said we should follow them."

"S'right. Follow dem," echoed Basic.

"So we did. We kept our distance and made sure they never saw us ..."

"Are you sure?" Tempest challenged. "Because staying out of sight is not a skill many people possess. Where are you now?" he changed tack and posed a question.

A little more snippily than he would usually employ, Hilary said, "On a small ridge looking down over the house. It's, um ... it's very gothic."

Amanda asked, "Gothic how?"

Tempest and Amanda were still challenging the speed limit when they could, hurtling south on one of the county's two main arteries. They had the phone on speaker, held between them in Amanda's right hand. At the other end, Hilary also had his phone switched to speaker mode, but he had the volume turned right down and was speaking in whispers lest he be heard.

He kept getting the sense that he was being watched and it was creeping him out more than everything else. It didn't help that the sun was dipping toward the horizon and the shadows were lengthening by the minute. It would soon be twilight and then dusk for a brief period before the darkness came.

Prior to meeting Tempest Michaels and finding himself drawn into his crazy world of killers, mental people, and outright lunatics, Hilary might have claimed he liked being out at night. However, the romantic connotations it once held had been irrevocably displaced by nightmarish scenarios where evil witches with giant electrode devices, genetically altered polar bears, and a host of other grim terrors lurked behind every bush. For Hilary, every shadow possessed the potential to be hiding a creature that, while arguably human, nevertheless wanted to suck out his liver.

To answer Amanda, he said, "Gothic as in it has lots of towers and is dark and in the middle of nowhere, and generally screams *go away or die* in loud and easy to understand words."

Tempest said, "If you are not going to head back to the pub ..." he let the suggestion hang heavy in the air.

Hilary craned his head to look at Basic.

"You go," Basic suggested. "Get me a pint of something hoppy. There are bad people. I'm going to help my friends."

Muttering that there simply was no way of arguing with sentiment of that nature, Hilary said, "We're staying where we are."

Tempest took it on the chin as if he'd expected nothing less and Hilary wished he could be disappointing, just for once.

"Okay, guys. Amanda and I will be there in just a few minutes. You won't see us coming because I'm going to kill the lights. I don't want them to have any idea there are other people in the area. I have your directions from the station. Look out for us and be ready to shine a light as I suggested earlier."

Hilary agreed to be ready and flicked the button to end the call. Tempest was tactical and calm and so in control it freaked Hilary out rather than make him calm. If he knew to shield his light behind his fingers so it made a thing that was visible over a space of just a few dozen yards but no farther, he might feel more comfortable, but the fact that Tempest had to talk him through how to not get spotted by the people in the house they were watching just made it worse.

Lying on the cold ground, imagining ants and beetles choosing to crawl into his pockets for warmth, Hilary listened and watched. Why wasn't he at home watching *Star Trek*? It was a question that begged an answer he was never going to get.

There were lights behind some of the windows of the large gothic house now. Should he call it a mansion? Or a manor? Hilary didn't know. Property wasn't his thing, though he suspected his wife would supply the answer; she seemed to know everything.

Whatever it was, it was big and either didn't have electricity, or the people in it were choosing not to employ it because the lights he could see were all flames.

There was a courtyard at the main entrance to the property. Enclosed by the building's wings as they wrapped around it, it looked to Hilary as though it was largely open on the fourth side at the front. From his vantage point looking down over the house, Hilary estimated the courtyard had to be close to fifty yards along each side. There were four or five trees growing that appeared to be deliberately planted and the floor was covered with ancient stone tiles.

It would have been very difficult to see at all were it not for the flaming torches being arranged around the periphery of the open area.

A sound made Hilary twitch his head around. Did something just snap a twig fifty feet behind him in the wood line?

"Did you hear that?" he asked Basic.

Basic said, "Yeah. Dat must be Tempest and 'Manda arriving."

Hilary was about to argue when he realised what Basic was hearing. It had been hard to hear before, but an engine had just shut off. His phone vibrated.

'*Turn on the tactical light and aim it south.*'

Perplexed, Hilary replied, '*How do I know which way is south?*'

His phone vibrated again. '*Check the stars!*'

Now unable to unknit his eyebrows, he sent Tempest a simple reply, '*!!!!!!!!!!???*'

A quarter of a mile away, Tempest mimed strangling himself and shooting his brains out with an imaginary shotgun.

The next message read, '*Just turn it on and spin like you're a lighthouse for two seconds.*'

With a shrug, Hilary got to his feet – it was getting dark now, so he wasn't so bothered about being visible – and did as Tempest requested. He got an odd look from Basic, but an almost instantaneous response.

'*Okay. I see you. Two minutes. Stand by.*'

Almost exactly two minutes later, Hilary jolly near had a heart attack when Tempest appeared from his blind spot.

"What can you see?" he asked, dropping to the ground to stare down at the manor house/mansion/whatever it was.

Amanda placed a hand on Hilary's shoulder. "You really shouldn't have put yourselves in this much danger. Thank you though. You might have really saved the day."

Her words swelled Hilary's chest, but when he tried to reply, he found she was on the grass next to Tempest.

In the dying light, the paranormal investigators had a set of binoculars and were scoping out the house. Nestling next to Tempest, Hilary pointed out the very obvious court-yard. Obvious because it was lit with burning torches that contrasted starkly with the ever-darkening landscape. The flames illuminated the stonework, giving it a spooky aura it really didn't need.

"Time to call the police?" Hilary asked hopefully.

Amanda twisted her head to meet his eyes, an apologetic slant on her lips, "Not yet. Sorry, Hilary. All we have right now is a bunch of people who went to a house and an accusation made by a man in the moments before his death. We believe the evidence points this way, but we must find something tangible to tie them to the murders. Our opinion isn't worth a thing."

Hilary continued to press, nerves driving his mouth, "Like what? What sort of evidence do you hope to find?"

"That symbol we found where they killed their victims would be nice," remarked Amanda flippantly.

"You mean that one right there," asked Tempest, aiming an arm at the house as he leapt to his feet. "I can do one better than that," he snapped, starting down the hill toward the gothic mansion. "Call the police!"

Amanda started forward, following Tempest, but straining her eyes to see what prompted him to move so fast. The flicker of light from the torches shifted when the breeze tugged at them, showing her the same symbol she'd found in Daniel McCormack and Amy Hildestrand's houses.

It was right there on the front façade of the gothic mansion, carved into the stonework. She was about to shout after Tempest when movement in the courtyard below drew her gaze and with an expletive, she started running too. Tempest was already hard to see, the darkness absorbing him, but slamming on the brakes, she reversed direction.

"Here!" she grabbed Hilary's arm and slapped her phone into his palm. "Call Ian Quinn! Tell him to send everything he's got!" she yelled as loudly as she dared, already running down the hill after Tempest.

Basic hadn't moved. Unsure what was happening or what he ought to be doing, his natural inclination was to follow Tempest and Amanda, but Hilary wasn't moving and Basic didn't want to abandon his friend.

Staring at Amanda's phone, Hilary called after her, "What … what do I tell him?"

Her voice drifted back up the hill, "There's about to be a human sacrifice!"

Rooted to the spot, Hilary couldn't believe his ears, yet there in the courtyard he could now see figures in black cloaks. Easy to pick out against the backdrop of flaming torches, they were positioning themselves around a black table – an altar, Hilary's brain supplied. Onto it, and wearing a white silk robe that clung to her naked body beneath, a young woman was being placed with reverential grace.

Understanding enough to make the right decision, Basic said, "Yeah, call the police!" Then he too vanished into the darkness, leaving Hilary alone.

Unable to believe how his day had gone, and feeling very exposed, Hilary found the number he needed and hit the dial button.

It's Britney, Bitch.
Wednesday, October
18th 1615hrs

N EARING THE OUTER EDGE of the house, I paused to listen, stilling my breathing as I searched the shadows for Tempest.

"Amanda," his whisper found my ears. "Over here."

I ran toward his voice, amazed at how well the man could blend with the shadows.

"Where are you?" I hissed into the darkness, putting all my effort into not screaming with shock when he touched my arm. "What did you do to your face?" I asked, reaching up to touch it. He was almost invisible in the moonlight.

"Dirt," he replied, grabbing my face and smearing it with cold, wet, sticky mud without even asking me. What was that going to do for my pores? "Put some on your hands and neck too," he advised, slopping a small handful into my right palm.

"Ewww," I complained, doing it anyway because camouflage is a good thing when you are trying to sneak up on people. Tempest usually carries a backpack containing his night-ops gear. Tactical Kevlar vest, fingerless gloves with hardened knuckles, plus black rip-stop trousers, combat boots and assorted accessories such as camouflage paint were weekly use items for him and Big Ben. I had my own gear, but rarely employed it.

Right now, it was precisely what we needed, but the bag of things I'd packed to bring on this case was back in London, and I was certain Tempest's would prove to be in Big Ben's car. What I wouldn't give for a couple of non-lethal weapons right now.

I saw Basic approaching and went to intercept him.

Together, the three of us were going to have to come up with a way to stop the cultists from killing the woman I'd seen. That she was being placed upon an altar by several dozen murderous mad people left little question that she was about to die.

We had to stop it. The police would come; I was sure of that. Hilary could be relied upon to get the message across and guide them to our location, but without the use of a teleportation device, they weren't going to show for twenty minutes or more.

Until they did, we were on our own.

"Dey are going to hurt dat girl?" asked Basic.

I placed a hand on his shoulder. "No. We are going to stop them."

"Okay," he rumbled, happy with my reply. "How?"

Tempest handed Basic more of the mud, helping him to remove the shine from his face while outlining a hastily concocted plan at the same time.

"There's too many of them to take in a fight."

"Way too many," I agreed.

"Even for Big Ben if we had him with us," Tempest said wistfully. Having the giant Adonis with us tonight would make us all feel more confident. "So we need to cause a delay; make them abandon their ceremony to deal with us."

"You know they will kill us in a heartbeat if we get caught," I pointed out. We were dealing with a satanic cult that was responsible for five deaths that we knew about. Goodness knows what the true figure might be. "The police won't get here for ages. So whatever we do, we need to either stay invisible, or make sure they can't catch or corner us."

Tempest said, "Let's start by setting fire to the building. You two head around the side, there must be a door open somewhere, but if not just smash a window. Get inside and let's get the place burning. Make sure it's visible."

I grabbed Tempest's arm. "What if they have more victims inside?" At the same time, though I didn't say it, I knew that if we burned up some of the cultists, we would be held responsible for their deaths. The fact that they were crazy killers wouldn't matter one bit in court.

Tempest cursed. "Okay, good point ..." His words trailed off and the only bit of his face I could easily see – his eyes – widened as he looked around. "Oh, dear Lord, where's Basic?"

I spun on the spot, twisting around to stare toward the courtyard. We were fifty yards away, looking at it from an angle. No one inside would be able to see us with all the flickering light playing around them so we were safe, but there was no sign of Basic and only one place he could have gone.

The courtyard was enclosed on three sides but there were old stone window openings on two of them. The side nearest to us was the open one, and directly opposite that was the building itself, the spires clawing at the sky.

I took a pace forward, and immediately spotted Basic as he passed in front of a 'window' blocking out the dancing flames from the torches inside.

My heart was in my throat, Tempest's too, I imagined as we both began running. We had no idea what he might try to do, but if he alerted the cult and they cornered him ...

Racing across the uneven terrain of the overgrown heathland and trying not to stumble or lose my footing, the unexpected sound of *Britney Spears* filled the air. Someone was playing her chart hit *Toxic* at high volume and that someone was Basic.

I caught a flash of movement to my right. Tempest saw it too – a bear-shaped black blob carving a circular path around and away from the courtyard.

"You utter genius," applauded Tempest.

Basic has a low IQ, no one would ever argue that, but it does nothing to diminish his value or his ability to think his way clearly to a solution.

Tempest and I stopped running, crouching low to reduce the chance of being spotted now that we were closer to the courtyard and the light from it might reflect off our clothes or eyes. A chunk of the cult was exiting the courtyard, some going through the window on this side though most simply came out the open end and ran around.

They were easy to spot in their black cloaks. Or they were until they stepped out from the lit area. After that they all but vanished.

"They'll be blind!" Tempest spat an urgent whisper as he grabbed the left sleeve of my coat and yanked me to my feet. He was already running. I knew what he meant – they had come from the light into almost pitch black so their night vision would be nil, their eyes filled with coronas from the brightness of the flames. Not only that, we were facing twenty of them at the most because Basic's genius tactic had drawn out a more manageable portion.

I like to think of myself as a girly-girl for the most part. I like pink things and I drink sparkling wine, but I had to learn self-defence as part of my police training, and I'd learned a good deal more since meeting Tempest. To get through our current situation in one piece, we could either run away – an option none of us would accept since there was a woman's life at stake, or we could do a thing that Tempest referred to as 'bringing violence to the enemy'.

With so many targets to choose from and the element of surprise on our side, it was no surprise when I heard the first cry of pain. The cult members had gathered around the phone, one of them picking it up and killing the music with a swipe of their finger.

That was when Basic hit them.

I could see them as a black blob, silhouetted by light coming from the window to their rear. Just before I got to them, they were all turning toward the sound of the fallen comrade. A tree branch, hefted into the sky by Basic I felt sure, hung in the moonlit air for a half second, before sweeping down to crush skulls like a sickle cutting corn.

The terror of the unexpected ambush was instant, but then even more so when Tempest and I hit their rear flank.

Fuelled by adrenalin and fear, and because I was running flat out, my initial assault consisted of jumping into the air to make an arrow with my feet. They hit someone in the middle of their back, folding them in half in a way that promised hospitalisation.

I'm not a naturally violent person, but I was prepared to be one if it meant I got to live through the next half an hour.

I landed, rolled, and sprung up with my right fist aiming at the first thing my eyes found. The blow stung my knuckles and jarred the bones in my forearm. Pain shot through them, but gasping from the exertion and the pace of my pulse, I spun to deliver another kick.

Between us we had to have taken ten or more out of the fight in under three seconds, but the rest were rallying, and the alarm had travelled to the main group. Just as before, some were coming through the window, that being the fastest route to get to our position, but the bulk were coming around.

They were going to cut us off!

I wasn't the only one who saw the likelihood of that scenario – Tempest was already taking action.

"Amanda! Basic! On me!" he yelled, abandoning any attempt at stealth now because the cat was well and truly out of the bag.

With a shoulder barge, I shoved another black cloak from my path and ran after my boyfriend. He was aiming for the window, and I saw why – it created a funnel, a pinch-point and only one person could get through it at a time.

Basic got there first, charging through the two men on this side with a thunderous roar that must have terrified those who heard it. His tree branch spun, scything down to fell another black cloak just as it rose to stand.

A shout from Tempest made Basic turn away from the window just as the next face appeared in it. I was right on his heels, running without knowing the plan, just trusting that Tempest had one.

He did. Sort of.

The black cloak at the window looked up, his face framed inside the hood for a half second – just long enough for me to see it was a woman, then she was gone as Tempest dived through the hole fists first.

Tempest was the kind of man who would never strike a woman, but all bets were off tonight.

I watched him tuck and roll, coming up into a fighting stance on the other side and went through after him. Out of breath, heartrate through the roof, and feeling shaky from all the adrenalin in my body, I felt a wave of relief wash over me when I saw how few of the cult were left in the courtyard.

The woman in the white silk robe was there, but she was no longer on the altar. She was being held up by two black cloaks – men, by their height and width, I judged. Behind them was the goat-headed figure I saw last night. In its right hand was the shepherd's crook from last night; the one that set fire to Statham.

Spread out across the courtyard were another dozen of the cult members. It left us severely outnumbered still, but our odds were improving.

Tempest hadn't slowed down and behind me Basic had come through the window and was now guarding it. In the torchlight I was able to see it better and what he held was closer to a tree trunk than a branch. A black cloak tried to get through the window, and I winced involuntarily when Basic donked them on the head with his half-a-tree weapon.

Tearing after Tempest, I lost ground when two of the cult members came at me. Blocking my path, I could see one was a woman. Short, petite, and probably weighing about ninety pounds, I jinked right to draw the man, then threw my weight left, barrelling through the smaller woman with not the slightest care for how she came off.

My sudden shift in direction threw the man off balance and I was by him and haring after Tempest before he knew what had happened.

Now there was nothing between me and the woman we wanted to rescue except the two goons holding her, and Goat Head. The remaining cult members would converge on us, but maybe we could grab the girl and get into the building. I could see the open doors begging to offer us refuge.

Tempest vaulted the altar, his legs kicking out as he came down and bounced up again. With the girl between them, the men holding her couldn't go anywhere fast enough to avoid the fight coming their way.

Tempest's right leg arced up and thrust outward. It struck the man on the left in his solar plexus driving the air from his lungs in a gush as he folded in half.

I screamed a warning, not that Tempest would have heard it or been able to react. Goat Head was swinging the crook at him, and I couldn't bear to see him get torched the way the Statham Wannabe had last night.

I needn't have worried. Such was Tempest's momentum that he carried on through the space where the man had been standing, and swung a haymaker of a fist at Goat Head before the cult's high priest could bring his or her weapon to bare.

Tempest's fist connected with the goat headpiece, knocking it clear off the person hiding inside it. As it spun away to land, bounce, and roll, the high priestess, or whatever she was, shrieked in horror.

The hood fell away and I couldn't stop the shock I felt at seeing Indigo inside the costume. Sure, Lucas told me she was behind it all, but I'd met her, and it seemed impossible until this very moment.

The shepherd's crook flew from her hand, hit the floor and ... I guess it must have cracked open because it burst into flames before it could bounce. It confirmed my suspicion that it contained a chemical designed to ignite when exposed to air. She was guilty of torching the Statham Wannabe last night and would do jail time if we survived long enough for the police to arrive.

The one man still holding the sacrifice was running, taking the woman in the silk robe with him. She ran alongside him, too confused or terrified to fight for herself. I might not have caught him had he not tripped on his robe, but his stumble was all I needed.

I ran right through him, knocking him over and leaving it at that because my focus was on the girl. She was the only priority and now that we had her, our focus had to be getting to the house.

Like it always does in a fight, time was passing slowly, but the time since coming through the window to where we were now had to be less than fifteen seconds. Basic still blocked the window, but his presence there was no longer worthwhile for they had given up trying to come through that way and it was largely blocked by unconscious bodies.

What we had achieved against such overwhelming odds was incredible, but with a small sea of black cloaks charging back into the courtyard from the open end, the effect of our efforts on their overall number was laughable.

"The house!" I screamed, yanking the intended sacrifice behind me. "Basic, get to the house!"

I ran as best I could, glancing to my left to find Tempest carrying Indigo over his shoulder. His pace was slower than it would otherwise be, but not much slower. In his hand, he held a knife, a foot long ornamental thing Indigo had undoubtedly planned to use for the sacrifice. She was screaming obscenities at him and pounding on his back with her free hand. Her other arm he had trapped in his grip.

The doors were ahead of us, and we were going to make it to the building.

Except we didn't.

Any Second Now! Wednesday, October 18th 1619hrs

I HEARD THE FOOTSTEPS thundering our way from within when we were still six or seven yards from the open doors. The light from outside shone in through the doors and windows, illuminating the interior of the building, but only to a depth of a few yards.

It was enough that we saw the black cloaks inside heading our way before they got to the doors. Our decision to aim for the building meant we were essentially trapped now. We either went through the men or it was all over.

However, a glint of something caught my eye. The black cloaks rushing toward us had just produced halberds and any thought of going through them to use the building as a refuge was instantly discarded.

There was nowhere to go!

We had the girl and we had Indigo to use as a bargaining chip, but changing direction in a panic took us into a corner of the courtyard. They were coming for us, and we stood no chance at all.

Seeing our plight, Tempest released Indigo, opening his hands so she fell from his shoulder to land in a heap on the flagstones of the courtyard. Turning to face the horde as they slowed their pace and stalked toward us, he beckoned for me to hand him the poor woman we almost rescued.

Basic came to stand beside me, the three of us bringing our tired arms up into fighting stances as we prepared to make a last stand. If Hilary was still on the hill, he would be able to see our hopeless situation and relay it to the cops, but the only thing that could save us now was a Regiment of Paratroopers.

Tempest gave the girl the knife he'd taken from Indigo. He was apologetic when he said, "Here. Stab anyone who comes near you. I'm sorry we didn't do a better job."

Indigo was back on her feet, dusting herself off and looking angry. To my great surprise, the black cloaks formed a barrier, pinning us in our corner, but did not attack. They had weapons now; more halberds getting passed around. I guess they felt they could take their time.

A black cloak emerged from the front row to give Indigo her goat head and then assist to position it correctly. When she was satisfied, she nodded to her acolyte who returned to the crowd and faced our way so he could watch.

Lifting her right arm, she beckoned toward me. At least I thought it was aimed at me until she spoke, the eerie voice cast by the goat head returning in place of her own.

"Come, Stephanie, return to your fold."

I blinked, confused by the request. It should have triggered me to react, but too late I caught the movement behind me from the corner of my eye.

The woman we had just saved swung the knife back to gain momentum before thrusting it forward. It was coming straight for me, her intent to skewer me as obvious as it was shocking.

Tempest lunged for her, but it was Basic who got there first, paying for his reaction time by taking the blade in my stead.

I heard him cry out in pain, the wound unseeable from where I stood. He fell to the ground carrying the blade with him, my heart tearing from my chest when he hit the stone tiles and stayed there.

The sacrifice victim's eyes were filled with bloodlust and mad venom, her lips drawn back in an excited leer.

Until I punched her lights out, that is. She tumbled away from me, her body going limp as she crashed to the floor. She wouldn't be out for long, but I had bigger problems. Dropping to my knees, I cradled Basic, my arms around his shoulder and my face against his head.

"Basic where did she get you? Is it bad? Can you stand?"

"Don't fink so," he wheezed, his reply drawing a cackle from Indigo that was echoed by the black cloaks around her.

"I warned you not to interfere, Amanda Harper. Now, come peacefully, child," she rasped in the goat head's inhuman voice. "Be honoured to give your life in sacrifice to Lucifer and accept him as your lord."

Tempest picked up the knife again, handling it in a menacing manner.

"We'll die here tonight, I can see that," he spat. "But be assured a whole bunch of you are coming with me." He meant it too. They were going to have to rush him and even then, he would get several of them.

It was little comfort.

Indigo sneered, "Take them. They can serve our master with their blood as an offering."

Huffing out a hard breath, I raised my fists and rolled my head from side to side as I told myself to stay loose and look for an easy shot. Maybe if I could grab one and get his weapon, we might scare them into holding back ...

It sounded like a long shot even in my head, but I couldn't see another play.

All the adrenalin was making me feel sick and lightheaded, but I was going to attack ... I just needed to pick a target.

A banshee scream filled the courtyard, making me jump. My heart skipped a beat and my brain told me the hooded figures were about to rush me.

It hadn't come from one of them though. The sound came from behind them and as I watched, Indigo and her black cloaks twisted their torsos through a hundred and eighty degrees to look back toward the open end.

There, silhouetted in the moonlight, was a man whose shape I recognised.

"Alright, ladies," he taunted them. "This sword," he lifted it into a guard position, "was first wielded by a Templar Knight in the 12th century. Worked into the steel is one of the original nails used to pin Christ to the cross. When I kill you with it, your soul will become trapped forever in a state of limbo until *He* rises again. Who wants to go first?"

As cool lines go, it was a good one, but when he stepped forward and the light from the torches illuminated him, the devil worshippers got a proper look at the man making the threats and I have to tell you, Frank Decaux just isn't all that imposing.

He's about five and half feet tall and might weigh a hundred pounds if he ate a big breakfast.

In the Goat Head's dreadful voice, Indigo said, "Kill him."

Frank, ridiculously brave, had of course, been bluffing. He wasn't about to kill anyone with a sword, and, honestly, it looked like he was struggling to keep it aloft. That didn't worry me too much because Frank travels with a team of four ninja warriors.

They were going to leap from the shadows any second now!

The army of hooded figures turned toward Frank.

Any second now there would be ninjas falling from the sky!

Frank backed up a step and in doing so prompted the hoods to charge. Not all of them though. Just more than half ran toward Frank. The rest remained where they were, keeping me and Tempest hemmed in.

Incredibly, Frank held his ground, refusing to flinch as they closed on his position. They were screaming and whooping, running straight for him. He was going to die for his foolish bravery.

When they got to within ten yards, Frank took his right hand from his sword and screamed a single word to the sky.

It sounded like, "Foraizze!" but whatever it was, the gibberish came accompanied by a sweeping hand gesture that created a wall of flame.

"I am the mighty hand of God," he roared from behind the fire. "I will smite you from this land!"

The flames had reached a height of ten feet, the heat from them enough to drive the cult members back.

Then the flames died again, almost as quickly as they came to life.

It left Frank staring at the line where they had been.

"Oh," he said, "They were supposed to last a bit longer than that."

With a mad cry that was repeated by more than half the black cloaks facing him, they charged.

We were not going to get a better chance. The number of people coming to kill us had been reduced by more than half and those who remained were momentarily distracted. With a weary nod from Tempest, I took two quick paces and hit the nearest hood with everything I had.

The punch stung my hand though it barely registered as I swung a kick to the midriff of the next hood in line. I snatched one of the halberds and swung it, but the black cloaks were dispersing, and I saw why when I shot a peek back toward the open end of the courtyard.

Frank's ninjas *were* here!

Dressed in nothing but black, they were nevertheless easy to spot. Frank's flames had created the distraction he needed to get them into place and now they were ripping through the devil worshippers like action heroes through a cast of low-paid extras.

Sandwiched between Frank and his ninjas at one end, and me with Tempest at the other, Indigo's people didn't know which way to turn and many of them, particularly, but not exclusively the women, were wailing in fear. Part of me wanted to berate the women for letting the side down, and the rest of me wanted to spit in their faces. The murderous scum were finally on the losing end of the equation and they didn't like it. Well tough.

Beyond the courtyard, where the woodland met the road about a quarter of a mile away, headlights appeared. They were distant, but my prayer that this might be the cavalry arriving was met a moment later when the flashing red and blue strobe lights ignited. There was a whole procession of them, cop car after cop car all coming our way at speed.

In answer to an unvoiced question, Hilary appeared through the haze of smoke left by Frank's fire line. He had my phone pressed to his ear and an overwhelmed look on his face, but he was guiding them in. From his vantage point looking down over the courtyard he must have been able to see Frank and the ninjas and to have known we were in dire straits until they showed up.

It was his sense of urgency hurrying the pace of the squad cars hurtling toward us now.

Some of the cultists were escaping; through the open 'windows' of the stonework or out through the open end of the courtyard because there just weren't enough of us to stop them. The greater percentage were on the ground, injured though their wounds were the kind that would heal.

The ninjas, Hatchet, Bob, Mistress Mushy, and Poison, were using blunt weapons, not the swords I so often saw them carry. They were doing their best to corral the black cloaks into the centre of the courtyard and by my count had more than half of them either on their backs nursing broken arms or bruised skulls, or on their knees in a pose of surrender.

With a jolt, I realised the one person I did not see was Indigo. Making a break for it, two of the devil worshippers ran for one of the windows. I wanted as many of them as possible – it was far easier to take them tonight than to try to sweep them up tomorrow. Tempest had seen them too, our eyes meeting as we both charged across the courtyard to cut them off.

It tore at me to leave Basic unguarded, I needed to get back to him and make sure he was ok. A glance aimed his way showed that no one was messing with him, but he needed proper medical attention right now. The moment it was safe to do so, he was getting all my care.

Right now, I was still awash with righteous judgement, and it showed when I tackled the nearest of the black cloaks from behind. Kicking his back foot as he ran, he tripped and went down hard, landing on his chest with a whoosh of air leaving his lungs. Winded, he didn't know the half of it, and I gladly educated him with a full elbow drop to his back.

Now he would think twice about getting up. I grabbed his right arm, bending it behind his back and doing so with distinctly more force than I ever would have gotten away with as a cop. I've got to tell you, there's a lot to be said for working independently. Just removing the rules that bind cops to permitted codes of behaviour was a gift.

I did miss the cuffs though. I was going to buy myself some the first chance I got. Or perhaps some of those cable ties they favour now. Yes, they would be most useful right now.

Hauling my prisoner – I was content to label him thusly – from the cold tile of the courtyard, I wheeled around to find Tempest dragging another by his collar. Whatever Tempest had done left the man he tackled unconscious.

The wailing sirens were right on us now, headlight beams striking the stonework at the leading edge of the courtyard as the squad cars covered the last hundred yards.

With a choked breath, I looked around for the four ninjas. True to their ancestral models, they had vanished. Frank remained, holding the giant sword aloft and promising swift retribution upon anyone foolish enough to try moving.

That there was no sign of Indigo irked me immensely, but less than a minute later, with cops flooding the whole area, I discovered she had been spotted heading across the heathland and had been caught. She appeared shortly afterward, her hands cuffed behind her back and a tirade of abuse pouring from her lips as she promised legal action against everyone present.

I could hear her, but alongside Tempest as the pair of us sat with Basic, I didn't bother to listen. The good news was that the blade had entered Basic's side at an angle and had missed everything but his obliques. He wouldn't be doing sit-ups for months and the wound would affect many other activities, but unless he bled out, which I didn't think he would, he was in no real danger.

Frank appeared at my side. "How's Basic?" he enquired, showing concern for our injured person.

Basic rolled to his side and gave Frank a thumbs up.

"He'll be fine," I reassured the bookshop owner. "Thank you for coming to save us."

Frank dipped his head. "You're most welcome. I think I almost gave Hilary a heart attack when I appeared."

"You were tracking us the whole time, weren't you?" Tempest accused him in a good-natured way.

Frank had little sympathy. "You gave me no choice, Mr Michaels. Sending me away this morning when you were proposing to take on a cult of devil worshippers? It could have gone so much worse."

"The ninjas are all okay?" I wanted to know.

Frank appreciated my concern. "They are. Mission accomplished you might say. You'll note I instructed them to use non-lethal weapons. I could tell we were dealing with humans and not supernatural creatures for once."

No matter how often we proved there was nothing paranormal going on, Frank would continue to insist the next case would be the one.

"I'd better make myself scarce," Frank said, rising to his feet again. "The cops are likely to ask some uncomfortable questions and I'd rather pretend I was never here."

Before he could extract himself, Tempest asked, "How did you do the thing with the fire?"

Frank grinned, continuing to back away when he said, "Magic, dear fellow. Magic."

Moments later, Hilary, acting as liaison and doing his best to explain the who, what, and why of the situation, brought a sergeant called Baxter to speak with us. He was the temporary situation commander until someone more senior turned up and assured us that was about to happen.

"Do either of you know Chief Inspector Quinn?" he asked.

Tempest laughed in a sad way. "I've met him," he replied.

"I used to work with him. I was a cop," I admitted. "I knew if I called him, he would react."

Sergeant Baxter took off his hat to scratch an itch in his hair line – I remembered how the hats had always made my scalp feel. Replacing the hat, he said, "You were not wrong. He'll be here any minute now. My advice: tell him the truth about all of this. There are thirty people with either broken bones or severe contusions. The paramedics tell me there's at least six showing signs of concussion. Some of your ... arrests," I guess he couldn't think of a better word, "claim they were hit with a tree."

"S'right," said Basic, speaking for the first time in over a minute. "Trees make good weapons."

Sergeant Baxter's face was a picture of disbelief though which part of what he was hearing and seeing he was struggling to believe I didn't know and chose not to ask.

"You really think these are the ones responsible for the string of Simon Slater murders in London?" he asked, his voice laced with doubt.

I pointed above my head to the carved stone inset on the front of the building above the door. "That symbol appears at two of the murder scenes. At least. It probably appears at all of them; we haven't had the chance to check that yet. They also had motive. The people in the black cloaks are, so far as we know, all members of the firm that published Simon Slater's works."

"Dang it," Baxter kicked at the gravel on the flag stones with an annoyed foot. "I rather liked the idea that he was back from the dead."

I wasn't sure what to say to that, but pushing off the ground I came back to upright. Dusting my palms on my jeans, a favourite pair that were heading nowhere but the bin, I nodded my head toward the circle of devil worshippers.

"You mind if I ask them a few questions?"

Sergeant Baxter hadn't expected that. "Only until the chief inspector arrives, okay? I'll supervise."

I crouched to touch Basic on the shoulder. The paramedics were finished with him, but with so many injured to transport to hospital, he was going to have to wait for his ride. Their triage process dictated that he wasn't the highest priority, and they didn't care that he was the only good guy with an injury.

Basic promised he was okay, and I believed him. I placed a kiss on his forehead and promised to see him before he went. We had to figure out who was going with him to the hospital and who was driving the van. There would be room for one of us in the ambulance; they wouldn't put any of the devil worshippers in it with him. If the guys didn't argue, it would be me travelling with Basic.

He saved me by diving in front of the crazy naked woman when she tried to stab me. That sort of thing sticks with a person. What was with that though? We were trying to save her, yet Indigo had addressed the woman by her first name and she tried to attack me with a knife.

STEVE HIGGS

I was almost at the gaggle of battered-looking cult members when Tempest caught up to me. He'd left Hilary with Basic, content that nothing was going to happen in the next few minutes while we got some answers.

It was all over. That was the headline news. It happened in a flurry of hasty activity none of us could have predicted, but that was how investigations go sometimes. I looked for Stephanie, the supposed human sacrifice. I'd last seen her when the paramedics covered her with a foil blanket, but she was nowhere to be seen.

"The nearly naked girl?" Sergeant Baxter sought to confirm. "She was one of the first to be taken away by the paramedics. They said she was suffering from the early stages of hypothermia."

That I believed. It was cold out. Not freezing, but certainly a temperature that would convince me to keep my clothes on.

"She'll be treated and transferred to the station for interview as soon as she gets the all-clear from the doctors. I sent two officers with her."

"She's under arrest?" I questioned.

"Well, yeah. She's one of them." He gestured with his head, nodding it at the faces looking lost and generally forlorn on the courtyard floor.

Tempest asked the question first. "She works for Kimble Publishing?"

"Apparently so," Baxter said with a shrug.

Now I was confused. Determined to find clarity, I found Indigo and sat on the ground so our eyes were the same height.

"Why were you going to kill Stephanie?" I believed it was a simple enough question though I expected her to either refuse to talk or to just pain lie. I was to be surprised.

"You are such an insignificant little speck," Indigo replied dismissively. "Stephanie was a willing volunteer, ready to give her blood for the dark lord. It is a blood-letting ritual, not

212

a sacrifice. The blood acts as a conduit, you see. It brings us closer to him. All the members of our church take their turn upon the altar."

It was bizarre, but not worth pursuing. If they wanted to carve each other up a bit, that was of no consequence to me. It was the people they had killed I wanted to hear about.

Pressing my luck, I asked, "Who killied Leslie Ashe, Indigo? Which of your 'church' members killed him? Did you send a team to recreate the scene from Simon's book and set the stage? Who did you use to pose as Simon?"

Indigo snorted an amused laugh.

"You silly girl. I begged the dark lord to end that fool's life. When I want people killed, I need only pray to my master."

She was trying to be clever, pinning the deaths on a force she proposed to wield. As a defence it would probably land her in the psych ward. Assuming, that is, that she was convicted at all. If the murders were all committed by members of the firm and the lawyers couldn't prove she was behind it all, maybe she would walk. They would get her for setting fire to the man last night, but that was hardly the same thing.

Changing tack, I asked, "What about Amy Hildestrand? I understand the motive for killing Leslie Ashe and Daniel McCormack, that was all about the royalties, yes?" Wisely Indigo said nothing, and I pressed on. "Why kill Amy? What was her crime against you? Was she a former member of the cult who tried to leave," I tried a longshot idea that occurred to me only as I was speaking.

Indigo frowned at me, her expression suggesting I was being particularly dense.

"We are not a cult, Amanda. We are all unified by our religion. When *his* time to rule comes, you will wish you had listened to *his* scriptures too. As for Amy Hildestrand, I haven't the faintest idea what happened to her. Trust me when I say she wasn't a member of our church; no one ever leaves. Why would they want to once they've heard the truth of *his* words? I'd never heard of her before her murder was tied to the deaths the dark lord was good enough to commit on our behalf."

My face was screwing itself up. Not because she was telling such elaborate lies, but because I wanted to believe her. Not the part about Satan perpetrating the murders, but about Amy. Indigo claimed she had no knowledge of her, and she made it sound true. She was admitting to the other murders ...

"What about Samuel Blake?" I pushed her to answer another question. "Is he one of the victims you prayed for the dark lord to take?"

"Time's up," Sergeant Baxter placed a hand on my shoulder. "Chief Inspector Quinn just arrived."

Pressing to get an answer, even as Baxter urged me to move away, I said, "Did you have Simon Blake killed, Indigo?"

She looked me dead in the eyes. "No."

No Escape.
Wednesday, October
18th 1705hrs

THE FIRST THING BIG Ben noticed was how much his head hurt. He opened his eyes and snapped them closed again just as quickly when the light hit his eyes like two lasers drilling a hole right through his head.

A wince of pain escaped his lips before he could suppress it and he squeezed his eyes tightly closed to limit the light coming through the skin over them.

His ankles and knees were bound, his chest too, he discovered, messages coming in from all over his body as his consciousness returned and he tried to move. His wrists were tied so that his arms were pulled apart and he was in a chair – a dining chair he decided, wriggling his hips to see if he could get up.

"I wouldn't bother," said a man's voice. The closeness of it startled Big Ben, and that made him mad. He hated being made to jump in fright.

Cracking his eyes just a fraction so he could see through his lashes without having to endure too much of the searing pain, he found a man sitting in the chair opposite.

The man said, "I'm really rather good at knots. I doubt you'll be able to get free."

Closing his eyes again, and giving himself a moment to think, Big Ben asked, "Who the heck are you?"

"That's not really something you need to know. The important thing is that you took something that belongs to me."

"Would you mind turning the lights down a touch?"

Big Ben's request caused a snigger to escape the man sitting opposite.

"I don't think so. Keeping you helpless is a far better idea. Have you read *To Hell and Back*? It is arguably Simon's best work."

"Can't say that I have." Big Ben rarely had time for books. I mean, really? He was going to devote his attention to the written word when there were ladies knocking on his door asking to come in? Not likely.

"Ah, well that is a little disappointing," the man remarked, the timbre of his voice a balance between annoyed and dispirited. "I suppose I'll have to explain."

"Or you could spare me the pain." Big Ben cracked an eye lid again, squinting up at his captor. "It's not like I give a damn about some book some bloke wrote."

"Some bloke!" Big Ben saw the man move, both eyes fluttering briefly open again just before his head was yanked back. "Simon Slater was a literary genius!" The words were bellowed into Big Ben's right ear, the man's breath hot against the side of his face as he gripped a handful or hair. He used it to pull Big Ben's head harshly to one side. "His death was a tragedy to the entire world!"

Despite the pain - the shouting and yanking were doing nothing for his headache, Big Ben cracked a smile. He wasn't about to be intimidated, it wasn't in his nature, and he'd just discovered his captor's trigger.

With a few choice words, Big Ben knew he could distract or anger the man. To prove his theory, he said, "Aw, that's sweet. You were in love with him."

The hand clutching his hair vanished though his head was thrown to the side in contempt first.

"Let's see how long you retain your sense of humour when you see what your future holds."

With no idea what that meant, Big Ben tried to open his eyes once more. Just as before, his eyelids fluttered, the pain from his eyes forcing them shut even as he tried to keep them open. When the lights in the room unexpectedly dimmed, the relief he felt almost demanded a grateful remark.

Not that he would have offered his thanks, but the sight that greeted him now that he could see was enough to stifle any comment.

The ropes around his wrists had been attached to nails driven through Genevieve's dining table. An experimental flex proved they were going to be hard to shift. They were not the real concern though.

The cross bow was.

Mounted on a jury-rigged platform, the crossbow was loaded with a steel-tipped bolt and prepared to fire. The tension in the 'string' – Big Ben wasn't sure of the correct term for it – was held in place by another piece of rope which in turn was anchored to the table with yet more nails.

"You're admiring my handiwork?" the man observed, watching Big Ben as he walked around the table. "Simon's ability to put the reader in the room made it possible for me to build this without the need for a picture or plans," he explained. "I apologise for its crude nature. Had I more time, I would have constructed something more elegant as I am sure Simon envisaged when he wrote this scene."

The man continued to babble, the words passing over and around Big Ben as he focussed on the device itself. The trigger mechanism of the crossbow had been removed which left the anchored rope as the only thing preventing the bolt from shooting across the room. A glance down at his chair revealed that the legs were nailed to the floor.

Could he shift it? If he threw all his weight in one direction with all his strength behind it, would he break free, or at least be able to move enough that the bolt might miss or at least hit him somewhere less fatal?

Another experimental tensing of his muscles threw the question into doubt.

The man twanged the rope, drawing Big Ben's attention back to it.

"It won't go off by accident," he promised. "That's not the point at all. Simon created tension and drama with this scene by forcing the reader to question how the victim would get free. He'd double crossed the wrong people, you see? They wanted him to know his death was coming, and to know he couldn't escape. The anticipation ... the knowledge that the rope would burn through ..." the man placed a small gas burner on the table under the rope which immediately began to smoulder, "was what sold the book in such high numbers. It really was his best writing."

Nervously licking his lips, his eyes on the rope, Big Ben asked, "How did the victim escape?"

His answer was a laugh. "He didn't. That's the point of the book. Sometimes in a person's life, they commit a crime against another person that cannot be forgiven. The rebalancing of the scales is as unavoidable as it is necessary."

Now unable to deny the rising panic he felt, Big Ben yanked on his ropes and tried to stand up. He was strong, stronger than anyone he knew. At the gym he attended, his bench press and deadlifts often attracted a small crowd. All that muscle had no impact on his bonds now though. The table and the chair upon which he sat refused to budge an inch as the ropes cut cruelly into his flesh.

Across the room, the man watched Big Ben's efforts with an air of emotionless detachment. That he seemed utterly unconcerned about his victim's attempts to break free unnerved Big Ben more than he cared to admit.

Straining and grunting, he twisted, pulled, and fought against the ropes that held him in place. If anything, they grew tighter in places.

Out of breath and perspiring, after five minutes of effort, Big Ben accepted defeat.

The man nodded his head. "Jolly good. Now perhaps we can move things along," he remarked, staring down at the burning rope. "We are up against a ticking clock, one might say."

For the second time, Big Ben asked, "Who the heck are you?"

Something Missed.
Wednesday, October
18th 1711hrs

"**W**E'VE MISSED SOMETHING," I stated it as a plain fact and Tempest's acceptance without argument made me more certain I was right.

We were back over with Basic, who was just about to be taken away by the paramedics. Half a dozen ambulances had arrived over the course of the last five minutes, enough to deal with the most seriously wounded, but still too few to transport all those who required medical attention. Some would go in the back of squad cars once the paramedics attending had splinted, immobilised, or otherwise performed basic first aid on their injuries.

"Everything okay?" asked Hilary, seeing the concern on our faces. "It's over, right? Case closed, moved on to the next one?" I think he could tell we were questioning the validity of that assumption.

"They might not have actually killed anyone," Tempest told him.

Hilary frowned and shook his head. "But the inverted pentagram? You said it was carved into the walls in the victim's homes. That directly ties them to the deaths." He jabbed a finger at the carved stone above our heads, the perfect inverted pentagram with the Sabbatic Goat enshrined within ought to be all the evidence we needed to have them locked up. But what about a conviction?

"It does," I agreed, unable to deny the same logic we had been following.

"So ... what?" Hilary pressed for us to explain why we looked so concerned.

I exchanged a look with Tempest. Everything pointed to Indigo and the devil worshippers. Kimble Publishing, the entire firm, was staffed by her cult members, entry to the cult forming the basis of employment. They stood to gain from the deaths of Leslie Ashe and Daniel McCormack, their share of the royalties from Simon Slater's books falling back into the pot to be divided by the remaining shareholders. To my knowledge only Genevieve and Kimble Publishing remained, but while they had motive, I believed Indigo's claim that she prayed for them to die.

Praying doesn't kill people, no matter how one asks. Then there was Simon's murder. Performed in the same style as the killings that followed, Indigo had nothing to gain from killing him. Unless they wanted to ...

A new thought slammed into my brain.

"Tempest if Indigo is telling the truth, that means the killer is still out there!" I already had my phone out to frantically dial Genevieve's number. Our client was completely exposed. Right from the start I'd suspected her of helping her husband to fake his death. I'd convinced myself she couldn't admit the truth of it because of the repercussions, public humiliation, and legal machinations that would follow, but I'd been wrong.

Her husband's body was still in his grave and if the people at Kimble Publishing weren't behind the murders, then whoever was probably still had Genevieve on their list.

I got no answer and when it switched to voicemail, I tried to get Big Ben instead.

Tempest was already calling him, and he wasn't answering either.

Rushing to get back to Indigo before she could be led away, I had to shout my question when two constables barred my way.

"Indigo! Indigo, did you or any of your ... congregation," I struggled to find the right word, "physically murder Simon Slater or any of the recent victims?"

"That's enough now, miss," warned the constable to my right. I didn't look his way, refusing to take my eyes from Indigo who was eyeing me curiously again.

"Did they?" I demanded to know, my tone shifting to one that sounded more like begging.

"Harper, just shut up!" roared Chief Inspector Quinn, his anger level predetermined when it came to me or Tempest. "You are not permitted to interrogate my suspects!"

I ignored him too, imploring Indigo with my eyes.

A smile played across her face. "You silly, girl. Why would I want to kill Simon Slater? He was one of the founding members of our church."

Rising to her feet as two more officers came to take her away, Indigo looked like a small and sweet older lady again. The kind who would bake cookies for her grandkids at the weekends.

Momentarily stunned by her revelation, I found my voice as they led her away.

"Indigo! Did your people physically murder anyone?"

"That's enough," snapped Chief Inspector Quinn, blocking my view when he stopped directly in front of me. "I want answers from you, not questions," he growled. "You too, Michaels. Like how is it that the two of you were able to overpower so many of them? I am hearing reports of a team of ninjas. I want to know who they are and where I can find them. No one starts a battle in my county and just vanishes into the night."

My head was filled with conflicting thoughts and urgent arguments, but with Quinn in my face there really wasn't a chance to deal with them now.

Smiling up at him as Tempest came to stand by my side, I said, "What a fanciful notion, Ian. A team of ninjas? Whatever next? Tempest dealt with most of the devil worshippers. He has a mean right hook, you know," I replied with a wink.

Tempest had served a jail term for knocking the chief inspector out in the middle of a televised press conference. Quinn could bluster and threaten all he liked, but we had done nothing illegal tonight, and he knew the press would have a field day if he arrested either one of us without an ironclad reason.

"Very well," he sneered. "I also have a description of a man with a sword who sounds remarkably close in height and features to a certain bookshop owner I know to be one of your associates. I shall be making enquiries. It might not be you going to jail *this* time ..." he put a lot of emphasis on the likely future event occurring, "but I wouldn't plan any holidays too far ahead."

With that, he spun on his heels and began barking orders.

Annoying Quinn was all well and good, but angry with myself for doing so, I realised we needed him.

"Ian," I called, jogging to catch up as he headed away from us. He refused to acknowledge that I had spoken, just as I knew he would. "Ian, our client is Simon Slater's widow, Genevieve Slater. She's not answering her phone and I ... she might be in danger."

Quinn slowed his pace to a stop, spinning around to peer down at me imperiously.

"Need my help, do you?"

"Genevieve Slater needs your help," I corrected him. Seeing his lip twitch and knowing he couldn't argue, I said, "The people you just arrested might not be the killers."

He jolted as if stung, his eyes flaring as he checked to see if I might be joking. Then he tipped his head back and laughed. His guffaws were loud enough that all around him the cops in the courtyard stopped what they were doing to stare.

Ian had tears in his eyes when he looked at me again.

"Seriously? You just brought down a battle in a privately owned house where members of a private and *legal* organised society were conducting a ceremony and you did so because you believed they were responsible for multiple murders. Now you want to tell me that perhaps you had it a teensy bit wrong?"

"Ian, she might already have been taken," I made it his problem to ignore.

He huffed a resigned laugh that had no amusement in it. "I'll speak to a colleague in the city. One of the senior officers heading up this case is already on his way down here. He believes you just cracked this case, but I'm sure he'll enjoy being told the killer is still at large. I can't wait to let him know," he replied with a wicked smile. "However, I'll make sure someone in London performs a check on Genevieve Slater's domicile." He turned away dismissively, shouting at one of his officers for not doing something he would never have known he ought to be doing before I could get another word in.

"Ian," I begged.

Without looking back at me, he snapped, "That's all you're getting, Harper. You've tied up enough police resources tonight already. If I can prove you entered the premises and attacked these people without provocation or just cause, I will be pressing charges."

I watched as he stalked away, but not for long. I had to get moving and my phone was already in my hand.

Massage Interrupted. Wednesday, October 18th 1727hrs

P ATIENCE, STILL BASKING IN the glow of post coital bliss, was barely awake even though the masseuse in the Ritz's exclusive spa was using an elbow to remove a knot of tense muscle from between her shoulders.

"Your phone is ringing," the masseuse, a tall, muscular black man called Eric, who Patience rather fancied, let her know.

"Let it ring," she murmured, her face pressed into the hole in the massage table.

With a shrug, Eric went back to his work.

The phone rang off, the voice mail engaging for a split second before the caller killed it at their end. It started ringing again, half a second later.

Patience ignored it. Nothing could be important enough to interrupt the sixty-minute session she'd booked. Only fifteen minutes into it, she was in heaven and didn't want it to end. It wasn't as if she would ever get to do it again. Unlike Amanda, the guys she dated didn't book rooms at the Ritz. The price of a massage had made Patience spasm when she first consulted the price list. However, Tempest had been good enough to leave her room tab open ...

The phone rang off again. Sighing thankfully, Patience let the tension flow from her body. She questioned if she had ever felt this relaxed before. The voicemail kicked in and this time someone spoke.

"Patience!" Amanda's voice burst from the phone, shattering the tranquil aura of the room. "Patience Woods, I don't care if you are having sex, having a poo, or dangling from a rope! Pick the phone up! I need you!"

Filling the room with obscene remarks, Patience tugged at her towel to keep it from slipping to the floor as she swung around to sit on the massage table. Then she though better of it and let the towel fall around her waist in the hope that Eric might notice her ample and enticing breasts.

"Oh, ah, I'll be outside," Eric backed toward the door and hurried through it. "Just let me know when you are ready to continue," he called through the final inch of space before he pulled it closed behind him.

Muttering about where she wanted to stick her phone when she caught up with Amanda, Patience thumbed the button to connect her.

"Patience! Where are you?" Amanda demanded with urgent breathlessness.

"Getting a massage," Patience growled. "At least I was." Her plan was to find out what Amanda wanted, promise to do it, and finish her massage first pretty much no matter what it was that Amanda wanted. The skinny white girl had already ruined her plans for the evening, solving the stupid Simon Slater case already, which of course resulted in Darius taking off when he got a call from his boss.

"Forget that," Amanda barked down the phone. "I think Genevieve might be in danger. She's not answering her phone, and neither is Big Ben."

"In danger from who?" Patience raged, annoyed that she was being called upon when there appeared to be no justification. "You just caught the devil worshippers behind the murders, didn't you?"

Amanda admitted, "We got them. We just don't think they were behind the murders."

"What? Darius ran out of here an hour ago yelling about you having found that symbol at their house in the country. You know they went back to all the other murder scenes and found it at every one of them, right?"

Amanda said she hadn't known that.

Curious, Patience asked, "Where are you anyway? It sounds like you are on the road."

"On our way back to you," shouted Amanda, gripping the roof handle above her head. Beside her, Tempest cranked the steering wheel as he shot the van between two juggernauts tracking north toward the capital. Leaving the house in Faversham in a hurry, they sent Hilary with Basic and took the van again in a bid to get to Genevieve before anything happened to her.

The cops probably would do a drive by of the house, but if they knocked and no one answered, Amanda didn't believe for one minute that they would see reason to forcibly enter. Ian Quinn wasn't going to place enough emphasis on it, just enough to cover his backside in case she turned out to be right about her client's imminent death.

"Well, you check on Genevieve then. I've already paid for this massage," she replied, omitting to reveal the part where she'd placed the charge to the room and not her personal account.

Amanda shouted loud enough that Patience had to pull the phone away from her ear. "We're an hour away! It's got to be you, Patience. Please!"

"They are having sex, Amanda. That's why neither of them are answering their phones." It was patently obvious. "Trust me on this. I *know* that man. Genevieve got back from the awful task of having her dead husband dug up. Feeling crappy and sad, all it took was one look from Big Ben's smouldering puppy dog eyes and the elastic in her knickers probably snapped of its own accord."

Amanda bit her lip. She'd considered the same thing and she prayed it might be the case. It probably was the case, she told herself.

But she needed to *know*.

"Please, Patience," she whispered.

Patience huffed out a hard and long breath, letting her shoulders deflate in defeat because she knew she was going to have to do it. Sliding off the massage table, and shuffling toward the adjoining changing room, she continued to argue, nevertheless.

"When I get there and they are still in bed or on the couch eating pizza to give them energy for the next round I'm going to be royally annoyed with you, Harper."

Amanda's reply of, "I'll buy you ten massages," did little to alter Patience's mood as she stuffed her feet into the cute ankle boots she'd bought in the Ritz's boutique. They went so well with the matching handbag the sales assistant helped her to find.

With her index finger hovering over the red button on her phone, Patience delivered a final line.

"I'll let you know when I am there."

Cutting Amanda's grateful response off because she was too irked to hear it, Patience stormed out of the spa, growled at the concierge when he wished her a pleasant evening, and shoved the doorman in his fine Ritz regalia out of the way so she could stick two fingers in her mouth and whistle for a cab herself.

Getting into the cab, she muttered, "Stupid dead people and their stupid cases."

No Chance of Ever Being Caught. Wednesday, October 18th 1736hrs

A FEW MILES AWAY in the home of Genevieve Slater, Big Ben found that he was left alone as the man cryptically commented on his need to fetch someone important.

Determined to break free now that he wasn't being watched, Big Ben threw his weight forward and then back. The effort tore at the skin on his arms. Gritting his teeth, he tried again, doing his best to ignore the pain it caused. When his efforts had no effect, he shifted to a side-to-side motion.

Given time, there was no way the nails employed to keep him in place would resist working free. Time though, was one thing that was definitely in a limited supply. The rope wasn't burning freely as he expected it might, the nylon strands resisting ignition, but they were melting. It was hard to see from his angle, but he judged the rope's girth to have been reduced by at least ten percent in the few minutes the flame had been touching the one spot.

Out of breath, he paused for just a second before sucking in a fresh lungful and trying again. The stupid chair wasn't budging, and his wrists and arms were beginning to bleed where he fought against his bindings.

The sound of the man returning gave him cause to stop which he was both grateful for and frustrated by at the same time. He wanted to wrench the chair from the floor, tear his arms free and use the man's head as a hammer to drive the nails the rest of the way home. Big Ben was not accustomed to losing.

Forcing still calmness to return, he faced the door just as his captor came back through it. The man wasn't first to enter the room though. That dubious honour went to Genevieve.

Tied into a wheelchair with duct tape, she was also blindfolded and gagged.

"Here we are," announced the man in a conversational tone when he parked her adjacent to Big Ben. Squinting at the knot holding her blindfold in place, he said, "I don't think we need this any longer."

Genevieve blinked, shooting her head around to look at the man even as he tried to take off her gag. It made the task impossible, forcing him to grab her head and hold it in place.

"Please, Genevieve. Give me a moment and I will explain."

"Explain!" she shrieked, though behind the gag it came out as a barely discernible mumble.

The gag came free, the man whipping it through the air with a flourish before putting it in his pocket.

Still twisting her head to see him, Genevieve begged, "Jeremiah what are you doing? Untie me, please."

"Oh, I can't do that. Not yet," Jeremiah replied with a warm smile. "I'll need a few guarantees first. You seem a little excitable at the moment." His tone was that of a teacher or parent talking to a child at the end of a tantrum.

A tear slid down Genevieve's cheek and she mouthed, "I'm so sorry," to Big Ben.

Her decision to talk to the other man in the room incensed Jeremiah instantly. His features darkened and his entire demeanour changed.

"Don't talk to him!" he screamed in Genevieve's face. "It's your fault he has to die!" There was spittle on Jeremiah's chin where his anger drove the words from his mouth. No sooner had his outburst taken life than it died again, and rage was replaced by heart aching disappointment. "Why Genevieve? Why him? Why not me? I've done so much for you?"

"Oh, yeah?" asked Big Ben, watching the rope nervously. "Like what? *I* made her scream my name," he taunted, discovering he had a second trigger. "What is it that you think you have done that's so great?"

Jeremiah's response was as immediate as it was predictable. He launched himself at Big Ben, landing punch after punch, the blows raining down on his victim's defenceless head.

When Jeremiah stopped, breathless and spent, Big Ben moved his jaw about, shifting it from left to right and accentuating the motion to get Jeremiah's attention before he asked, "I've got an itch. It's right by my nose. Could you get it for me?"

Before Jeremiah could answer with his fists, Genevieve interrupted.

"Jeremiah, please! Why are you doing this? What has come over you?"

He stepped away from Big Ben, his eyes lingering on the man sitting opposite the cross-bow for a second. In a move that made it look as though he'd just remembered where he was, Jeremiah looked down at himself and seeing his tie was skewwhiff, he straightened it.

"I'm sorry, Genevieve, but your recent behaviour is far from acceptable. If things are going to work out between us, this has to be the last time. I'll not forgive you again."

Genevieve had to search through his words to explore their meaning, though she needed only a second to figure it out. She took the rest of the time before she spoke to figure out what to say.

"You're ... you're in love with me?" She had known he was infatuated, or had a crush on her; a woman learned early in life to notice the signs. It had been easy to dismiss though. Jeremiah was so much younger – almost two decades her junior and she expected his feelings would find a new outlet soon enough. His work on Simon's books was almost done and she had been waiting for him to move on, both physically and emotionally, while choosing to keep her distance as much as possible.

Jeremiah dropped to his knees, taking her right hand in both of his, though her arm was still taped to the wheelchair.

"Yes! Yes, my darling. I have been from the first moment I saw you. You are the moon and stars to me. That's why I have been doing all I can to protect our future."

Genevieve didn't want to hear it, but she already suspected the truth. "What? What have you done, Jeremiah? Did you kill those people?"

Rising to his feet and dropping her hand, his words were snippy when he replied.

"You should be more grateful, Genevieve. None of them had a fair claim to your money. That thief Leslie Ashe had earned over a hundred thousand pounds over the years for a few easy pieces of rubbish cover art he designed. He'd been paid a thousand times over and still the greedy git wanted more. His death was glorious and the books sales ... oh, the book sales, Genevieve, haven't they been magnificent over the last few weeks?"

"It's not my place to judge," remarked Big Ben, "but are you aware that you are stark-raving mad?"

Jeremiah spun around, flinging out an arm that hit Big Ben in the face with a back-handed slap.

Big Ben wrinkled his face and wriggled his nose from side to side by manipulating his top lip.

"That's much better, thanks. I'll let you know if the itch comes back."

Genevieve cried out, "Stop provoking him, Ben! He's going to kill you!"

"Yes!" Jeremiah's eyes danced with excitement. "Yes, I am! Do you recognise the scene, Genevieve? Isn't it exactly how you imagined it?"

She didn't answer his questions. "Jeremiah, this has to stop. You need to turn yourself over to the police."

"The police?" he scoffed, chuckling at the suggestion. "Why ever would I do that? They are never going to catch us. The police are chasing Simon's ghost. Dressing in his old clothes – it was so good of you to leave them in his wardrobe – proved to be a touch of genius. A wig, a pair of prop glasses the same style he used to wear, and everyone thought it was him. I even found some fingerprints to lift and place at one of the crime scenes. They were on a sterling silver hipflask I found in his desk. It still had some Irish whisky in it. It was so simple to just leave it at the crime scene."

Big Ben was staring at the rope. It was more than halfway through now and he was starting to sweat. At what point was there insufficient strength left in the rope to stop it from snapping. It was halfway down and that had taken about fifteen minutes. Did he have five minutes left? More?

His attention swung back to Genevieve and Jeremiah when she asked, "What about Amy Hildestrand and Samuel Blake? They had no claim to Simon's royalties as I understand it. Did you kill them too?"

Jeremiah spat, "They deserved it! Not just them, of course. I have another twenty-seven on my list and Simon was good enough to leave us with plenty of source material. His books have proven to be endlessly entertaining: you can read them, or you can recreate the scenes in them," he chuckled.

"Twenty-seven," Genevieve repeated, "Twenty-seven what? Who are they? Why did you kill Amy Hildestrand and Samuel Blake if they have nothing to do with the royalties?"

Jeremiah's face darkened again. "They are literary agents and publishers, book promoters and influencers in the world of fiction. Not one of them possessed the vision to see what my books could become."

"Your books?" Genevieve questioned with a mystified expression.

Jeremiah thundered, "Yes! Yes, my books. They rejected them. They told me the manu-scripts needed work. They took my money and promised me they could make me a star only to apologise later when their attempts to launch my career failed. They deserve to die, and they will. Every last one of them. Don't worry though, the police will never catch me. They will continue to think it is Simon."

"But he's dead," wailed Genevieve, adrift on a sea of overwhelming emotions.

"Yes!" exclaimed Jeremiah. "Don't you see? That's the beauty of it. At each of the murders I have left a little calling card. The inverted pentagram from the front of Simon's books. I was always curious about what it represented. I asked him about it a few times – why he had it on all his books, but he never would tell me. Do you know?"

Genevieve shook her head.

Jeremiah accepted her response, his desire to know the truth, but recognition that he might never, clear in his expression.

"Well, whatever it means, I don't think the police found them yet, but they will. It will tie all the deaths together just as much as the re-enactments of Simon's best scenes. They will believe they are looking for a killer who has risen from the grave, his spiritual form claiming souls as recompense for their crimes."

"But their crimes were not against Simon," Genevieve questioned Jeremiah's logic. "He didn't even know them. I doubt he was ever in the same room as Amy Hildestrand or Samuel Blake. The police will figure that out, Jeremiah."

Jeremiah huffed a small snort of amusement. "No, they won't. You give them far too much credit. I'm going to have to kill that Harper woman from the paranormal investigation agency though. I did advise against hiring them if you remember."

The sound of a phone ringing stopped his run of words, and frowning, he pulled it from his inner jacket pocket.

Pursing his lips, he said, "Talk of the devil," then laughed at his choice of words. "I'll just take this in the other room." He started to walk away, then stopped. "Whoops." he retraced his steps, reaching across the table to move the flame out from under the rope. "I wouldn't want to miss the fun part." He gave Big Ben a wink and hurried from the room, closing the door to lessen the chance of his caller hearing a cry for help.

The Lie. Wednesday, October 18th 1741hrs

"J EREMIAH, IT'S AMANDA HARPER," I blurted an introduction the second he answered the call. "Have you got any idea where Genevieve is?" I was holding his business card in my right hand and thanking my stars that I had it. He could go to the house and let me know if there was anything amiss. I ran the risk of him discovering the object of his affection was shacked up with Big Ben, but Jeremiah's emotions regarding Genevieve were the least of my concerns.

"Genevieve? Goodness, no. Why?"

"She's not answering her phone. I'm worried about her."

"Golly, I wish I could help. I'm away doing research again I'm afraid. I drove up to York first thing this morning. Simon set his very last book there and I want to get a feel for the city before I start filling in the parts he didn't get to finish."

I felt the frown form, my forehead creasing and my eyebrows bunching together.

"York? You went to York this morning?"

"Yes. Why?"

"Because Genevieve told me you were at her house this morning." I delivered my response as an accusation, but when the words left my mouth, I was only calling him on his lie. The moment they were in the air, I saw what they meant. "It's you," I murmured, speaking to him, but not saying it with any conviction. It was like I was trying the idea on for size which was ridiculous because I already knew I was right.

It … it just fit.

At Jeremiah's end there was a pregnant pause, my brain screaming that he was trying to think of something to say.

"What's me?" he asked after what had to be four or five seconds. He managed to voice the question causally, like he was doing something else and hadn't really heard what I said.

"It makes perfect sense. You're a writer. The random victims that make no sense are both literary agents. Did they reject your work? Oh, my God! Jeremiah what have you done with Genevieve?"

"No, I ah …" Jeremiah struggled to answer my question coherently, then realising that he only sounded guiltier by trying to deny it, he hung up. Jeremiah sensed he was busted and chose to end the call.

My chest was heaving, my breaths coming fast and shallow. I'd met the killer yesterday morning and I shook his hand. He'd been working in Genevieve's house for months and I even noted how infatuated he looked. That it was him even explained the appearance of the symbol. It was nothing to do with the devil worshippers, they just wanted to scare me off because they believed they were summoning the devil and he was killing off the people they wanted dead. Jeremiah hadn't carved the inverted pentagram at the sites to implicate them, it was to further the suggestion that Simon was behind it all.

I gripped my phone, squeezing the life out of it as I lifted my hand to bash it against my forehead.

This morning outside the Armenian restaurant I was looking at a photograph of a man wearing Simon Slater's clothes. Where had he got them from? Out of Simon Slater's wardrobe! How had I been so blind? He was too tall to be Simon Slater, I even made that observation, but knowing Jeremiah had all the connections and the access he needed, it still hadn't occurred to me to look at him. Heck he probably even had his own key!

Tempest hadn't said a word during my exchange with Jeremiah or since. What he had done was put his right foot down. He'd been breaking the speed limit since we left Faversham, now we were entering the city and soon the option of going faster than we otherwise might would be denied to us by the evening traffic.

The clues had been right there under my nose, and I cursed myself for not seeing them.

"How long?" I asked.

Tempest didn't need to seek clarification.

"Twenty minutes. If we don't hit traffic."

I punched the dial button on my phone. Jeremiah knew he was busted. What he did next came down to how crazy he was. He might just run. Terrified of being caught, it was possible that he was packing his bags and hoping to get on a plane before I could get the alert out.

It was possible, but I didn't believe it. Waiting for Patience to answer her phone and praying she would because I needed to warn her, I let the most likely scenario play out in my mind. He was going to clean house. If Genevieve and Big Ben were still alive, he would kill them both, and believing I would be racing to save her, he would lie in wait to kill me too.

Well, I *was* racing to save her – I reached across to place a hand on Tempest's leg – but I wasn't alone.

Staring at my phone, I begged, "Pick up, pick up, pick up."

Level Five Clinger.
Wednesday, October
18th 1743hrs

S TILL SPORTING A FROWNY face because her massage got cut short, Patience was peering through the windows of Genevieve's house when the call from Amanda came in. It went unanswered because she had her phone on silent.

"Damned fool errand," she muttered, standing on her tiptoes to look in. "If I interrupt Big Ben having sex, what's he's going to think, Amanda?" she asked the air. "He's going to believe I'm some bunny boiler, level five clinger, who is all in love with him and can't be cool."

Patience moved to the next window. "And I am cool, Amanda. He and I had a thing for a while. It was fun, but it's done. No big deal, let's not make a big deal out of it."

Cupping her hands to the side of her face to block out the streetlight reflecting off the glass, she looked around. The downstairs lights were off – because the people in the house were upstairs in bed, she told herself.

"And they're not playing tiddlywinks," she muttered.

A shadow passed in front of a doorway just when she dropped her hands. It was only there for a fraction of a second, but it had been tall and male and wearing clothes. That had to make it Big Ben, but a nagging voice inside her head argued that it wasn't. The shape she'd half seen wasn't the right shape for it to be Big Ben.

Grumbling that she was going to get caught and that would be even worse than knocking on the door, because she truly would look like a psycho stalker if Big Ben caught her snooping outside, she moved to the next window.

This one showed that there was a light on inside. It wasn't in the room she was currently staring into, but she was able to make out a thin line of dim light coming under the room's door.

Moving cautiously now – she did not want Big Ben to ever know she was here, she moved on again.

Seconds to Live. Wednesday, October 18th 1745hrs

B IG BEN WAS CERTAIN he'd never felt so helpless. His rage level was off the charts, though he recognised filling his head with dark, violent thoughts would do nothing to make them come true. He needed to be like Tempest – detached and calm so he could clinically assess his assets to find the opportunity when it came.

That lasted for roughly three seconds. Nothing came to him in that time, and rather than sit quietly, he started thrashing again. It was only when Genevieve begged him to calm down that he stopped fighting against the ever-constricting ropes.

She assured him there was no point in shouting for help because their cries would not be heard. Not unless they opened a window first and neither could manage to move from the spots they were in.

Speaking in hushed, but urgent whispers, they each searched the other for a weakness in their bindings. Anything they could exploit to get free. Then they tried to wriggle free again. Genevieve had the most success, fighting against her duct tape until she managed to get her right arm to start moving. It cost her all the hair on that arm; a small price to pay, but an inch was all she got before angry footsteps heralded Jeremiah's return.

The door behind her flew open, hitting the stop with a loud thump and flying back to slam shut again. Jeremiah stormed into the room, shifting the flame back under the rope before he started speaking.

"Where were we?" he asked, the question aimed not at either of his captives, but intended to jog his own memory.

Big Ben caught movement from the corner of his eye and flicked his gaze toward the window. He tore it away again for fear Jeremiah might also look and begged his brain to work at triple speed.

"Ah, yes, I was lamenting about the need to kill Amanda Harper. Another person who has to die because of you, Genevieve. If you want things to work out between us, you are going to have to listen to me when I talk. You do want things to work out, don't you?"

Expected to answer, and replying to a stone-cold serial killer, Genevieve did what almost anyone would do. She lied.

"Yes, Jeremiah. I do hope we can work through this."

The crossbow made an ominous creaking sound. The thinning rope was beginning to stretch.

Going for broke, Big Ben sniggered.

"Right. You think you're going to follow me, do you? Good luck with that. I hope you're a better lover than you are a writer," he laughed again.

Predictably, Jeremiah couldn't resist rising to the bait.

"I am a brilliant writer!" he roared. "I could have been a god in the literary field if just one of those short-sighted fools had given me the slightest chance."

"Yeah, right," Big Ben started to really laugh. "That's what all the losers say. I could have been great, they just never gave me a chance," he spluttered in a sing song voice. "Hey, Genevieve, how do you fancy life with a loser?"

Jeremiah ran around the room, shunting Genevieve's wheelchair in his haste to get to Big Ben.

"I'm going to enjoy watching you die!" he screamed, going around behind Big Ben to grip his throat and begin to strangle him.

Through the pain, Big Ben rasped, "Just so long as you don't bore me to death by reading your terrible books aloud."

Jeremiah bellowed his rage, Big Ben's tactic working perfectly. He wanted to mask the sound of Patience breaking in.

It almost worked.

Almost.

"What was that?" Jeremiah's grip on Big Ben's throat dropped away. The sound of a window breaking could not be confused with anything else and his question was rhetorical.

Everyone held their breath to listen. Except actually they didn't. Genevieve and Jeremiah had done precisely that, but Big Ben wasn't straining his hearing. He knew what the sound of breaking glass meant, just as he knew the sound of the crossbow shifting again meant he was almost out of time.

He was moments from salvation and seconds from death. Which would arrive first he could not guess, but with Jeremiah distractedly looking toward the dining room door, he dipped his head and sunk his teeth into a hand.

Jeremiah was just starting to move when it happened. He couldn't hear anything, but he hadn't imagined the sound of someone smashing a window. Was it that Harper woman? Was she here already? How did she know to come to Genevieve's house?

It required investigation and whoever he found was going to have to die, but just as he pulled away from the fool about to get a crossbow through his heart, excruciating pain tore through his left hand.

He tried to tear his hand away, but the dumb muscular brute wouldn't let go. Blood was running down his palm and onto the cuff of his shirt. Jeremiah swung a punch with his right hand. It connected on Big Ben's right eye socket, but for all the force he put into it, no benefit came. If anything, Big Ben was biting harder now.

Swinging his right arm back for another attempt, pure shock registered when someone caught it. Gripped by fear, Jeremiah shot his head around to see who was there and couldn't believe his eyes. Genevieve had one arm free and was fighting to hold on to him.

Fighting to hold on and knowing she was about to lose her grip, Genevieve put everything into her desperate scream, "Help us! We're in here!"

Big Ben yelled, "Grayshience!" his voice muffled by the hand jammed into it.

For the second time in two minutes, the dining room door flew open to smash against the stop. It didn't shut again though as it had before. Instead, it struck Patience as she charged headlong into the room.

She could hear the struggle, however finding her way through the house had been trickier than she could have imagined. Even though she'd been in it last night, the place was huge and confusing.

Patience had no idea who the man in the middle of the room was, but Big Ben and Genevieve were tied up and fighting him as if their lives depended on it. That was all the information she needed.

Running straight at him, Patience intended to knock the wind from his sails, and she hadn't really thought beyond that tactic. With a banshee shriek, she charged.

Jeremiah had no idea who the new woman was. Another person he was going to have to kill was the dominant thought in his head. Kicking out, he toppled Genevieve's wheelchair, his right arm coming free as she squealed and fell, then he ripped his left hand free of Big Ben's mouth, leaving flesh behind as he aimed a blood-soaked punch at the newcomer's head.

Patience ducked under it, driving her right shoulder into Jeremiah's ribcage to send him back into the dining table.

Spitting out a piece of Jeremiah's hand, Big Ben's terrified eyes knew what was going to happen.

He yelled, "Patience! Look out!" but it was too late to stop the inevitable result.

Jeremiah fell backward, Patience following him down to land on his chest on top of the dining table. The impact jolted the entire structure, sending a shockwave that the final strands of burning rope could not hope to withstand.

The sound of the crossbow bolt firing was one Big Ben would never forget. The same could be said of the sight that came with it.

Unable to breathe, Big Ben looked down at his chest. The tip of the crossbow bolt was touching his shirt and would leave a bruise where the final drops of its energy had dissipated against his flesh. It had gone right through Jeremiah, entering his ribcage on one side, and exiting on the other, only to stop before it was all the way out.

"You're under arrest, dirtbag!" yelled Patience, bouncing up and off Jeremiah's lifeless corpse. "Move and I'm gonna kick you in the nuts so hard you'll sing like Mariah!" Landing on her feet, she brought her hands up in a fighting stance the way she'd been taught to but rarely, if ever, used in her career in the police. "Oh, did I knock him out?" she asked.

Case Closed?
Wednesday, October
18th 2003hrs

"**A** MANDA!"

I looked up to find Patience waving her arm in the air to get my attention.

By the time we arrived, the private street outside Genevieve's house was lit up like a Christmas tree. Strobe lights from a dozen police cars bounced off the walls of all the nearby houses and a small crowd of neighbours were gathered to chat, point, and speculate at the edge of a hastily erected cordon. I knew to expect it because Patience had called me immediately after calling police dispatch.

I'd already dialled nine, nine, nine, myself. Making the call from the car when I was unable to raise Patience. Explaining the need for them to get to Genevieve Slater's house in my most urgent terms, the dispatcher had calmly explained to the hysterical woman that a patrol car was already scheduled to perform a drive by of the property. His inability to grasp the severity of the situation led to an argument and a warning that I could be charged with phone abuse if I refused to calm down.

Tempest drove faster.

We were still ten minutes away when Patience called me.

Learning of Jeremiah's death removed some of the urgency we felt, but impatience to see it all for ourselves and make sure Big Ben was okay – Patience told us about a crossbow and a beating Big Ben took, but she was known for embellishing her stories.

We made good time in getting across London, but even so the police got there before us. A uniformed constable approached Hilary's van, waving for us to stop.

"Are you residents?" he asked before Tempest's window was even halfway down. "I'll need you to clear the street either way."

I leaned across and ducked my head to make eye contact with the man in uniform. "We're going in there," I pointed to the house and to Patience who was now at the edge of the cordon. "We're with her."

He looked about for somewhere we could park. "Okay, um. Put it ..."

"I'll park in front of the owner's garage," Tempest suggested congenially and pointed to where he wanted to go.

Two minutes later, we were walking through the front door, Patience making sure we got through the cordon without hassle.

I wanted to find Genevieve and Big Ben; that was my priority, but I expected to have to answer some questions first and I was not wrong.

Patience told us the senior officer at the scene was Detective Superintendent Gary Smith. He was in the lobby of Genevieve's house, speaking on the phone when we entered. I could tell he was a senior officer from his demeanour and commanding presence – one gets a feel for such things quite quickly in any uniformed service.

When I glanced his way, I inadvertently caught his eye and he spoke his next words rapidly, wrapping up his phone conversation and covering the phone with his hand so he could give a softly spoken order to a nearby sergeant in uniform.

Reacting just as swiftly, the sergeant moved to block our path.

"Sorry. The superintendent wants a word." That was all the explanation we got, as he forced us to wait.

It was only for a few seconds, the superintendent's body language making it clear he was trying to get the other person off the line.

"Tempest Michaels?" the senior officer stuck out his hand. "Superintendent Gary Smith. I believe I have you to thank for solving the case."

I rolled my eyes and kicked Tempest ever so gently in his left calf.

No one else saw the move, but they all saw Tempest flinch and then laugh, his unexplained actions causing a few confused looks.

"I helped at best," Tempest assured the superintendent. "The bulk of the investigative work and the leaps that led to successfully identifying the culprit were made by my colleague, Amanda Harper," Tempest took a pace to his right to make sure the focus fell on me.

I blushed a little at the sudden attention.

"We were very lucky," I admitted. "The result tonight could have been entirely different if Constable Woods hadn't answered the call. She is the one who tackled the serial killer. Constable Woods forced entry to prevent loss of life and tackle a known murderer single handed."

"Oh, stop it!" Patience blushed, loving every word.

"Without her intervention, the killer would almost certainly have killed both Genevieve Slater and Benjamin Winters before escaping. All I was able to do was identify him, and I was jolly slow in doing that."

Superintendent Smith nodded his head thoughtfully, his eyes focused on Patience.

"I shall be speaking to my boss about you, Constable Woods. A commendation is clearly in order. I shall need to know the name of your supervising officer. I hope he or she knows how lucky they are to have officers of your calibre under their command."

I almost spat out a laugh imagining Chief Inspector Quinn having to listen and smile while Patience was being praised and applauded. His bosses would likely seek to make a public example of her, promoting her image as a successful young black female officer. I could picture it all in my head. Best yet, this wasn't her first major bust in the last couple of years.

Turning his attention back to us, Superintendent Smith said, "If you had asked me this morning, I would have claimed I had seen it all. The Simon Slater case was one that fell under my remit, but even the bizarre nature that came with it was nothing too far from the ordinary. I've been in this business for more than thirty years and I have to tell you, the last couple of hours are going down in my memoirs as the craziest I've ever witnessed or heard of. The dead author's publishing firm were a devil worshipping cult? The man employed to finish his final works was a serial killer selecting his victims based on their claim to a portion of the author's royalties or their denial of the killer's own career as a writer. Inverted pentagrams, people dressing up with goat head costumes? My report is going to read like a work of fiction and that was before I found out the dead author's wife had hired a team of paranormal investigators who solved the whole case while my own team was scratching their heads." He looked around the room as he made his last remark, the officers gathered to hear him speak all refusing to make eye contact.

I felt a little sorry for them.

Sensing that he had more to say, I spoke first. "If you'll excuse us, we really want to check on our friend and Mrs Slater."

"Of course," he set off to lead us through the house. "We set them up in the living room."

Flashes illuminating the hallway ahead were coming from the dining room where I imagined several crime scene officers were already working. They would have plenty to keep them busy as they went back over the previous murders to correlate evidence and confirm Jeremiah was responsible for them all.

His death this evening meant he could not be questioned or give a confession. The admission he made to Genevieve and Big Ben, which I knew about from talking to Patience, would be recorded, but wouldn't be enough by itself to close the case file. For that to happen, they would have to go all the way back to Simon Slater's murder and prove without doubt Jeremiah was behind that too.

Big Ben looked comfortable but tired in a large reclining chair in the corner of the living room. A paramedic was talking to him, audibly recommending he not drink the tumbler of dark liquid Big Ben held in his right hand.

"I'm sure you're right," Big Ben agreed, taking a sip. "But when *you* have a brush with death like the one I just had, you will understand."

The paramedic threw an arm in the air and shook his head.

Big Ben smacked his lips together. "Best painkiller on the planet."

He looked like he needed it; his face was a mess. He had a black eye and a dozen cuts to his face, plus a nasty lump on his forehead where it met his hairline.

Tempest went to him, making sure he was doing okay, and I made a beeline for Genevieve.

Like Big Ben, she'd chosen to have a stiff drink. Her tumbler was empty. She was staring into space, her eyes seeing nothing while her mind went around in circles trying to unpick what had happened to her.

I placed my right hand on top of hers, causing her to snap her eyes across to look at me. I don't think she'd even noticed I was there until that moment.

"Have the paramedics checked you over?" I asked. She had a nasty welt on her arm where some skin was missing, but other than her clothes looking ruined, she appeared to be unharmed. The damage was in her head.

She nodded, moving her mouth like she was going to say something, only to stop before any sound came out. Her eyes were back to looking at the carpet, but she tried again, this time forming a sentence.

"He was in my house. Jeremiah had been in and out of my house for nine months. I even gave him a key. He said it was easier for him to complete Simon's unfinished manuscripts if he sat in Simon's chair. He told me he felt some kind of connection to him. I mean, I knew it was nonsense just as I knew he had a crush on me. I thought the crush would pass. Is it my fault he killed all those people?"

"Goodness, no, Genevieve." She was going to need a bucket of therapy. "You mustn't ever think that. You are blameless here. You couldn't have known about Jeremiah's past – his failure as an author or that his obsession with you would drive him to such murderous lengths."

"That's just it," Genevieve murmured, "I actually did question it."

That made my eyebrows rise.

"When the police first asked me about the CCTV footage of Simon not far from Amy Hildestrand's house, I thought then that it looked a bit like Jeremiah. He had an alibi for the time of the murder though. He was conducting research – getting the feel for the area he was describing and was staying at a B&B in Bristol. I remember now that I raised the subject casually, like I was asking how the books were going and was his trip worthwhile. He'd made a big point of telling me about how he was taking the trip. I didn't think anything of it at the time. Now though, I realise he was staging his alibi. When I started the conversation, he produced receipts for his stay and even showed me a few selfies he took in Bristol. It's all so obvious now. I bet he has alibis for all the other murders too."

I would not be surprised to discover she was entirely correct. He'd said he was staying in York. Would there be a room booked somewhere to make it look true?

"He killed Simon too, didn't he?" Genevieve asked, though it was a statement rather than a question. I chose to offer no opinion. I could see why he would. Simon was a successful author writing in Jeremiah's chosen genre. By removing him, he got the job finishing Simon's work. Plus, he was in love with Simon's wife. In love to the point that he would kill for her.

My line of thinking was interrupted by Big Ben.

"That doesn't sound right," he challenged Genevieve's assumption. "When I disrespected Simon, Jeremiah tried to take my head off." He pointed to his bruised and battered face for emphasis. "He loved Simon. Worshipped him even."

"That doesn't mean he didn't also kill him. Stars have been killed by their fans before, Benjamin," she argued, sounding a little annoyed at having her beliefs questioned. "Isn't that what happened to John Lennon?"

I didn't know what had happened to John Lennon; he was some musician who died before I was born, but I didn't need Genevieve or Big Ben to be getting excited or agitated at this time.

"The police will be able to prove what happened and whether Jeremiah was behind it or not. There's nothing to be gained by discussing it now," I did my best to diffuse the situation.

"Well, I'm sure it was him," Genevieve insisted.

Big Ben was not of a mind to argue.

The next hour went by swiftly. Police officers came and went, Jeremiah's body was removed, statements were recorded, though we would all be required to give them again later when some of the dust had settled.

Big Ben wanted to leave and was given the freedom to do so just before ten o'clock. Tempest was going to take him home, driving Big Ben's big truck to get it and him there. That left me with Hilary's van. Tomorrow would involve some do-si-do-ing of vehicles, but I was fairly sure Tempest and I were going to take the day off to relax and recover.

I followed Tempest to the door so I could kiss him goodnight without a whole bunch of people watching.

"You're going to follow shortly?" he sought to confirm.

"I just want to make sure Genevieve is okay. She seems a little fragile."

Tempest could only nod his head in agreement. "It's not surprising. It will take her a while to find peace, I expect, but she has closure now on her husband's death."

Big Ben, hovering by the door while he waited for Tempest, said, "I've just remembered something."

We looked his way.

"There's a brick wall in the basement."

I stared at him, recalling that he mentioned it earlier and questioning why he had brought it up.

"It's behind a door," he added, expecting that to hold some meaning for us. "Don't you think that's a little odd?" he prompted.

Tempest's phone beeped before either one of us could answer. It was in Tempest's left hand, Big Ben's car keys dangling from his right.

"It's from Hilary," Tempest let us know, squinting at the screen to read the message. There were no words though, just a picture. Tempest turned the screen for me to see.

It brought a smile to my face. Hilary had taken a snap of Basic. He was lying on a hospital bed in a busy accident and emergency ward. Grinning madly and giving the camera a Fonz-style double thumbs up, it was a typical Basic pose and I felt great relief to know he was fine.

About to go back to whatever point Big Ben was trying to make about the brick wall in the basement, something in the background of the photograph caught my eye and my blood froze.

The Tattoo.
Wednesday, October
18th 2211hrs

"**T**HE TATTOO," I BLURTED, snatching the phone from Tempest's hand. Using two fingers I stretched the screen, zooming in on what I had seen.

My heart had stopped beating and I was holding my breath. Just behind Basic were two members of the satanic cult. Each was wearing a hospital gown, the kind that fails to cover anyone's bottom ever. Cuffed by their right hands to a pair of uniformed cops, they were facing away from the camera, but taking the phone in as close as I could, losing focus and having to come back out a bit, I knew I was right.

At the base of their spines was a tattoo. An inverted pentagram, would you believe?

Tempest and Big Ben were staring at me, their expressions begging an explanation I didn't give. I wanted to, I just felt tackling a killer came with a higher priority.

"Babe?" asked Tempest, when I twisted off my right foot and started running back through the house.

Most of the cops were gone now and the few that remained were packing up a final few things and getting ready to leave.

I threw myself back into the living room, my accusation already on my lips. It died there for Genevieve was not where I left her.

"Genevieve!" I screamed her name and waited for her to respond.

A tentative, "Yes," returned.

Tempest, eyeing me with a questioning look, said, "Babe?" again when I started running.

I burst into the kitchen where I found Genevieve unloading her dishwasher. It was a perfectly mundane thing for a person to do. The cops had made hot drinks and someone had loaded the dirty cups into Genevieve's machine.

"You almost got away with it," I wasted no time in getting to my point.

Pausing with a coffee mug in each hand, she gave a small shake of her head. "Got away with what? Whatever is the matter, Amanda?"

"How did it happen?" I asked. Tempest and Big Ben had moved to flank me. They had no idea what was happening, but were willing to back me without needing to know more. "Did Simon trick you into getting the tattoo?"

Genevieve turned away, continuing her task of replacing the clean crockery into a cupboard.

"I've no idea what you are talking about," she replied dismissively. "I don't have any tattoos."

"No, you wasted no time in getting it removed once you found out what it represented. He was trying to recruit you, wasn't he?"

Genevieve had returned to the dishwasher to retrieve the next two mugs but froze with her back to us.

"The inverted pentagram tattoo you had at the base of your spine. I thought it was funny that a model at your end of the business would ever have a tattoo, but it was recent, wasn't it? A little more than a year ago, I would guess. Simon had one too, didn't he?"

I thought I was going to have to keep going, but Genevieve's shoulders began to shake, and she turned around to face us, tears flowing from her eyes as huge racking sobs shook her.

"He never said what it was for!" she wailed. "He lied to me. Right from the start he was lying! Only when I got the tattoo did he show me the room in the basement. There was a shrine to the devil in my house and I never knew! He was evil!"

"Is that why you killed him?" I asked, my voice softening.

Patience drifted into the room. "What's happening?"

Genevieve sobbed, "Yes. He showed it all to me and explained about his success. Simon believed the devil was helping him to be a great author. He believed that only through following the satanic scriptures could we be truly happy. He was so pleased to have finally revealed the truth to me."

"How did you kill him?" I asked. I was on a roll and genuinely believed she was going to continue talking. I was right, too.

"We were in the basement still. He'd just revealed what was in the room. I remember just feeling so terrified. And angry. I was so angry. I asked him to get me a glass of water and he skipped away back up to the kitchen like it was the happiest day of his life. I followed him, taking off my shoes so he wouldn't hear me approach. Honestly, I don't really remember picking up the sword ... it was in the basement too, but the next thing I knew, he was pinned to the wall with the blade sticking out of his chest."

"So you posed him?"

Genevieve's eyes had been locked firmly on the kitchen tile, but she looked up now to meet my eyes.

Making it sound like an apology, she said, "No, I went out to dinner." I recalled that her statement at the time said she came home, couldn't find her husband, assumed he was writing and didn't wish to be disturbed. She told the police and the press that was his regular habit, so she went to bed and only found his body the next morning.

It was a cleverly concocted alibi; the time of death getting less exact and harder to pinpoint with each passing hour. Once a body has completely cooled, temperature can no longer be used to give a precise time of death, so her dinner out could easily be argued to have covered the period when he met his end.

"I posed him when I got home," she admitted, her voice quiet. "The idea came to me while I was eating dinner. I had no idea anyone would ever copy it."

I understood it all now. Genevieve had vehemently denied any suggestion that her husband had been involved in devil worship, passing it off as a rumour started as a promotional stunt to sell his books. She was guilty of murder, but when the recent killings so closely resembled her own and came from the publishing community associated with her husband, her guilty conscience told her Simon was back to take his revenge.

It wouldn't have helped that he'd been spotted. She hired us to catch her husband's unresting spirit, and in the end ruined her own perfect crime. Had she stayed quiet, I questioned if she would have ever been caught. Jeremiah was never going to hurt her; she was the object of his adoration, the reason he started his murder spree.

While Patience took Genevieve into custody and Tempest went to find a cop with some cuffs, I leaned against a wall and felt my whole body deflate.

Now it was over.

A New Case. Thursday, October 19th 0855hrs

J UST AS I PLANNED, Tempest and I did not go to work the next morning.

We slept in, recharging our batteries, until sunlight and natural body rhythms woke us a little before nine. Tempest went downstairs to make tea, leaving me in bed, and he donned joggers, flipflops, and a sweater to retrieve his dogs from his neighbour, Mrs Comerforth.

I could hear Bull and Dozer, Tempest's pair of miniature dachshund boys going nuts in their excitement to have him home. The combination of warmth and lingering drowsiness almost had me asleep again by the time Tempest reappeared with the mugs of tea. The dachshunds arrived on the bed with their usual gusto, Dozer ensuring I was fully alert by landing on my bladder.

He was heading for my face, intending to give it a thorough wash which I only avoided by picking him up. His tail whizzed back and forth like a metronome, and I liked that he was just as happy to see me.

It was like getting familial approval.

After a leisurely breakfast, we took the dogs for a walk through the vineyards around the village and discussed stopping for a pub lunch somewhere. That was for later – we'd only just had breakfast and as we chatted back and forth, it soon became apparent that we were both trying to avoid talking about work.

I asked, "Shall I just send Jane a message and make sure she's okay without us still?"

"She would let us know if she was snowed under."

I challenged Tempest's statement with my right eyebrow: we both knew that wasn't true. As a team we worked hard and did our best to support each other. Sometimes that meant carrying the burden because one or more of the others was hip-deep in a case or recovering at the end of one.

Our cases had a habit of being rather demanding in terms of time and energy.

Jane had been alone at the office for days and Tempest, due to his international rescue operation to help Patricia Fisher, hadn't been into the office all week.

"Okay," Tempest laughed, "Let's pop over there and spend a few hours catching up on things. There will be new cases to start."

"There always are," I agreed. "Bet you a pub lunch we have something new for the board." It made Tempest smile.

A while back he'd chosen to create a sort of leader board with our names on it and a long list of supernatural creatures. Jane was the only one to have chalked up dragon and swamp creature so far, but we all had werewolf, ghost, and vampire ticked off.

Basically people are a bit bonkers, and each time we think we've hit the crazy ceiling, someone manages to top whatever we've seen before.

We took Tempest's car, parking it behind the office in his usual spot. Bull and Dozer led the way, nudging at the door with their little wet noses until Tempest opened it. Then they charged down the corridor to do the same thing with the next door.

Jane was in what had originally been my office. When we moved into the premises – a plush place in Rochester's historic High Street – it was just me and Tempest and I was employed by him, not a partner in the business. Now there were three of us, we hot-desked. It worked out because it was rare for all three of us to be in the office for very long.

"Oh, hey, guys!" Jane said, looking up. "I wasn't expecting to see you today. I was just about to go out."

"Meeting a client?" Tempest asked, walking backward as he aimed toward the fandango coffee machine he'd bought for the office. He'd never admit it, but I think he'd missed it the last few days.

Jane rose from behind the desk, joining us in the main room. The dogs finished fussing around Marjory's feet (she's the lady running our reception) and raced across the carpet tiles to get to the one person they hadn't bothered yet.

Jane knew well enough to crouch. It was that or have her tights shredded when the little dogs tried to run up them.

"Yes, a client," she replied to Tempest's question. "They want you though." You might have been able to guess, but she wasn't talking to me.

Tempest was loading the coffee machine, his focus on that when he asked, "Any particular reason why?"

Jane sucked some air between her teeth. It made us both look at her.

"Weeeellll," she drawled, really drawing us in. Now I needed to hear what she had to say. "Remember that Live Action Role Play club I was part of way back in the day?"

Tempest put down the porcelain cups he held and crossed the office to get back to where Jane and I were standing.

"Yes."

Of course he did. That was the case where he and I met. He, I, and Jane actually although she wasn't called Jane then. At the time – more than eighteen months ago – Jane was part of a LARP (Live Action Role Play) club organised specifically for people with a vampire fetish. Demedicus, as Jane, or rather, James, had been known at the time, left the club when Tempest killed the master vampire they served.

Not that it was a real vampire, you understand.

"Well, they reformed some time ago. I got a message from them. James did at least," explained Jane, who rarely dressed as a boy anymore. "They are being targeted by someone. They don't know who." Jane turned to look at me. "Remember I told you someone got staked the other night?"

I nodded. "Yes."

"Well, that was Tom Davies. I know him. Turns out he was the third one at the club to have been chased. Tom survived by the way. I was just on my way out to see him. The stake poked a hole in his heart, but I guess they fixed it. He's still in the hospital, obviously. Anyway, the club wants to hire us, or more specifically, you, to figure out who is behind the attacks. What do you think?" Jane enquired, pulling a face that said she wasn't sure if Tempest would want us to take the case or not.

"Someone staked him?" Tempest wanted to make sure he had it right.

Jane nodded her head. "Yup. Used a sharpened piece of wood and everything."

I couldn't help but say, "How very Buffy of them."

Tempest was frowning. "I need to speak to Frank," he announced, heading for the office's front door.

I called after him, "What for?"

He paused with one hand on the door handle. "To find out where Vermont Wensdale is." He opened the door and went through it.

Jane shouted after him, "Are we taking the case?"

His voice echoed back from outside. "Damned right we are!"

The End

Author's Notes

Hello, Dear Reader,

Thank you for reading this book. For me this has become a mature series. Now five years old and twenty-one books long, it is also the series that started my career as a writer.

I have plans for this series that include spin-offs, where a new branch or branches of Tempest's successful business will open. This is something I am exploring now. If it goes ahead, there will be some crossover between the characters you know and love and new ones to be introduced. Also, characters such as Vermont Wensdale, who has appeared three times in the series thus far, could easily pop up in America, Australia, Germany, or wherever a new office begins to tout for business.

I guess my advice is to sign up to receive my newsletter if you want to be in the know. You can do that from my website or from the links you will find on the pages to follow. You will also find a teaser for the next book in this series if you keep scrolling.

In this book, I have a little fun with James 'Basic' Burham and his wonderful range of fad gifts. I'm sure many people roll their eyes and comment on how ridiculous they are to whoever is within earshot. However, I assure you these are all real products you can find online. Examples of them have been posted by my readers in my Facebook group.

Better yet, I will remind you that such unexplainable behaviour on the part of the consumer is not a new thing. Who remembers the *Pet Rock*? If you don't then please type it into your search bar. In the eighties, the inventor sold millions of ordinary rocks just by putting them in a box.

Air guitars are a real thing. You can even buy second hand ones.

Did you pick up on the line from *American Werewolf in London*? I like to slip in a little Easter egg every now and then, just to see if people pick up on it.

I sent Tempest and Amanda to the Ritz and stayed there myself with Gemma in what proved to be a memorable getaway a few years ago before our first child came along and ruined everything. I jest of course. The kids have only ruined most things.

If you are ever going to The All England Club – better known as Wimbledon, then be sure to get on the right tube line. If you head for Wimbledon station, you have several miles to walk to get there. I was fortunate enough in my military career to attend the club as a steward. Basically, we were there to look pretty and control the crowds. It was enormous fun and I got to watch a lot of tennis stars parade their prowess.

I want to ask if you spotted the inclusion of Albert's Smith eldest son, but if you are unfamiliar with my series *Albert Smith's Culinary Capers*, the reference will mean nothing. If you have read, and thus obviously now love Albert and his dog Rex Harrison, then you could not have failed to see it.

Toward the end of the book, I gave Big Ben searing pain in his eyes due to the blow to his head. This light sensitivity is one of the worst things I have ever had to endure. It happened to me when I caught a minute bullet fragment in my right eye. Unable to do anything but sit in a dark room with my eyes closed for days, I developed a new appreciation for my friends because I lived with two Labradors and couldn't hope to walk them until the sun went down.

I hope I was able to truly capture how seriously painful such an experience can be.

Language differences is a subject that crops up semi-regularly with English readers complaining about my use of Americanisms. I understand the argument, but there are a couple of very good reasons why I do it. The first is because globalisation and the proliferation of American TV has melded many American terms into our daily lexicon. I will announce that I am, "Taking out the trash,". That's not something my father would have ever said, but I believe it would be commonplace among the characters I am writing. More importantly though, I embrace American spelling for certain words, and one occurred in this book. Instil and instill – two acceptable ways to spell the same word depending on where you live. The first is British and I suspect also Antipodean, the latter is American and every last one of my American proofreaders wanted to correct it.

Here's the problem. If I leave it alone, a ton of American readers will highlight what they believe to be a typo directly to Amazon through their Kindle. The people at Kindle will in turn force me to address it with the threat that my book will be removed from sale if I fail to comply.

Why not publish English and American versions? At this time, it doesn't work like that. There may be a way around it, but I'm too busy writing the next book to worry that much over a single letter.

That's it for now, I am wrapping up this book. It has taken longer to write than any book in the last two years. Mostly this comes down to mental fatigue due to my beautiful two-year-old daughter refusing to sleep. She finally permitted me to get into bed at 0300hrs this morning only to then be woken by Hunter when he got up at 0600hrs.

Being creative and keeping a complex story on track in these conditions is difficult. I'm not complaining though, not to you at least. I am very lucky to be able to get to do what I do.

I'm off to write another one now.

Take care.

Steve Higgs

What's Next for the Blue Moon Crew?

Monsters Everywhere

T EMPEST MICHAELS HAS A vampire problem.

He's an old hat at this game and dealing with cases like this are his speciality. Except this time ...

... the vampires are his clients.

When someone starts targeting members of the local vampire Live Action Role Play club, there's only one person they can think of to turn to – their old nemesis, Tempest Michaels.

Unfortunately for Tempest, when he takes the case, he doesn't realise they automatically assume that means twenty-four-hour protection. All too soon he has vampire wannabes camping on his lawn, he has vampires wannabes sleeping in his shed, and as for his office ...

He needs to solve this case and fast and it's not the only one demanding his attention.

Hold on to your butts because this one's going to be a thrill-ride!

MONSTERS
EVERYWHERE

BLUE MOON INVESTIGATIONS BOOK 22
STEVE HIGGS

More Books By Steve Higgs

Blue Moon Investigations
Paranormal Nonsense
The Phantom of Barker Mill
Amanda Harper Paranormal Detective
The Klowns of Kent
Dead Pirates of Cawsand
In the Doodoo With Voodoo
The Witches of East Malling
Crop Circles, Cows and Crazy Aliens
Whispers in the Rigging
Bloodlust Blonde – a short story
Paws of the Yeti
Under a Blue Moon – A Paranormal
Detective Origin Story
Night Work
Lord Hale's Monster
The Herne Bay Howlers
Undead Incorporated
The Ghoul of Christmas Past
The Sandman
Jailhouse Golem
Shadow in the Mine
Ghost Writer

Felicity Philips Investigates
To Love and to Perish
Tying the Noose
Aisle Kill Him
A Dress to Die For
Wedding Ceremony Woes

Patricia Fisher Cruise Mysteries
The Missing Sapphire of Zangrabar
The Kidnapped Bride
The Director's Cut
The Couple in Cabin 2124
Doctor Death
Murder on the Dancefloor
Mission for the Maharaja
A Sleuth and her Dachshund in Athens
The Maltese Parrot
No Place Like Home

Patricia Fisher Mystery Adventures
What Sam Knew
Solstice Goat
Recipe for Murder
A Banshee and a Bookshop
Diamonds, Dinner Jackets, and Death
Frozen Vengeance
Mug Shot
The Godmother
Murder is an Artform
Wonderful Weddings and Deadly
Divorces
Dangerous Creatures

Patricia Fisher: Ship's Detective Series
The Ship's Detective
Fitness Can Kill
Death by Pirates
First Dig Two Graves

Albert Smith Culinary Capers
Pork Pie Pandemonium
Bakewell Tart Bludgeoning
Stilton Slaughter
Bedfordshire Clanger Calamity
Death of a Yorkshire Pudding
Cumberland Sausage Shocker
Arbroath Smokie Slaying
Dundee Cake Dispatch
Lancashire Hotpot Peril
Blackpool Rock Bloodshed
Kent Coast Oyster Obliteration
Eton Mess Massacre
Cornish Pasty Conspiracy

Realm of False Gods
Untethered magic
Unleashed Magic
Early Shift
Damaged but Powerful
Demon Bound
Familiar Territory
The Armour of God
Live and Die by Magic
Terrible Secrets

About the Author

At school, the author was mostly disinterested in every subject except creative writing, for which, at age ten, he won his first award. However, calling it his first award suggests that there have been more, which there have not. Accolades may come but, in the meantime, he is having a ball writing mystery stories and crime thrillers and claims to have more than a hundred books forming an unruly queue in his head as they clamour to get out. He lives in the south-east corner of England with a duo of lazy sausage dogs. Surrounded by rolling hills, brooding castles, and vineyards, he doubts he will ever leave, the beer is just too good.

If you are a social media fan, you should copy the link below into your browser to join my very active Facebook group. You'll find a host of friends waiting there, some of whom have been with me from the very start.

My Facebook group get first notification when I publish anything new, plus cover reveals and free short stories, but more than that, they all interact with each other, sharing inside jokes, and answering question.

 facebook.com/stevehiggsauthor

You can also keep updated with my books via my website:

g https://stevehiggsbooks.com/

Printed in Great Britain
by Amazon